DEDICATION

For all the munitionettes who risked their lives and their health working in Britain's munitions factories during both world wars.

.

ACKNOWLEDGMENTS

Devil's Porridge was not an easy book to write, and the period it covers was one of great anguish for the British people. I hope I have done the subject justice.

I first came across references to Gretna Munitions Factory during my research into the origins of women police in Britain, and was fascinated to find out that women police were sent to munitions factories through an arrangement with the Ministry of Munitions. My research into women police led to the creation of Kirsty Campbell, Dundee's first policewoman. I intended to carry on with more Dundee books using this character, but the interest in Gretna would not go away.

This interest turned my research in a different direction, to Gretna itself. In the process of doing this research I learned a great deal about the First World War on the home front, munitions, and the factories involved. However, because of the passage of time and the secrecy around munitions factories, not all information was available and I had to use my imagination, therefore any historical inaccuracies in this story are my own.

However, I did find a lot of information and I am indebted to the people who facilitated this for me.

I consulted many books and documents which enhanced my research, and I would like to thank the writers and academics who published the following: Gordon L Routledge, for his two books – *Gretna's Secret War*, and *Miracles and Munitions*; Chris Brader, for his thesis *Timbertown Girls: Gretna Female Munitions Workers in World War 1*. These publications were of great value to me in understanding the life style and working conditions of the munitionettes.

I am also indebted to Devil's Porridge Museum in Eastriggs for their help with my research and allowing me access to their archives.

My initial research into women police commenced after reading Joan Lock's, book *The British Policewoman*. This is one of the best books I have read on the subject and it is full of information on these early pioneering women. It was after reading this book I realized that the first women police came from the suffragette organizations.

I must not forget to thank all those selfless writers in ALLi (Alliance of Independent Authors) who offered advice on my book cover and blurb, in particular Dave Sivers who helped me to compile the perfect blurb, the most difficult piece of writing imaginable for writers. And Cathy Helms of Avalon Graphics who has surpassed herself with the cover design for Devil's Porridge.

And before I go, I must express my deepest thanks to my two brilliant readers, Betty Doe, and Liz Strachan who never hesitate to tell me where I am going wrong.

1

Friday, 19 January 1917

Oily smoke rose from the smouldering bundle of rags. He covered his mouth and nose with a handkerchief. He should leave. It was dangerous here. But he had to be certain the fire took hold before he left.

He stepped over the girl lying at his feet and prodded the rags with the toe of his boot. A small flame flickered, quickly multiplying into more and larger flames, spreading, looking for fuel to feed their hunger.

They had been walking out for several weeks before he asked her to let him have a look inside and, at first, she said no. 'It'd be more than my job's worth. Nobody's supposed to know what we do.'

'You are a silly.' He laughed and pulled her around to face him. 'Everyone in Silvertown is aware of what the factory does.'

'That's as may be, but it don't mean I have to let you see inside.'

He took her into his arms and kissed the point of her nose. 'What harm will it do?' He kissed her right eye, then her left one.

'For all I know you might be a German spy.'

He held her back from him and looked into her eyes. 'Do you think I am a spy?'

She looked away and mumbled, 'How do I know what a spy looks like?'

'Well, he wouldn't look like me, I'm sure,' he said, a hint of exasperation in his voice. 'I am only a news reporter trying to do my job. Nobody got in Conan Doyle's way when he wrote about a munitions factory. *The Annandale Observer* published his Moorside article last month, so I could do the same as he did, and give it another name.' He gave her a slight shake and released her from his arms. 'If that's how you feel, perhaps we shouldn't see each other any more.'

'I'm sorry, I'm sorry. I've never met any reporters before, and I thought it strange you wanted to get into the factory.'

He relaxed and pulled her into his arms again. 'I will be able to write a better article if you show me where everything takes place, and there's been so much in the newspapers about us not having enough ammunition for our men at the front. It's bad for morale that, so I need to prove we are doing something to increase the supply.' He hugged her tight. 'But if you don't want to do your bit and help – well, the public will have to go on believing we can't provide our fighting men with what they need.'

He whispered endearments to her, stroked her, made love to her. By the end of the evening, she agreed to do what he wanted.

'It will have to be Friday,' she said, 'after everyone's finished for the week. The chemist on duty will be in the lab, and Albert, the night watchman, should be in his hut. If you sneak past him, I'll make sure the side door's unlocked.'

Friday was dark, the moon obscured by clouds, which suited him nicely.

'This is the melt-pot room,' she said after she let him in. 'This is where the trinitrotoluene is melted before they pour it into the casings.'

'Isn't that dangerous? TNT is an explosive.'

She shrugged her shoulders. 'Not according to the bosses. They say an awful lot more heat would be needed before that could happen.'

'You're a very brave girl.' He pulled her into his arms and kissed her long and hard before he strangled her.

With a last glance at the fire, he turned and ran for the door. It slammed shut behind him. He kept on running until he rounded the side of the building and passed the watchman's hut, where Albert lay slumped on the floor, before slowing to a fast walk when he reached the road. It wouldn't do to draw attention, but he wanted to get as far away from the factory as he could before the blaze became an inferno.

He had timed it well. The factories had closed for the weekend. The shopkeepers had pulled down their shutters. And most folks would be having their evening meal or enjoying a pint at one of the many pubs.

He hurried on and had just passed the Fire Station on North Woolwich Road when the crackle of flames, and the heat searing his neck and arms, forced him to look back. The windows of the factory glowed red, the flames behind them flickering and spiralling in a macabre dance.

A distant shout alerted him to the danger he was in, and he darted up a side street where he would not be so easily observed. The clang of the bell on the fire engine beat in his ears, getting louder and louder. Doors opened. Men, women and children tumbled out of their houses onto the pavement, staring aghast at the factory a few streets away.

Men rushed from door to door, banging and shouting, 'The factory's on fire.'

More people joined them and soon there was a crowd of panic-stricken people, all running. He ran with them. There was safety in crowds.

Yellow, orange, and red flames leapt from the roof. Sparks rose and fell back to the ground, like shooting stars, smoke billowed upwards in great clouds, and the stink of burning chemicals stung his nostrils. But still he ran. While behind him the blaze increased, turning the evening sky crimson.

Victoria Dock was on his right when the first explosion came. The ground shook, buildings collapsed, and sparks showered the area, starting smaller fires where they landed. A fiery glow bathed everything in a blood-red vision of hell, silhouetting the houses left standing against the inferno. Then the second blast, louder, more spectacular, filled the sky with a display that would put Guy Fawkes to shame. A sizzling lump of flying metal flew past his head, singeing his hair and embedding itself in the road in front of him. The flour mills in the Victoria Dock crumbled under the force of the blast, and a gasometer at the other side of the river on the Greenwich Peninsula exploded, sending a glowing fireball sky-high.

His lungs felt as if they were exploding but he turned and ran. Ran for his life.

2

Sally

'Be a love, and pop out the back and get some milk from the food safe.' Sally's mother wiped her floury hands on her apron.

It was Sally's sixteenth birthday and her mother was baking her a cake, although goodness only knows where she obtained the flour and eggs. But Silvertown was a place where neighbours helped each other. No doubt they rallied around to find the necessary ingredients.

She grasped the iron hook resting in the fireplace and swung the trivet hob towards her. Soup, bubbling in the pot, spat angry droplets on the burning coal. The hook, which she dropped into the fender, left a residue of soot on her fingers, and she rubbed her hands with the towel draped over the fireside chair.

'You coming with me?' She held a hand out to the toddler playing with a wooden train on the rag rug. Molly's fascination for fire worried Sally who feared her sister might burn herself if left to her own devices.

Molly's face lit up. Still holding the toy, she scrambled to her feet. Sally leaned over and picked her up, enjoying the feel of the squirming body in her arms. How was it possible to love a child so much? Particularly someone so tiny and doll-like, with her mass of red-gold curls, blue eyes that melted her heart, and a curiosity any back-alley cat would find hard to match.

'An afterthought,' said Dad when she was born, 'another mouth to feed and clothe.' This was at a time when the family was struggling to survive. How were they to know that soon they would be at war with the Hun and everything would change.

Sally missed her father after he left home to join the fighting. She didn't know where he was, except it was somewhere foreign, but she feared it was France. 'Don't worry,' he said when he boarded the troop train. 'It should all be over by Christmas.' That was more than a year ago, and two Christmases had come and gone.

Pushing thoughts of her father from her mind she hoisted Molly into a more comfortable position on her hip before stepping outside the back door. Mum was waiting for the milk.

The food safe in the dark corner to the right of the door, was illuminated by a strange light. The sky above glowed crimson, and smoke tickled her nose and caught in the back of her throat. A bell clanged in the distance, and the sound increased until it seemed the noise came from the next street.

All thought of the milk left her and she rushed back into the house. 'Fire,' she gasped. 'The sky is the strangest colour of red I've ever seen, there's a horrible smell of burning, and the fire engine bell is deafening.'

'Is it the factory?' Her mother grabbed the edge of her apron and scrubbed the flour from her hands.

'I don't know. But we can see it from the front of the house.' Sally wrenched the door open, unable to suppress a gasp of terror at the sight of flames leaping from the factory roof.

'Best get out of there, lass.' Geordie, their next door neighbour ran past her brandishing a stick which he used to thump each door he passed, shouting, 'Fire, fire. The factory's on fire.'

'Mum, Mum, we have to leave.' Her words tumbled out in a rush. 'Before it blows.'

'I'll get the coats,' her mother said.

'We don't have time.'

But she was already returning with them over her arm.

'Hurry, hurry!'

Her mother turned to lock the door.

'There's no time for that.' She grasped her mother's hand. 'Don't you understand. If the factory blows there won't be any house left. Now run.'

Men, women and children erupted from houses. Fear permeated the air like something visible you could reach out and touch. The crackle of the blaze, the clanging bell of the fire engine, and the screams and shouts of the panicked crowd combined, heightening the urgency to flee from the conflagration.

Sally dragged her mother along the street while she balanced Molly on her hip. Her breath whistled out of her chest in painful gasps but she kept on running. She'd worked in the factory long enough to understand how dangerous this fire was. At any moment it could explode, taking all the houses and everyone in the vicinity, sky high.

They must have run more than a mile before she was forced to stop. Unable to retain her hold on Molly, the child slid down her hip to the ground. Sally bent over, hands on her knees, she no longer had enough breath to keep on running.

'Have we come far enough? Are we safe?' Her mother hoisted the toddler into her arms and cradled the child's head against her neck.

Sally straightened. 'I don't know, but my legs are like jelly and I had to stop. We'll go on in a minute.'

She leaned against the wall, out of the way of the mass of people continuing to run, and that was when she saw him on the opposite side of the road. He'd stopped to look back at the inferno. But Rosie wasn't with him. Her friend had talked about her date with the reporter tonight. 'Ever so posh, he is,' Rosie said. So, where was Rosie?

The force of the factory exploding pushed all thoughts of Rosie and her boyfriend from Sally's mind.

3

Kirsty

Ixworth Place Section House, two miles further east from the headquarters of the Women's Police Service at Little George Street, provided bed and board for London's women police. This was the place Kirsty Campbell called home. She had been a policewoman for more than two years, ever since the two main suffragette societies abandoned their militant activities, at the start of the war, to form England's first women's police service. Her move from the Women's Freedom League to become one of London's first policewomen, had been effortless.

Today's patrol had been uneventful, evening and night ones were more exciting. Darkness lent itself to all kinds of disreputable activities. However, whether or not the patrols were uneventful, it made no difference to the effect on her feet.

With an effort, she forced her unyielding leather boots off and massaged her toes. Next, she removed her skirt and jacket, rubbing her body vigorously to relieve the itch of the coarse material. She didn't mind the roughness of her uniform, nor the itch. She was proud to wear it as a serving woman police constable.

Before the war, such a thing would have been unthinkable, but now, women were doing all sorts of jobs usually reserved for men.

The wooden floorboards chilled her bare feet, but she resisted enclosing them in shoes until she was ready to leave her room to find something to eat. There was a kitchen in the section house, and Kirsty shared the cooking task with three of her friends because the warden in charge of the building did not provide meals.

Martha grinned at her when she entered the room. 'I managed to persuade the butcher to part with four meat pies,' she said. She ladled potatoes onto a plate beside one of the pies.

Kirsty nodded her thanks, grabbed a knife and fork, and pulled a chair over to the table. She sliced the pie in half, savouring the aroma, before cutting a smaller section and popping it into her mouth.

'What do you think about our new orders?' Martha sat down opposite her.

She waited until she finished chewing. 'It should be exciting.'

'Where is Gretna anyway?'

'I don't think we're supposed to mention the name,' Kirsty said, 'but it's on the west coast of Scotland.'

'Interesting. I haven't been back there since we left in 1911. Will you take time to visit your parents in Dundee?'

Kirsty frowned. 'What would be the point? What would I say to them? I'm sorry I left six years ago! That would be a lie because I'm not.' She pushed a potato around the plate. 'They disapproved of me then, they will disapprove of me now.'

'Maybe they've changed. Maybe they'd like to see you now.'

Kirsty snorted. 'And pigs might fly.' She was unable to keep the note of bitterness out of her voice.

She had hardly finished speaking when there was a rumble and the building shook. Her plate slid towards the edge of the table forcing her to make a grab for it. 'That was close,' she said to Martha who was retrieving the contents of the sideboard from the floor.

Ethel, who had eaten her evening meal earlier and had gone to polish her boots and belt in readiness for her early shift the next day, stuck her head around the dining room door. 'Who's with me to go and see where the bomb landed?'

Kirsty laid her plate on the table. 'It must be nearby, the house shook with the impact.'

She pushed past the cluster of policewomen congregated at the open front door and stepped outside, but was unable to see any damage nearby, nor any Zeppelins hovering overhead; however, the sky was an eerie red colour like nothing Kirsty had ever seen before.

'What's happened? We thought it was a bomb.'

One of the women said, 'It's an explosion of some sort. I was coming off shift when the blast almost knocked me off my feet and the whole sky lit up. Whatever it is, seems to be in the east of the city, over by the dock area.'

'Zeppelins, do you think?'

'Probably, although I didn't notice any.'

They stood for several minutes watching the deep red glow spread over the entire city.

'The docks must be on fire,' someone said.

'That's more than ten miles away.' The speaker shrugged. 'No danger of it spreading here.'

Kirsty remained at the door and watched long after the group dispersed, wondering what kind of blaze was big enough to redden the sky over all London. She couldn't help wondering what size of a bomb would be capable of doing that, and how much damage had been left in its wake.

Eventually, she returned inside to eat the remainder of her now cold meal and to throw herself in bed afterwards, where she tossed and turned for the rest of the night.

Kirsty woke with a start the next morning. She looked at the clock and groaned, roll call was in ten minutes. She'd never be ready in time and she hated getting black marks.

There was no time to wash so she grabbed the facecloth from the wash stand next to her bed and scrubbed her face. A cat's lick her old nanny had called it. At least she'd folded her clothes last night so they wouldn't be creased, and her boots and belt were shining. She scrambled into her shirt, lifting her chin to button it tight to the neck, then secured her tie under the collar before stepping into her skirt, nearly overbalancing as she did so. Her stiff leather boots were a struggle to pull on, and the laces insisted on tying themselves in knots. She was still fastening her jacket buttons as she raced down the corridor.

She stopped at the duty room door. Blast, her hair wasn't combed, but her hat should hide it until she had a chance to attend to it later on.

'I am glad you could join us, Campbell,' Sergeant Gilbert said in a withering tone.

Kirsty slid into position at the end of the line of policewomen. 'Yes, ma'am,' she mumbled.

'Don't let it happen again.'

'No, ma'am.'

The sergeant picked up a piece of paper from the desk behind her. 'Those of you allocated your shifts will proceed as normal, but Campbell, Fairweather, Stewart, and Dakers, you will proceed to Silvertown where there has been an explosion. Your main task will be to document the fatalities and list those injured in the blast, but you will also provide support and assistance to the population wherever it is needed. You will work in conjunction with the rescue teams.' She laid the paper back on the desk. 'Dismiss.'

'Anyone got a comb?' Kirsty asked, removing her hat as soon as the sergeant left the room. She took the one Ethel held out, and dragged it through her short auburn hair. 'Thanks,' she said returning it. 'Now, who knows anything about this explosion at Silvertown?'

'I'm just off night shift and there's a lot of talk on the streets.' Doris yawned. 'Apparently the munitions factory went up, and most of Silvertown has been flattened. I don't envy you your job this morning.'

Kirsty shivered. She would prefer to be out on patrol.

4

MI5

Captain Vernon Kell winced as he eased himself out of his chair. His back was playing up again. It was always at its worst when sitting. Thinking about the events of last night, the frown between his eyebrows deepened. No intelligence reports had been received concerning the Silvertown factory, but that did not necessarily rule out enemy action.

He crossed the room and opened the door to the outer office. Melville, his senior detective and the best investigator in his employ, was leaning over the clerk's desk examining one of the cards from the index.

Melville was a good man, no longer young, but showing no sign of seeking retirement. He was tall, as befitted a former police superintendent, but stocky with it. His bushy moustache and receding hair were grey, the only real indication of his age. Despite his height, he had the ability to blend in and remain unnoticed when he wanted to. This made him a successful agent.

Superintendent William Melville, the former head of the Special Branch, left the Met in 1903 to become an investigator for the War Office. This was six years before the Secret Service Bureau, now known as MI5, was established with Kell in charge, and he had proved his worth many times over.

'Ah, Melville,' Kell beckoned him into his room. 'You've heard about the Silvertown explosion, I take it.'

'Yes, sir. Terrible business. I sent Fitzgerald to see what he could find out and he got back not long ago. His report states that much of the district was wiped out.'

Kell stroked his moustache. 'The Prime Minister asked for a briefing. What can I tell him?'

'Fitzgerald reported back that it's difficult to make sense of what happened because the situation is still confused. However, the emergency services are starting to move in, and First Aid stations have been established. Shelter is being provided for people at churches, boys clubs and the Seamen's Missions. Apart from that, there's not much to tell, sir. We were not aware of any activity in the dock area, most of the intelligence has been coming from the ports recently.'

'Did he discover anything else of interest, William? What are the people saying?'

A flash of pleasure lit up the older man's face because Kell rarely used Melville's first name. 'It's not good, sir. Fitzgerald reported more than a hundred people were killed, and thousands of buildings damaged, some of them just ruins now. Rumours are widespread – some are blaming it on a Zeppelin bomb, others that it was the work of a German spy. Most likely, it was an accident.'

'We can rule out the Zeppelin theory, there were no air raids last night. It could have been a German spy but there is no information to confirm that. So that just leaves accident as the cause. I hope to God that's what it was. The last thing we want is a spy running amok and blowing up munitions factories.'

Silence fell while the two men thought.

'Do we know where Dietger Leclercq went after he left Falmouth?'

'No, sir. We lost track of him.' Melville fiddled with his watch chain. 'It's a possibility he is responsible, sir. But it doesn't seem his style.'

'Nevertheless, worth considering.'

'Yes, sir.'

'You say you've dispatched Fitzgerald to the disaster site, but I want you to visit as well. Find out everything you can. We need to know whether or not this is the work of a saboteur.'

'Yes, sir. Right away, sir.'

Kell waited until Melville left the room, then selected a folder from his desk and put it in his attaché case. He straightened his uniform jacket, plucked his cap off the coat stand and placed it carefully on his head. The time had come to attend to the Prime Minister's briefing.

Kell made an imposing figure as he left his office in Charles Street and strode in the direction of Downing Street. His erect bearing gave no indication of the pain radiating from his spine, while his purposeful expression masked his inward trepidation. He was a shy man and, although he never experienced problems with leadership, he had to make an effort to communicate on a social level. Not that his meeting with the Prime Minister would be a social one. He would expect a briefing on what MI5 could offer in relation to the spy problem, and how something like the explosion at Silvertown might be circumvented in the future.

The last time Kell briefed a Prime Minister on the work of MI5 was at the Committee of Imperial Defence in March 1914, before the start of the war. At that time, he presented exhibits, lists of foreign agents arrested and prosecutions made. The outcome had been that his staff doubled by the end of the year. He was less hopeful about this meeting following the Silvertown disaster.

Part of his nervousness arose because Asquith was no longer Prime Minister. When he was ousted in December, Lloyd George took his place. Kell had not got the measure of Lloyd George yet and this led to uncertainty on how to present his report.

On arrival at Downing Street, he was shown into the Prime Minister's study. A large oblong room with four beige upholstered armchairs filling the space at one end, and a round polished table, surrounded by eight cloth-covered straight-backed chairs at the other. Three long windows lined one wall while bookcases were positioned against the remaining walls.

Lloyd George sat at the table studying some papers spread out in front of him. He did not look up immediately, but when he did, Kell, struck by the piercing nature of his gaze, felt even more insecure.

'Sit, sit.' He pointed to one of the chairs. 'I plan to visit Silvertown today, so what can you tell me about this explosion? Is it sabotage?'

'There are rumours to that effect, sir.' Kell shifted in the chair trying to find a comfortable position. 'These are yet to be clarified. I have dispatched two agents, Melville and Fitzgerald, to Silvertown to investigate.'

'Hmm. Don't know Fitzgerald, but Melville's a good man.'

'One of my best, sir.'

'What information do we have about foreign agents operating in Britain at the present time?'

'We have identified several suspects, but there is insufficient evidence to make arrests as yet. The Port Control section, established last year, is producing results and agents are either being picked up or put under observation when they land.' Kell hesitated, reluctant to tell the Prime Minister about Dietger Leclercq, but he had no option. 'One agent arrived at Falmouth several weeks ago. We put him under surveillance but he managed to evade us.'

'You are not aware of where he is?'

'No, sir, but we think we know where he might be heading. Hinchley Cooke, my agent at Falmouth, interrogated the young woman he had been residing with. According to her, Leclercq talks in his sleep and he mentioned Greta. She thought he meant another woman and told him to leave. We think she misheard, and what he said was Gretna.'

Lloyd George thumped the table and jumped to his feet. 'He must be stopped. That is our biggest munitions factory.'

'The matter is in hand, sir. I intend to dispatch two of my best undercover operatives to Gretna. I am sure we will manage to prevent anything happening.'

'You had better be right.'

5

Kirsty

The scene at Silvertown turned out to be worse than anything Kirsty imagined. Along the river bank, stumps of buildings pointed fingers to the sky, and she found it hard to think the wreckage, which seemed to stretch for miles, had once been homes where workers lived, ate, and slept. Some houses furthest away from the blast site still stood, either as empty shells or ruins, but all with roofs in various stages of collapse, and black holes where once there were windows. Even the worst bomb sites didn't match the destruction here, and Kirsty wondered if this was what a battlefield looked like.

'I've never seen anything like it,' she said.

Trickles of smoke rose from isolated areas, and firemen directed their hoses on anything that looked as if it might be smouldering. Men shouted to each other as they searched derelict properties. Some of them sobbed as they tore at heaps of rubble. Further down the road, WRI women dispensed cups of tea from an open-sided truck.

Kirsty laboured for breath. She tried to convince herself it was the smell of smoke and burning affecting her, but that wasn't true. The desolation of what lay before her, the drama and desperation permeating everything like a physical entity, grabbed her mind and her heart. Tears weren't far away, but she suppressed them. She must be professional. She had to do her job.

'The town hall must be around here somewhere,' she said, in a voice, shaky and subdued and lacking confidence, reflecting how the scene affected her.

'I can see Red Cross trucks and ambulances over there.' Florence also sounded shaken.

Martha and Ethel had not said a word since they got off the omnibus, and Kirsty could only imagine they were similarly affected by the aftermath of the explosion.

Turning her back on the ruins of what was once a thriving community, she walked in the direction of Florence's pointing finger.

An ambulance, with blaring siren, screeched past them as they drew nearer, other ambulances clustered around the front of the building. Red Cross workers unloaded boxes of supplies from their trucks and carted them inside. A variety of other vehicles squatted in front of the official looking building which was a hub of activity outside and chaotic inside.

'Do you think we are in the right place?' Ethel seemed overwhelmed by what she saw.

Trestle tables loaded with blankets, clothing and food, filled the large open room while harassed women attempted to deal with the demands of desperate families. Bewilderment and confusion hung over everything, easily seen in the dazed expressions of the men, women, and children seeking to survive, following the loss of their homes and possessions.

Kirsty strode to one of the nearest tables. 'Is this the town hall?'

The Red Cross worker nodded without looking up. 'I think there is still space at the scout hall.' She handed a blanket to the woman in front of her.

The woman grabbed it with one hand and a toddler with the other before hurrying off.

'Sorry,' the Red Cross worker said. 'The situation here is manic. So many people have nowhere to go.'

Kirsty nodded. 'I can understand that. I would like to help with that side of things but we've been instructed to document the fatalities and injuries.'

'That's an impossible task. Many people who have been injured or killed are still lying among the wreckage, and many of those taken to hospital haven't been identified yet.' She gestured to the door. 'I suppose the best way to go about it is to talk with the survivors. They will be aware of who is missing. And you'll find them scattered throughout the borough in churches and halls. I wish you luck.' She picked up some blankets and offered them to the next family in the queue.

'I take it you heard,' Kirsty said.

Florence, Ethel, and Martha all nodded.

Kirsty sighed. 'We'd better find someone to give us a list of the places where people have been sent, and then we can divide them between us. That way we will cover more ground.'

'I'll stay here and set up a station where people can report,' Florence said, 'and I'll find something to make a notice board where we can post the names of those missing.'

'Good idea,' Kirsty said. 'Shall we get started?'

After two days talking to the survivors, listing the dead and documenting the missing, exhaustion overtook Kirsty making her long for some time to herself to recover. She'd witnessed grief, sorrow, and despair, but overriding that was the overwhelming optimism and bravery of the Eastenders.

Sergeant Gilbert, normally brusque and forbidding, nodded her approval of their work at Silvertown. 'I've pinned up next week's duty roster,' she said, 'you might want to check it.'

Kirsty joined Martha at the notice board in the front hall.

Martha squeezed her hand. 'I see we've been given the day off tomorrow.'

'Thank goodness for that,' Kirsty replied. 'I'm on the verge of collapse. It will give me time to get my strength back so I'll have enough energy to catch the train for Gretna on Tuesday.'

Martha nodded. 'I wonder what it will be like.'

'An adventure.' Kirsty grinned despite her tiredness. 'Something different.'

'Don't forget it's a munitions factory, and after what we've seen, it might not be the safest place.'

'I don't think we enlisted in the Women's Police Service to be safe,' Kirsty said.

The front door clattered open and two policewomen hurried in, slamming the door shut behind them.

'Oh, good,' Doris said. 'The roster's up.' She frowned. 'I'm on duty at Silvertown tomorrow.' She turned to Kirsty. 'You've been there, what's it like?'

'Tragic, you want to help, but you don't know how. But the little you can do is appreciated, and each expression of thanks leaves you with a warm glow.'

'The talk on the streets is that the King and Queen, and the Prime Minister went to the disaster area today.'

'Yes, I heard that too, but I didn't see them. I was too busy visiting the various places where people sought shelter. I found it heartbreaking.'

Kirsty thought of the final place she visited. The gaping hole in the front of the church left the roof tilted at a dangerous angle, but the hall at the rear was intact. Women and children sat and lay on the floor, with what little possessions they'd managed to save piled around them. Most of them seemed dazed and bewildered: however, a small group had gathered around an organ and the chorus of *Keep the Home Fires Burning* echoed around the hall. Kirsty had to smile at their choice of song, it was typical of the Eastenders' sense of humour.

'In some ways, I wish I could go back.' She turned away from the notice board to hide the tears in her eyes. The help she'd given had been minuscule.

6

Dietger

Dietger Leclercq sealed the envelope which he addressed to Mevrouw Agnete Claessens in Rotterdam. Should it fall into the wrong hands it was simply a letter from a devoted son to his mama. The message gave no clue that Mama was actually Hilmar Dierks, a name familiar to England's intelligence community. Dierks and his partner Heinrich Flores were responsible for most of the German spies operating in Britain, although they remained safely out of reach in Rotterdam.

The envelope nestled, out of sight, in his inside jacket pocket when he left the hotel. On the reverse of the letter to Mama, the report of his visit to Plymouth and the Devonport Dockyard was inscribed in invisible ink.

He merged with the flow of people on the pavement. Experience had taught him the best place to hide was in the midst of a crowd. Several of his counterparts had been caught because they preferred more secluded areas, and Dietger had no intention of risking his freedom and his life by making this mistake.

The barber shop, situated in a side street, was popular with men from the area which made it safe. Dietger grabbed a newspaper and sat in one of the leather chairs lined up along the back wall. He riffled through the pages but they contained no mention of last night's disaster at Silvertown. The English were good at censoring information they did not want made public. It made no difference, the news always got out and several versions of the explosion were circulating already. Rumour had that effect, magnifying and elaborating the truth.

At last, it was his turn. 'A hot shave,' he said. 'Make it a close one.'

'As you wish, sir.'

He waited until the barber was tucking the dry towel into the collar of his shirt, before slipping him the envelope. The man, adept at sleight of hand, turned to hold another towel under the hot tap and the envelope was nowhere to be seen. Wringing the excess water out, he wrapped it around Dietger's face and neck until only his nose was showing. 'Is that hot enough for you, sir?' he said.

Dietger mumbled his assent.

After a few moments, the barber removed the hot towel and set to work with the open razor. 'The meeting is arranged,' he murmured. 'The information is in your pocket.'

Dietger, resisting the urge to hurry, strolled back to the hotel. Once inside, in the privacy of his room, he examined the folded piece of paper, memorized the time and the address, then placed the paper in the grate, struck a match and burned it.

The Irish Republican Brotherhood had been useful in the past, but like him, they preferred to keep a low profile and their meetings frequently moved venues. Arranging to meet could be complicated. But he needed their assistance. It was essential to have an inside man to help him access the Gretna munitions factory.

Several agents had provided reports on England's other factories. Their geography, size, what type of munitions they produced and a lot of the finer detail.

Information on Gretna was less available, and the problem arose because the establishment was not like other munitions factories. Instead of being a single factory building or even a cluster of buildings grouped together, it was a facility, stretching from Longtown in the north of England to Dornock in Scotland. As far as he knew, the factory site stretched along the coast of the Solway Estuary for nine miles, and munitions were manufactured in buildings hidden from general sight.

The last agent who tried to get inside the site had been

detained and the difficulties inherent in gaining access seemed insurmountable.

With the Irish Brotherhood's help, he might succeed where others failed.

7

Aidan

Aidan Maguire never told Mary about his meetings with The Irish Brotherhood; what she didn't know wouldn't hurt her. This was why he always waited until after she left for her job as a barmaid at The Black Lion before he slipped out of the house.

Tonight was no different. As soon as he thought it safe he pulled on his jacket, stuck a flat cap on his head and adjusted the peak so that most of his face was in shadow, before he ventured outside.

The streets were in darkness but he walked close to the wall where the shadows were even denser. He had been in London less than a month but knew his way around better than any alley cat, which was just as well, because the Brotherhood never met in the same place twice.

The narrow passage between two semi-derelict buildings yawned in front of him. Unable to see where he walked, he trailed his fingers along the wall until he came to a door. This must be the place. He rapped on the door, three slow knocks then two fast ones. After a few minutes, the door creaked open and he slipped inside.

He followed a shadowy shape up a flight of stairs and into a room almost as dark as the street outside. Some of the Brotherhood were paranoid about being seen and recognized. He felt his way into a chair and sat.

'Welcome, my son,' said the shadow on his left. 'This will be our last meeting before you leave.'

Aidan nodded.

'Your friends at Gretna, you experienced no trouble contacting them?'

'None,' Aidan said. 'They've fixed me up with a job and

a room.'

'Good, good,' the voice said. 'I have someone here I want you to meet. He has business in Gretna.'

The man beckoned to someone standing in front of the window.

Aidan, unable to distinguish anything, apart from the fact he was well dressed and younger than anyone else in the room, narrowed his eyes in an attempt to see better.

'I am pleased to make your acquaintance,' the stranger said.

The handshake, short and gentle with fingers lacking warmth, riled Aidan. Although he had nothing to base it on, it reminded him of an outmoded Irish upper-class who treated working men like dirt. Everything about this man made him uneasy, his dismissive handshake, the way he held himself, and the stink of his hair pomade. This was no working class man. With difficulty, he resisted the urge to crush the man's hand in the firmest shake he could muster.

'What do I call you?'

The man shrugged. 'That is immaterial. I answer to many names. You will know me when I come to you.'

Aidan tried to place the accent. It wasn't Irish, nor was it English.

The brother next to him said, 'Our friend has helped the Irish cause in many ways. In return, we provide assistance to him when he requires it. He will contact you in Gretna when the time is right.'

'What will I have to do?'

'Whatever he asks. The thing to remember is that it will benefit the cause.'

'When do you wish me to go?'

The brother gestured to another shadowy shape at the opposite side of the room. A man shuffled forward and placed a brown paper parcel tied with string, on Aidan's knee.

'You will find what you need inside.' He reached into the pocket of his jacket and pulled out an envelope. 'This contains train tickets for Gretna and money for your expenses. You travel on Tuesday. Details and instructions are in the envelope. You will leave now and prepare for your journey, and you will tell no one where you are going.'

Aidan rose and followed his guide down the stairs. He stepped out into the stygian blackness of the alley.

'God go with you,' the man mumbled before he closed the door.

Aidan stood for a moment, the parcel tucked underneath his arm. The Brotherhood had been vague about the job they wanted him to do in Gretna. He fingered the envelope nestled in his pocket hoping the instructions inside made his task clearer.

Dietger Leclercq waited until Aidan left the room before asking, 'Is he the right man for the job?'

'He is the best we can offer.'

Dietger frowned. He had sensed Aidan's unease when they shook hands and wondered if he could trust him.

'He is a patriot,' the man continued, 'he will do anything for the cause. He fought on the barricades at the Post Office in Dublin last Easter and spent time imprisoned at Frongoch. I have it on good authority that Michael Collins trusts him.'

'Will he keep his head in a crisis?'

The man shrugged. 'He is fanatical about the cause which makes him volatile. But I believe you can trust him.'

'I hope you are right.' Dietger picked up his hat and coat. 'A lot depends on his reliability.'

Aidan wasn't entirely comfortable with his new task. However, he had come a long way since he fought on the Post Office barricades, and he believed fervently in the cause. Ireland must be freed from England's yoke, no matter the cost. And despite his imprisonment by the hated English, he was proud to have been part of the fight for Ireland's freedom.

In common with most of the others, released on the same

day, Aidan had nowhere to go except back home to Ireland. But he couldn't bear to return so soon after the failure of the rising. They had hoped for so much, a free Ireland, one no longer crushed into submission under the domination of the English. How did everything work out so horribly wrong? Many of his friends were dead, or like him, incarcerated in Frongoch or Reading prison.

Frongoch hadn't been so bad, though. The prison camp was where he met Michael Collins and became a member of the newly formed Irish Republican Army. Already the IRA was more organized than either the Irish Citizens' Army or the Irish Voluntary Force. There was hope for Ireland yet.

Chaos reigned on the day of his discharge from Frongoch. The Irishmen were excited at the prospect of returning home, but Aidan did not share their enthusiasm. What kind of life would he have on his return? He couldn't imagine the British authorities would allow him much freedom. He would be under observation all the time, one false move would be an excuse for the military to shoot him, and he desperately wanted to continue the fight. Besides, he had no one waiting for him, only his mother who was old and demanding and provided no love or protection for her son. Her voice, thick with complaints, sounded in his head. 'A son's duty is to look after his mother when there's no father left to do that.'

Father, that was a laugh, the old bugger had made his life a torment from the day he could walk and talk; a big man, ready with his fists and always spoiling for a fight, Aidan was glad when he dropped dead from a heart attack. His da didn't die immediately, though. Aidan still dreamed of that hand held up to him, and the plea, 'Help me, son.' But Aidan didn't help, instead, he walked away leaving his father lying in the snow at the side of the road. It was morning before the body was found.

The Irish Citizens' Army had been his saviour. The men became his family, and he often wished their leader, James Connolly, had been his father. He would never forgive the British for executing the man he idolized.

On that last day at Frongoch, Michael Collins pulled him aside, separating him from the other men busy gathering their belongings into bundles. The chatter carried on, the men laughing and joking at the prospect of leaving this bleak place.

'You sure you don't want to go home to Ireland?' Michael's hand on his arm was tight and unyielding.

'There's nothing for me there.'

'But you will carry on the fight here, in England, like we discussed.'

'Yes.' Aidan had never been more certain he wanted to strike back at the English. Pay them back for what they'd done to James Connolly and a lot of his friends.

'Good lad. I knew I could rely on you.' Michael Collins slapped his back. 'Now you know what to do when you get to London. You contact the Irish Republican Brotherhood, and they will supply you with funds and everything else you need.' He handed over a piece of paper. 'Memorize the names and addresses on that and then dispose of it.'

Aidan thrust the paper into his pocket. 'I'll be sure to do that.'

'You need to find your own place to stay. It's better for you to remain anonymous, and it wouldn't be safe to billet you with any of the IRB members in London.'

The two men shook hands, and Michael Collins left Aidan with a muttered, 'May the luck of the Irish be with you.'

The orderly line of discharged prisoners broke ranks when they reached Frongoch railway station, where the train taking them to freedom, panted, shuddered, and belched smoke into the damp Welsh air.

'On board! At the double!' The sergeant with the bristly moustache marched up and down the platform, seemingly as keen to get rid of his charges, as the Irishmen were at the thought of returning home.

Steam hissed menacingly as the men hurried to board the train, and sparks flew upwards from the engine's funnel, floating down again to land sizzling on top of the wet carriages. Aidan couldn't help thinking that the British would be pleased if the train, with its dilapidated wooden carriages, relics of the last century, were to catch fire and cremate everyone inside.

The men, desperate to leave Frongoch, pushed and jostled, fighting to get on and claim their space, while the soldiers poked and prodded, forcing them into the carriages.

Aidan could hardly breathe, rammed up against the end of the carriage into which the soldiers insisted on packing in more and more of the released captives. The sound of a multitude of Irish voices filled the air with their excitement at going home, an excitement Aidan didn't share, although he was delighted to have left Frongoch behind.

The journey from Wales to London seemed to take forever, and Aidan's ribs were crushed and sore long before it ended.

Exhausted after he left the train, he longed for somewhere he could relax and get his breath back. Outside in the street, he looked around for a handy pub, and The Black Lion seemed as good a place as any. It was there he had the good fortune to meet Mary, and she obviously fancied him, so he'd gone home with her.

But he never told her he would be moving on once he got his instructions from the Irish Republican Brotherhood. The less she knew about his plans, the better.

8

Beatrice

The locks snapped shut. Beatrice Jacobs slumped on the edge of the bed with her hand resting on the plain brown case, the memory of the last time she clicked a suitcase shut almost too painful to remember. It had been over two years ago and her mother had been telling her to hurry.

'We have to go now. There is no time to lose.'

Beatrice had never heard such a high level of anxiety in her mother's voice before, and it alarmed her.

'Calm down, Annemarie, you are much too agitated,' her father said in a soothing voice.

'But the Germans are only 26 kilometres away at Leuven, and the Jannsens, our next door neighbours, have already left. It is only a matter of time before they are here.' Annemarie grabbed her case with one hand and her hat with the other. 'Hurry, Beatrice. Hurry, Paul.'

'This is exciting,' Paul whispered to Beatrice. He was only fifteen and the German invasion, to him, was a big adventure.

Hugo Jacobs removed his rimless spectacles and glared at his son. 'We leave now, but we do it in an orderly fashion as we have always done.'

'Yes, Papa.' Paul's voice sounded meek, but Beatrice could see the sparkle in her brother's eyes, and hoped he would not get up to one of the tricks he was so fond of playing.

'Come, Annemarie.' He replaced his spectacles and took the case from her. 'Put your hat on, we must maintain standards after all.'

Annemarie donned her bonnet and inserted a hatpin through it and into her brown hair, although her fingers trembled so much she was in danger of piercing her head. Once her hat was secure she grasped her daughter's hand, and they stepped outside into the bright August sunlight.

Beatrice narrowed her eyes against the glare and flicked her dark hair away from the collar of her light blue jacket. As she waited for her father and Paul to join them she wondered how old her mother had been when she put her hair up. Perhaps she would ask permission to put hers up when they reached Paris. After all, she was twenty-two now, no longer a child.

'What will become of the house?' She watched her father turning the key in the lock.

'We will come back after the Germans are defeated,' he said, pocketing it.

The street was deserted. Houses, usually bustling with life, appeared strangely empty. It seemed to Beatrice that everyone had fled and they were the last to leave.

'We must hurry now,' her father said.

He picked up the suitcase and strode down the middle of the road. His pace increased until he was on the verge of running.

Beatrice walked faster to keep up with him, but the oppressive heat weighed on her and she found it difficult to ignore the stabbing pain in her chest with each breath she took. Sweat trickled between her breasts and her corset tightened. She glanced at her brother prancing along with his shirt collar unbuttoned and his jacket flying open. Momentarily envying his freedom, she fingered the neck of her blouse and, although aware it was not ladylike, she loosened the two buttons at her throat.

Turning the corner to the main boulevard was like entering a different country. A sense of panic and chaos enveloped the hurrying crowd as they battled past anyone who got in their way. The desperation they felt was plain to see on their faces. Dust from their feet spiralled upwards in a choking cloud. A group of young men fought at one side of the road, fists and clubs drawing blood, while the crowd, showing scant interest, continued to surge around both sides of them. Women grabbed their children, pulling them along, keeping a wide berth of the fighting youths. Old men hobbled past on sticks, others dressed in hospital gowns followed them. In the midst of the bedlam, families struggled with piles of belongings on handcarts and wheelbarrows, men shouting and women crying with the effort, while their distressed children sobbed and screamed as they tried to keep up.

Beatrice's hand tightened on her suitcase handle. She had never felt fear before, but now it was something tangible, she could sense it all around her and her breathing quickened. She drew closer to her father, almost pushing him over. He put his arm around her shoulders. 'It will be all right,' he said, hugging her. 'It will be all right.'

Beatrice believed him. He was Papa and the head of the family.

The street leading to the station was filled with hurrying people and their luggage. They pushed into the throng and were carried along with a tide of those determined to escape. But the building sense of hysteria, which turned normal law-abiding people into savages, scared her, although her father looked calm and in control.

Beatrice's heart was thumping in an alarming fashion by the time they arrived at the station entrance. She had heard horror stories of what the Germans did to women unlucky enough to fall into their hands. And the Germans were at Leuven. It would not take them long to arrive in Brussels.

The mood of the crowd turned ugly. People, who would normally be polite and pleasant, battled to reach the station's entrance doors. Fists flailed, walking sticks and parasols battered off heads and poked painfully into ribs. The strong prevailed, the weak were shoved aside.

Beatrice observed the worry etched into her father's face when he frowned at the melee in front of them, but he remained composed.

'Hold on to each other, we must not get separated.' He thrust the edge of his jacket into Beatrice's hand. Then, his natural reserve forgotten, her father barged through the mass of people thronging the station. She grasped the back of his jacket and followed, choking with the heat, the soot and smoke, and the sickly smell of sweat. When he reached the steaming locomotive he grabbed a carriage door, heaved her suitcase on board and pushed her after it.

Her mother was pushed on next, squeezing between the bodies already inside. But there was no sign of Paul.

Her mother fought her way back to the door of the carriage. 'Paul,' she screamed.

'You stay, I will go find him,' her father said.

'I am coming with you.' Her mother struggled out to the platform.

'No, you stay on the train.'

It was too late. Several men fought their way on, one of them throwing Beatrice's case out. 'No room for that,' he growled, and Beatrice did not argue because of the menacing look on his face. She was hemmed in now. No room to move and hardly any room to breathe, so all she could do was watch as her mother and father were swallowed up by the crowd.

That was the last time she saw her parents and her brother.

The journey was a nightmare which was about to get worse because her father had the tickets and money, and the angry ticket collector at Paris was shouting at her. No one had ever shouted at Beatrice before and she did not know what to do.

She was hot and tired. Her smart blue jacket and ankle-length skirt were creased and stained, her white, high-necked blouse stuck to her skin, and her hat had been lost on the train. Knocked from her head and trampled on. Tears trickled down her cheeks.

'Can I help you, Mejuffroux Jacobs?'

Beatrice looked up into the eyes of a dark-haired young man, not too much older than herself. He was handsome, with a pencil moustache, soft brown eyes, and a commanding appearance. Flustered, she glanced away again, but the only place to look was at the fat ticket collector whose walrus moustache waggled furiously as he gesticulated at her.

'I saw what happened in Brussels and you have no need to be alarmed. First, I introduce myself. I am Dietger Leclercq, I am from Antwerp, and a few years ago I was a student of Professor Jacobs at Leuven University, so I recognized him. He is your father?'

Beatrice nodded.

'He was a good tutor. He took time and was popular with his students, so I would like to help his daughter.' He gave a small bow and turned to the ticket collector. 'This young lady's father is following with the tickets so kindly let us through the barrier or it will be the worse for you, my man.'

After several more minutes of argument with the walrus moustachioed man, they were standing on the street outside the Gare du Nord.

'My thanks, Meneer Leclercq.'

He waved his hand. 'A pleasure, Mejuffroux Jacobs. May I now presume to ask what you plan to do?'

Beatrice hesitated. Without her parents to advise her she did not know how to proceed. At last, she said, 'My parents will be on the next train. I should wait for them.'

His expressive brown eyes saddened. 'I fear there will be no more trains. I rather think we were on the last one out of Belgium.'

'Oh!' Beatrice's shoulders slumped and despair swept through her. She shrugged helplessly. 'I will remain in Paris, then. Surely I will be safe here?'

'Not a good idea, I am afraid. The Germans will be intent on invading France. Paris will not be a safe place. Besides, now that there are no more trains to France, your parents will probably try to leave the country through Holland. My advice would be to travel to London and meet them there, and if it would not offend you, I could accompany you part of the way.'

Dietger left her when they reached Calais. 'I must go now,' he said, bending and brushing her fingertips with his lips. 'You will be safe in England.'

'But how can I repay you?' Beatrice felt the burden of the obligation she owed him weighing upon her.

'When we meet again you may be in better circumstances. We can think about repayment then. Until that time comes you must not worry about it.' He kissed her fingertips again. 'Bon voyage, Beatrice, the time has come for you to go.'

She struggled up the gangplank, one of the many refugees crowding onto the boat. Pausing on deck her eyes followed Dietger as he vanished into the throng of people below, and there was an unfamiliar ache in her chest.

'He does not come with you?' The stocky man with the bushy grey moustache was obviously not Belgian.

'Pardon,' she said, 'you are not comfortable with our language so we can speak in French or English, whichever you prefer.'

'I was simply observing that your man friend has not accompanied you.'

Beatrice shrugged. 'He is only an acquaintance who was kind enough to escort me to the boat. I have not travelled alone before.'

'You have friends in England?'

'Alas, no.' Beatrice shivered. She did not know what she would do when she landed in Britain, or what would become of her.

'A large number of refugees travel to England and arrangements have been put in place, so you have little need to worry.' He pondered for a time. 'You speak English well – there is hardly a trace of accent. You say you also speak French.'

'Yes, sir, I speak four languages, Dutch, English, French and German.'

'With so many refugees, I have need of an interpreter from time to time. I will contact you at the refugee reception centre, Alexandra Palace, which is where you will be taken on arrival in England. Until then, I wish you good day.'

Beatrice sighed. So much had changed in the two years

following her arrival in London. The man from the boat, William Melville, had been as good as his word. He sought her out, arranged for her billet with two elderly spinster sisters, and gave her regular work as an interpreter.

She owed him a lot, so when he suggested she go to Gretna, to work at the munitions factory, she agreed.

She heaved her suitcase off the bed. It was time to go, time to become William Melville's eyes in Gretna.

9

Aidan

Aidan Maguire tucked the edge of the farewell note behind the clock on the mantelpiece. Through the bedroom door, he glimpsed Mary's tousled hair, the only thing showing above the blankets. It would be an hour or two before she woke up, and by that time, he would be long gone. He hated goodbyes.

Ash spilled from the grate into the fender and coal shifted in the fireplace – the faint glimmer of a struggling flame already in its death throes. He took a last look around the room that had been home for him since his release from Frongoch prison camp.

When he arrived in London, Mary took him in and shared her bed. She would do nicely until it was time for him to move on, he'd thought at the time. But now that he was leaving he would not miss her, or even think about her, nor would she miss him. He would be replaced within the week with someone else willing to provide solace to her while her husband fought at the front.

Aidan strode through London's streets. It was a fair walk to the railway station but he was glad of the fresh air, although London's air was far inferior to Ireland's. Keeping his head down, he acknowledged no one. He disliked Londoners and detested London, maybe Gretna would be better. At least he would be joining more of his fellow countrymen there.

'There are good wages in Gretna,' Dermot's letter said. He'd known Dermot since they'd been at school together, and he didn't hold it against him that he left Ireland to work in England, instead of carrying on with the fight. After he wrote that to Dermot, his friend responded indignantly that Gretna was in Scotland, not England.

36

Arriving at the station he fought his way through the crowds on the platform. Most of the carriages were full, but he found space in the second carriage behind the engine. He threw his case on the rack, undid the buttons on his jacket and prepared to sit down.

The young woman in the corner seat moved nearer to the window to give him more room, but the elderly woman in the opposite corner glowered at him, perhaps she took umbrage because he unbuttoned his jacket. The woman's husband patted her arm and smiled politely at Aidan.

'You do not wear a uniform, sir,' he commented. 'You have a furlough, perhaps?'

Aidan bit back the retort that he would rot in hell first before he would join the British Army, and instead smiled pleasantly. 'I fear I am otherwise engaged in other important war work, sir.'

He settled back in his seat. They would have been outraged if he explained his war work was Ireland's fight for freedom from British rule, and that the two guns, given to him by the Irish Republican Brotherhood, nestled in his suitcase in the rack above their head.

10

Dietger

Dietger Leclercq put the scent and the talcum powder in his toilet bag, rolled the fine pens in a handkerchief which he then pushed through a hole in the valise lining, and last of all, he placed the lemon in his jacket pocket.

The lemon was a problem. He would have to get rid of it, but not here where it could be linked to him. It would not be the first time an agent had been arrested on the basis of the invisible writing materials he carried, and the lemon was a giveaway.

He fastened the catch on the top of the leather bag and checked the room one last time for anything he might inadvertently leave behind.

There was only the letter which he sealed in an envelope and tucked into his breast pocket.

The letter to his mama in Rotterdam mentioned his visits to see a Barrie play – 'Barrie is such a small, insignificant looking man,' he had written, 'but his plays are excellent.'

His news included the shows he had seen and the music halls he visited.

He added his impressions of Vesta Tilley and Marie Lloyd – 'lovely ladies, although Marie Lloyd is a bit saucy.'

No, there was nothing in the letter to arouse suspicion, however, his report, written on the back of it in invisible ink, was detailed

After paying his bill in cash he left the Savoy Hotel. Turning right, he dropped the lemon in the gutter and walked towards the barber's shop which acted as one of the postboxes he used to send information to his handlers in Rotterdam.

He would leave the envelope and have his moustache

shaved off before he went to catch his train.

Dietger Leclercq watched Beatrice until she vanished into the railway station. He thought back to the time he first met her, flustered and anxious, and being bullied by the ticket collector at the Gare du Nord. She had been beautiful then, and was even more beautiful now, with an air of self-assurance and maturity she had not possessed at the time. Back then she brought out his protective streak, but the feeling, this time, was less protective.

She passed him so close he could have reached out and touched her. But she did not recognize him and he did not want to startle her. She might think him a stranger molesting her and scream for help. The last thing he wanted to do was draw attention to himself.

Today, he was unrecognizable as the dapper and charming young man who rescued Beatrice in Paris. Gone was his moustache, and his clothes were those of a working man rather than the stylish suits he preferred to wear. His hair, no longer slicked back and shiny with pomade, was tousled and hidden beneath a flat cap. No wonder Beatrice passed by without a hint of recognition.

Dietger hurried after her. The suitcase she carried indicated she was heading for a train, and if he obtained a seat in the same carriage it would give them time to become reacquainted.

Despite his hurry, he hesitated before he entered the station. Over the years, he had learned to be cautious when entering crowded places. And it was just as well he did because leaning against one of the pillars was William Melville, one of Britain's most wily spycatchers.

Melville turned.

Dietger froze, expecting the spycatcher to inspect everyone arriving or leaving the station. Worried that his disguise would not be good enough he slipped behind the luggage trolley parked inside the entrance.

However, to his relief Melville was not paying attention

to the crowds. The secret agent seemed to focus on the fair-haired woman a few paces to his left, and when their eyes met, Melville gave an imperceptible nod towards Beatrice hurrying down the platform. The woman nodded and followed in Beatrice's wake.

Why was Melville having Beatrice followed? Dietger would have been aware if she was part of the spy network. Information had a habit of dribbling down, and he always ensured he was well informed. It was necessary in order to stay alive.

Mysteries intrigued him, and he determined to get to the bottom of it.

'What you doing skulking behind there?' The voice was harsh and female.

Dietger smiled. The special smile he used to charm women. 'I was checking my suitcase was here,' he said.

'And is it?' The voice was less harsh this time.

He tapped one of them. The label said, Carlisle. 'Yes,' he said, 'it is here, all safe and sound.'

The girl porter studied him. 'That's all right then. But I need to get these cases to the train, it'll be leaving soon.'

'I can help, if you like,' Dietger said. 'The trolley must be heavy to push, and I am catching the train in any case.'

'If it's not too much trouble.' The girl took hold of one side of the trolley's front bar.

Dietger grasped the other side and, after throwing his valise on top of the pile of suitcases, he started to push. 'No trouble at all,' he said.

Melville never gave them a second glance as they passed, but Dietger made sure the porter remained between him and the spycatcher. Nevertheless, he heaved a sigh of relief once they were on the platform.

As soon as they were level with the train's rear carriage the girl brought the trolley to a stop. She slid the doors open, revealing a large storage space evidently intended for baggage. Dietger jumped in, aware that this would take him out of Melville's line of vision.

'Pass the suitcases to me,' he said, 'and I will load them

in here.'

After he stacked the cases in the luggage van he stood in the door considering whether it was safe to emerge. Crowds of people still thronged the station, but he saw no sign of Melville.

'I had better find a carriage now.'

He jumped to the platform and kissed the tips of her fingers. Smiling to himself he left the bewildered girl and strode up the platform to find a seat as far away from Beatrice as possible. Sitting beside her was no longer a good idea because she was being followed, and he had no desire to reveal himself to one of Melville's cohorts.

11

Kirsty
Kirsty Campbell wriggled, trying to find a more comfortable position on the polished oak settle. It seemed hours since the court convened, and Florence seemed to have lapsed into a trance.

'I don't know why we bother,' Kirsty said, 'Mead will never allow us to give evidence.'

Florence shrugged. 'The Commandant expects us to come, even if only to make a point.'

'It's just so tedious. We do this over and over again when we know full well that Mead will never change his mind about allowing women into the courtroom.'

Leaning back, she rested her shoulders on the wall. She thought it laughable. As suffragettes the magistrates and judges showed no compunction in bringing them before the court to castigate and sentence them, yet as women police officers they were considered too sensitive to be allowed inside. Kirsty grimaced, remembering Mr Mead, the Marlborough Street magistrate announcing in his pompous way, 'No woman will ever be allowed inside my court.'

Florence lapsed back into her trance. Kirsty glared at the closed courtroom doors then turned away in disgust and concentrated on watching a sporadic sunbeam dance across the marble tiled floor of the large, echoing, entrance hall.

Constable Burns had already been called to give evidence. He was one of the few decent constables in the police force. However, his evidence would be worthless because he had been chatting and joking with one of the doxies when Kirsty and Florence found the two men cavorting in the bushes at Hyde Park. By the time Burns caught up with them, the men's clothing had been adjusted and they were protesting they had only been taking an evening stroll.

The double doors to the court opened and Burns exited. He shook his head.

'I knew it,' Kirsty snapped. 'They've got off with it.'

The two men she had last seen in the bushes at Hyde Park, emerged. The taller one looked over to the two policewomen and smirked. He raised his hat and said, 'Ladies!' They paused in front of the doors leading to the street and he said something to his friend. Both of them looked back smiling broadly, and their laughter could be heard after they vanished out of sight.

Kirsty suppressed her anger. 'Waste of time charging them.'

The wall clock chimed reminding her of the time. 'Oh, blast. The train, I must dash.'

Clasping a hand on her pudding bowl hat, she sprinted out the door.

No cabs or taxis were to be seen, so she continued to run. While she ran, she scanned the streets for some form of transport, but she traversed several streets before a taxicab trundled towards her.

She leapt onto the road, waving her arms.

'Reckon you must have a death wish, missie.' The cab driver leaned over and looked down at her.

'Train – station – late,' Kirsty gasped, each breath another knife piercing her chest.

The cabbie descended from his perch. 'In you go, missie. I'll get you there in time. Which railway station you going to?'

'Thank you.' Kirstie collapsed into the cab. 'Euston, please.'

Martha was waiting at the station entrance when Kirstie tumbled out of the cab.

'I thought you weren't going to make it,' she said. 'Better hurry, the train's almost ready to leave.'

'Sorry.' Kirsty thrust a shilling into the cabbie's hand and followed Martha into the concourse. 'The trial went on longer than I thought it would.'

Her friend stared at her in disbelief. 'You gave evidence?'

'You know as well as I do that's never a possibility when Mead's presiding? "No woman should be subjected to that kind of language",' Kirsty mimicked him. 'Even when the only witnesses are the women who observed the perverted behaviour taking place,' she continued bitterly. 'And, of course, the accused got off because there were no other witnesses.'

'Waste of time going to court when we all know we won't be allowed inside.'

'I know, but the Commandant insists we make the attempt.'

Martha grabbed her arm. 'This way,' she said, pulling Kirsty along. 'The train's due to leave so we'd best put a spurt on.'

Kirsty trotted behind Martha, dodging trolleys and piles of suitcases. A group of chattering soldiers blocked their way and they detoured around them. The whole world seemed as if it was either coming back from or going to some place. It had never been as busy as this before the war started.

Martha sped on in front and Kirsty ran faster to keep up. Smoke caught in her throat, and she could taste soot on the back of her tongue. At last, they reached the platform where a guard stood with his whistle and flag at the ready.

'Wait, wait,' Martha screeched at him. 'Our carriage is up near the engine.'

He made a show of looking at his pocket watch. 'One minute,' he growled, 'can't keep the train waiting for ever.'

Soldiers leaned out of windows whistling and cheering them on. 'There's room in here,' one of them shouted.

The train let out a belch of steam and smoke, seeming to judder on the rails. But they could see Ethel now, leaning out of the carriage window. She waved and opened the door, and the two of them scrambled inside to the sound of the guard's whistle.

Clutching their sides they looked at one another and laughed.

'God, I'm sweating after that,' Martha said.

'You should not take our Lord's name in vain,' a disapproving voice said. 'And besides, ladies do not sweat, they glow.'

Kirsty turned to look at the speaker; an attractive but prim looking young woman, clearly a new recruit whose uniform had obviously not yet seen any service.

'If you joined the Women's Police Service expecting it to be an organization of ladies, Lydia, then I hate to tell you, you're in the wrong profession.'

The young woman flushed. 'Just because I became a policewoman it does not mean I have to give up my values.'

Muffled laughter sounded behind Kirsty and she turned to see Ethel stuffing her fist into her mouth to smother the sound.

'Oh, rats,' Kirsty said. She tossed her hat into the rack, ran her fingers through her short auburn hair, and sat down beside her friend.

12

Beatrice

Beatrice heaved her suitcase onto the overhead rack before settling into her seat. She rested her elbow on the sill of the window frame, cupped her chin in her hand and surveyed the men and women on the platform. The crowds were thinning now as people boarded the train, and for a moment she thought she saw a familiar figure from her past. She blinked, and he was gone. She must have been mistaken.

Further down the platform the running figures of two lady police transported her back to when she first arrived in London.

The ferry from France had been crowded and the thought of going below decks repulsed her. With so many bodies it was bound to be even worse than the conditions on the train from Brussels to Paris. She found a corner on the deck where the engine fumes were not so strong and pulling her collar up she wrapped her hands around her body, and sat down.

The train from Folkestone to London was no better and by the time she arrived at St Pancras her clothes were sticking to her skin. Her hat had not survived the journey, and her long brown hair straggled over her face and onto her shoulders.

The platform was a heaving mass of people and the crowd pulled her along with them towards the station exit.

Bewildered, she stood outside wondering what to do and where to go. She had no money and no belongings apart from what she wore. Previously, there had been no time to think, she had been too busy running from the desperate situation in her homeland and travelling to safety. But was this safety? The direness of her plight struck her; the energy that kept her going seeped away, and despair set in. Her shoulders slumped and she leaned against the wall, watching her fellow travellers who all seemed to be going somewhere.

'Can I help you, dear?'

The smartly dressed woman's face showed concern.

'You look lost.'

Beatrice smiled at her. This was the first time anyone had spoken to her, or shown her any kindness, since the brusque man on the boat at Calais.

'It is my first time to London, it is somewhat overwhelming.'

'Ah, you've just come from the boat train then.'

Beatrice nodded.

'You are not British, although your English is excellent.'

'I am Belgian.'

The woman seemed to think for a few moments. 'Maybe I can help. A friend of mine has one of the restaurants near here, and I think he is looking for someone to serve tables. I am on my way to see him now. If you would care to accompany me you could make enquiries.'

Relief swept through Beatrice. It felt as if a physical weight slid off her shoulders, and fresh energy surged through her.

'Oh, I forgot to introduce myself,' the woman said. 'I am Mrs Baker. And you are?'

'Beatrice.' She held her hand out. 'I am Beatrice Jacobs and I am so happy to meet you Mrs Baker.'

Looking back now, she was amazed how gullible she had been. It was only the intervention of the two lady police which saved her from what her mother would have said was 'a fate worse than death'.

The women police running up the platform drew level with her carriage. Now she could see them more clearly, she realized that the younger one was the same person who had saved her on that terrible day two years ago.

William Melville hid behind a pillar to avoid Beatrice seeing him when she arrived. Blake followed close behind her and would soon be on board as well. He would not leave the station until after the train left.

His plan was working well.

Beatrice posed no problem when he met her at the Lyons Teahouse.

'I require you to do something for me. It would help me greatly,' he said as he offered her a cake from the cake stand. Cakes were a luxury in wartime London, but Lyons Teahouses always seemed to obtain a supply.

Beatrice nibbled a madeleine cake. 'Another translation job?'

'No something different this time. Perhaps if we walk in the park after you finish your tea I can explain to you. I would not want to be overheard.'

Melville escorted Beatrice along the busy street. He was not immune to the charms of an attractive woman, and he took pleasure in the many admiring glances cast in their direction. When they reached the park he pushed open the ornamental gates and stood back to let her pass through.

'This is most pleasant,' he said. 'A quiet oasis in the midst of busy streets.'

She nodded in agreement.

A breeze rustled through the trees bordering the path. He shivered and thrust his hands into his pockets because, despite the winter sun, a smattering of frost covered the grass.

They walked in silence following a meandering path until they found a park bench out of the main flow of walkers.

'We can sit here while I explain what I want you to do,' he said.

She sat, and although she said nothing her eyes were full of curiosity.

Her stillness discomfited him and he waited a few moments before he spoke.

'What I want you to do is be my eyes and ears at Gretna munitions factory.'

'I see. You want me to spy for you?'

'Yes. Will you do this for me?'

'What will this spying entail?'

'I think a nest of Irish revolutionaries operates at Gretna, and I want you to keep an eye on them.'

'Irish, not German!'

'That's right.'

'I am not sure how good a spy I would make,' Beatrice said, 'there are some things I would not be prepared to do in order to get information.'

'Ah!' Melville exhaled, his breath misting in front of him. 'But the revolutionaries I speak of are female.'

'I did not realize that women could be involved in revolutionary activities!'

Melville thought he detected a note of relief in her voice.

'You will do it?'

'You need to tell me more. What you want me to do and how I go about this task. I have never spied before.'

'These girls and young women I want you to keep an eye on are all members of Cumman an mBan, which in turn is an offshoot of the Irish volunteers. Their aim is to cut Ireland off from Britain so it can be an independent country and they are not averse to fighting for what they want.'

Melville plucked a fob watch from his pocket. 'I must go,' he said, 'another meeting.' He stood up. 'I have your consent?'

Beatrice nodded.

'I will be in touch with the arrangements and a list of names,' he said. 'You leave on Tuesday.'

Pleased about the success of his meeting with Beatrice, he smiled as he strode off in the direction of the park gate. His plan was working, because not only would Beatrice be keeping an eye on the Irish contingent, but she would be in a prime position should Dietger LeClercq decide to focus his activities on Gretna.

Now all he needed to do was set Blake up to follow Beatrice.

13

Sally

Sally Scott hugged her suitcase close when she saw the mass of people milling about on the station concourse. Trains letting off steam added to the noise battering her ears.

She had never been away from home before. She thrust her arm through her mother's. 'How do we know which train is the right one?' She shouted to make herself heard.

'Platform three, my love.'

Sally's head buzzed, with the racket, the fumes, and people hurrying here, there and everywhere. There seemed no pattern, but everyone seemed to know where they were going. Not like Sally, who relied on her mother to put her on the correct train.

They pushed through the milling crowds and at last arrived at platform three. They detoured around a trolley where a young woman unloaded cases and trunks to be stashed in the luggage van. Sally gripped her suitcase even closer to her body. She didn't want to let it out of her sight because it contained everything she possessed, which wasn't much, after the terrible explosion at Silvertown.

Her mother hustled her along the platform, ignoring the wolf whistles and catcalls, shouted by the soldiers leaning out of the windows of the first carriages they passed. But when they reached the final carriage, just behind the engine, her mother finally stopped.

'You will be safe in this one,' she said. 'The lady police won't let anything happen to you.'

A whistle blast signalled the train's imminent departure, and Sally hugged her mother for the last time, holding her in a firm grip.

'I'll be all right, Mum. We need my wages more than

ever now.'

She blinked her eyes in quick succession, determined to suppress the tears that threatened to force their way out. Her mother did enough crying for both of them and her tears would just make things worse. But now the moment had come, the stiff upper lip they tried to maintain, wobbled and shattered.

'You will be so far away.' Sally's mother scrubbed her eyes with the back of her hand. 'And you will be doing such dangerous work. After what happened ...' Her voice tailed off.

'Shh, Mum. You're not supposed to know where I'm going. They told me this munitions factory is a big secret. And the work's no more dangerous than what I did at Silvertown.'

'But I'm worried for you.'

'I know, but I will write, and I'll send some of my wages home every week.'

Another whistle blast pierced their ears.

'I need to go, Mum. Give Molly a hug from me and tell her I'll soon be back.' Sally thrust her shabby case into the carriage, hugged her mother for the last time, and jumped aboard. Tears pricked her eyes as the platform receded until she could no longer see her mother. She was starting a new life, embarking on a new adventure. She should be happy. But everything she had suppressed, over the past few weeks, now rose to fill her with misery.

Her life changed when the factory exploded, her best friend died, her home reduced to a heap of rubble, her family destitute, and now she had lost them as well. She remained standing and leaned her forehead against the window, feeling more alone than she had ever been before. The tears overflowed and trickled down her face.

'Move up the seat a bit and make room for the lass.' Kirsty touched the girl's elbow. 'Squeeze in here beside me, it will be a long journey and you can't stand all the way.'

51

Ethel and Martha shuffled along the seat to make space, although Kirsty heard a faint 'Tut' from Lydia, in the corner. Probably too much of a lady to welcome a working-class girl into their midst, she thought. Well, it wouldn't take long to sort her out once they got to Gretna.

Kirsty leaned over and put her hand on the girl's knee. 'Your first time away from home?'

The girl used her thumb to wipe a tear from her cheek. She nodded. 'The Ministry got me a job, but it's such a long way from home.' She sniffled.

'Munitions?' The faint tinge of yellow in her skin did not escape Kirsty's notice. 'I bet you're going to Gretna.'

'I'm not supposed to talk about it. They said I'm not to tell anyone where I'm going.'

'Don't worry,' Kirsty said. 'We're headed there as well and we will look after you.'

Kirsty wriggled into a more comfortable position. 'You seem young for the War Ministry to send so far away.'

'I'm sixteen,' Sally said. 'I've been working for the past two years, so it isn't anything new.'

'Have you always worked in munitions?'

'Yes, but the factory blew up and put us all out of work. I'm lucky to get this job, but I wish I'd been given one nearer to home.'

Lydia leaned forward and looked along the carriage to Sally. 'That must have been awful.'

'Awful doesn't describe it,' Kirsty said. 'I went to Silvertown the next day and I'll never forget the devastation the explosion caused. The place obliterated, the houses in ruins, and the people with nowhere to go. Most of them wound up sleeping on the floors of churches and halls, packed in with hardly room to move. Goodness only knows where they will find a home.'

Fresh tears trickled down Sally's face. 'My mum and little sister are in the church hall. I didn't want to leave them.'

Kirsty put her arm around the girl's shoulders. 'I am certain things will be sorted out for them before too long.

You just concentrate on the job you're going to. I am told the girls earn good money at Gretna, and with your help, they will soon be on their feet again. That's all you can do.'

Sally nodded. 'I feel so helpless, though.'

'I am sure you are doing all you can for them, and at least they are safe where they are.'

14

Dietger

Dietger squeezed into a seat in a rear carriage. 'Pardon,' he said as he sat down.

The woman in the opposite seat scrutinized him through her pince-nez and whispered something to the man sitting next to her.

The man cleared his throat. 'You are not from London? I cannot quite place your accent.'

Dietger frowned. He prided himself on his impeccable English. 'I am from the north, sir,' he said.

'You do not sound as if you are from the north.' The man leaned forward for a closer inspection.

Dietger restrained himself from running his finger around his collar. In situations like this, it was important to remain cool and bluff things out.

'Ah, that is because I was educated at Eton, sir. Accents do not serve well there.'

'You have come upon hard times, sir,' the man said.

Dietger had forgotten he was wearing workmen's clothes. He must be slipping. 'Indeed, sir. The bombing took care of that. I lost everything, my belongings, my clothes, my uniform. I was lucky to escape with my life. Thank goodness for the Salvation Army.'

'Your uniform, you say? You are in the armed forces?'

'Yes, sir. I am on sick leave at the moment. I thought I would head north to see mater and pater before I am sent back to the front.'

'Good for you, good for you.'

The man whispered something to his wife, before concentrating on his newspaper.

Dietger relaxed. That had been a close call, but it would

be better if he did not have to converse further with anyone else. He closed his eyes and feigned sleep.

Before long his thoughts turned to Beatrice, so near, and yet so far away. He remembered the first time he saw her, long before their most recent encounters, on one of the open days at Leuven University. He looked out of the library window and was entranced by the girl skipping alongside her father, her eyes shining with excitement. She could not have been any older than fifteen, but showed signs of becoming a beauty even then. He recalled watching them, fascinated by her exuberance, and wishing his relationship with his parents had been just as carefree, instead of the formal, stilted one they had. It was all down to his mother's Germanic roots, of course. She was much stronger than his browbeaten Belgian father, for whom he had no respect.

When he encountered Beatrice in Paris and came to her assistance, he had felt it was fated, and his intention had been to accompany her to London. Melville put paid to that, the spymaster's presence on the boat forced him to leave her at Calais and wait for the next ferry. He could not risk coming up against Melville, the man was too astute.

He kept track of Beatrice after her arrival in London and even met her a few times when a safe opportunity presented. He knew she provided a translation service for Melville, although he doubted whether she was part of his spy network, somehow or other he did not think that likely. And over the past two years he observed her from a distance, resisting the temptation to contact her more often because it was far too risky.

He smiled, imagining how she would react to him contacting her again. It was such a pity Melville was having her followed, otherwise, that contact could have been made today.

Dietger feigned sleep for most of the journey. It was safer than getting into conversation with his fellow travellers, but now they were approaching Carlisle it was time to prepare for his departure.

He tensed, worried something would go wrong. Worried in case he would be recognized, even though he excelled at remaining anonymous. The heavy sensation in his abdomen worked its way up to the familiar tightness around his chest.

It was imperative no one knew of his arrival in this part of the country, and that meant avoiding Beatrice who was in one of the carriages further up. There would be too much risk if she became aware of his presence.

Dietger removed his valise from the rack and placed it at his feet so his hands would be free to open the door. He pulled the leather strap, lowered the carriage window, and leaned out to grasp the handle. He turned it but held the door closed until the train slowed. The minute it stopped he jumped out, pulled his cap low over his forehead, and keeping his face averted, he hurried to the exit. The street outside was quiet but would not remain that way for long once the train disgorged all the passengers. He slipped into a convenient arched alcove near to the station entrance, hunched back into the shadows and waited for Beatrice.

15

Arrival at Carlisle
Beatrice checked her handbag yet again. It contained money, the note with her contact's name and all the other details, and the address of the hotel for her overnight stay. She memorized the address and returned the note to her bag.

The train shuddered to a stop and she stood up to retrieve her case from the overhead rack; however, a final jolt threw her back into her seat.

'Allow me.' The Irish gentleman reached up to the rack and pulled the suitcase free. He opened the door, got out of the carriage, laid the case on the platform and turned back to offer her his hand to help her alight.

'Thank you, sir.' Beatrice wondered whether she should say more, but the man was already turning away from her.

'My pleasure,' he said, before striding off to join a bunch of young men and girls, chatting and laughing among themselves.

They greeted him with hugs and laughter and were still there when Beatrice passed them on her way out of the station.

'Aidan!' Dermot broke free from the group and rushed to meet him. The two friends clasped hands and thumped each other on the back, before being swamped by the rest of the men.

'Silly buggers, they're like big bairns.' Shannon shot a disapproving look at them, but her eyes sparkled with mischief.

Aidan wilted under the barrage of thumps. 'Canny up lads, or you'll manage something Frongoch never succeeded in doing.'

'What's that then?' Cormac thumped his back again.

'Beating me to my knees, that's what.' Aidan grinned so they would know he was joking.

'Takes an Irishman to do that.'

'Sure, and the English wouldn't have the muscle now, would they lads?'

'Too true, they wouldn't. It takes an army of them to get the better of us. If we had as many men as them we'd never have been defeated in Dublin.'

'Aye, a sad day for the whole of Ireland.'

The men lapsed into silence.

Fergus crossed himself and muttered, 'In the name of the Father, and the Son, and the Holy Ghost.'

Dermot was the first to break the silence. 'Enough of the troubles for now. The pubs will soon be shut and time is wasting, we need to celebrate Aidan's arrival.'

'Sounds good,' Aidan said. After a few drinks, the others might be amenable to his plan to disrupt the English and strike a blow for Ireland.

Kirsty grabbed her hat from the rack and rammed it on her head.

It was every woman's dream to be doing something useful for the war effort, and the invitation to provide a service at one of the country's most important munitions factories was an indication that women police were starting to become accepted.

In many ways, it helped to make up for the difficulties experienced during her first two years in the force and having to put up with a lot of abuse along the way. It hurt when insults were thrown by the bobbies on the beat, and the girls they were trying to help weren't much better.

Over time, Kirsty, as well as her colleagues, had been forced to learn how to retain a professional attitude and conceal their distress. But now, the recognition that women police had something to offer, and were valued, made all the obstacles they'd had to overcome, worthwhile.

She jumped out of the carriage into a shower of soot and sparks from the engine in front of her. She blinked, and was glad she had a spare uniform in her suitcase. This one was bound to be spotted with soot. But where was her case? It had been such a mad dash to catch the train this was the first time she'd given it any thought.

'Martha?'

Her friend turned at the sound of her name. 'Yes?'

'Have you any idea where my suitcase might be?'

Martha laughed. 'The luggage van, of course. Where else would it be?'

'Thank goodness for that. I had visions of it left behind on the platform at Euston.'

By this time all the policewomen had alighted, but the young girl still sat inside.

Kirsty got back into the carriage. 'I think you have to get off here to change trains for Gretna. Did the Ministry give you a travel warrant? It should tell you what to do.'

Sally rummaged in her pocket and produced the piece of paper. 'I don't know where we are,' she said, giving it to Kirsty.

'This is Carlisle, and that seems to be as far as this takes you. Did the people who arranged for you to come here provide any instructions?'

'They gave me a letter. I put it in my suitcase.' Sally bent over, snapped the locks open, pulled out an envelope, handed it to Kirsty, and shut her case again.

'It says that you will be met here. You are to stand beside the ticket office and wait for a welfare worker named Miss Brown.'

She folded the paper and replaced it in the envelope. 'Would you like me to wait with you? Or will you be all right.'

'I will be fine, miss. Thank you for your help.'

Kirsty watched the forlorn figure walk away.

'Done your good deed for today, then?' Martha prodded Kirsty in the ribs. 'You can't take care of every waif and stray, you know.'

'Yes, I know, but I can't help feeling I didn't help her enough.'

'By doing what, exactly?'

Kirsty shrugged. 'I suppose you're right.'

'Now that your conscience is salved, it might be a good idea if we sought out our transport. They said an army truck would be waiting to take us to our base at Gretna.'

16

Spies and Saboteurs

Alice Blake readied herself to leave her carriage as soon as she saw Beatrice pass. Several minutes later she alighted and slotted herself into the crowd behind her quarry. Her grip tightened on the small bag she carried. She always travelled light, and she threaded her way expertly through the throng of people, never once taking her eyes off Beatrice. Melville said the Belgian girl was not a suspect, but because of her previous acquaintance with the German spy, Dietger Leclercq, there was a possibility he would either contact her or that she would recognize him.

'If that is the case, would it not be easier for Beatrice to report back if she suspected Leclercq was at Gretna?' Alice queried.

'Beatrice is unaware he is a spy,' was Melville's only response. It left her wondering if he doubted the Belgian girl, although she understood Beatrice hated the German occupation of her country.

But Melville was a devious man, and his instructions to her had been clear. 'Watch Beatrice, but do not allow her to suspect she is under observation. And check out anybody who approaches her. Remember, Leclercq is expert at changing his appearance. Many times we have been on the point of apprehending him, but he has always slipped through our fingers. Beatrice may be his downfall.'

Alice loitered outside the Station Hotel to give her quarry time to register and be shown to her room. After a few minutes, she peered through the door in time to see Beatrice half way up the imposing staircase. It would now be safe for her to enter.

The woman positioned behind the reception counter in

the gloomy foyer towered over her in a less than welcoming pose. Alice supposed the extra trade generated by the war and the proximity of the munitions factory made a servile nature unnecessary. 'You have a reservation?' The tone was even more unwelcoming than the woman's posture.

'Yes,' Alice said, 'I made it by telephone yesterday.'

'Hmph, you're the second one today. Can't be doing with them newfangled telephones.'

Alice forced a smile. 'I had to be sure there would be a room for me.'

'Number 13, first floor,' the woman said. 'I hope you're not superstitious.'

Alice shook her head and grasped the key held out to her. 'Are there many guests?'

'Hotel's full. You were lucky to get a room. That's what I told the other young lady. She's in the room next to you.' The woman sighed and her shoulders slumped. 'You'll have to carry your own bag. All the porters have gone off to fight, and I'm left to do everything on my own.' Her forbidding expression softened, and a weary look flitted over her face.

'I will manage, it's only a small bag.' Alice picked it up and headed for the stairs.

From his vantage point, Dietger watched Beatrice emerge from the station.

He drew further back into the shadows until she passed him. Several yards behind her he spotted Aidan Maguire in a boisterous group of young men and girls headed in the same direction. He tucked himself in behind them, Beatrice would not see him here, and if she did he would appear to be part of the group because he dressed in a similar fashion. It was unlikely she would identify him as the dapper young man she met in France.

He did not have to follow her for long. She turned into the doorway of the Station Hotel, an impressive looking building, adjacent to the station. Satisfied that he knew where she was, it would be easy to avoid her. He continued on along the street, behind the chattering group and followed them into a local hostelry.

The inn was bright, cheery, and noisy. A good place to meet and rub shoulders with workers from the munitions factory.

His feet crunched on the sawdust covered floor, and after watching the drinkers for a few moments he joined the throng at the bar.

'A pint, please.'

He did not like beer and would prefer a glass of wine, but that would single him out as being different, and he wanted to blend in.

'You were following us.' The voice behind him had an attractive Irish lilt.

He turned, and looked into a pair of mischievous blue eyes. She was petite and shapely, and a smile lingered on her lips.

'Ah! That is because I did not know where I was going and you looked as if you did.'

'You're not from around here then?'

'No, and neither are you,' he said. 'I reckon you are a long way from home because I detect an Irish accent.'

'And what would you be knowing about Ireland?'

Dietger hesitated wondering how much to tell her. But the Irish were all rebels so he thought it safe to reveal something, although not too much, of his previous contact with Irish revolutionaries. 'Let me just say, the English would not welcome me in Ireland at the moment,' he said.

'Nor would they welcome some of our group.' Her eyes sparkled with mischief. 'What's your name?'

'Derek,' he said, 'Derek Clark.' He was used to using this name. It was his favourite alias when in England.

'Derek, is it? Well, maybe we'll meet up again sometime, Derek.' She leaned close to whisper in his ear. 'Sometime soon.' With a flounce of her skirt and a mischievous look she was gone.

Dietger, ignored the plate of biscuits and sipped his beer, suppressing a shudder at the rough taste of the alcohol. But his eyes never left the girl who was now laughing and chatting to one of the young men in the group. She might prove useful.

Shannon linked arms with Peggy. 'What have I missed?'

'Not much by the look of it. I noticed you flirting with the young fellow at the bar.' Peggy moved closer to Shannon and whispered in her ear. 'You wouldn't be trying to make Aidan jealous, by any chance?'

Shannon's smile broadened. 'Chance would be a fine thing,' she said.

She glanced at Aidan, but he was deep in conversation with one of her brothers, discussing the troubles, no doubt.

As if sensing her gaze, Aidan turned. His serious expression lightened, and a slow smile uplifted the corners of his mouth. He was less muscle-bound than the other navvies, but his wiry frame radiated pent-up energy.

Shannon did not smile back.

Her brothers, Dermot, and Cormac, had been so excited when they got the letter from Aidan, saying he intended to join them at Gretna.

Fergus Murphy hadn't been so sure. 'He'll bring trouble with him, mark my words,' he'd said. But Fergus hadn't been involved with the Post Office rebellion, although the rest of them had been there, fighting on the barricades. Aidan had been the one caught, and he was the one who paid a heavy price.

The warning was ignored, and because Fergus was the only dissenting voice in the group, plans were made for Aidan's arrival. A job would be ready for him, he would bunk in with his friends, and they would give him a welcome fit for a hero.

Shannon was as excited as any of them. Aidan was her childhood sweetheart. She had been proud to stand on the barricades with him, and fight at his side. And it was Aidan who engineered her escape when the English overran the Post Office, and she had taken her brothers with her. But he had been ignoring her ever since they all met at the railway station.

How did he think he could get off with that, and then thinking if he smiled at her she would come running?

She unlinked her arm from Peggy's and looked across the room to where the stranger, Derek, stood. Their eyes met and he lifted his glass in a salute. She smiled at him. But before she could make a move in Derek's direction strong fingers closed around her wrist, they tugged her back and she whirled around to meet Aidan's gaze.

'You wouldn't be thinking of taking up with anyone else now, would you?' His dark brown eyes fixated on hers and she felt their mesmeric pull.

'Why would I be thinking that? And, in any case, what business is it of yours?'

'You're mine. That's why.'

'Since when? Besides, you haven't given me two looks since we met at the station.'

'I had business to discuss first.'

'Dirty business, I'm sure.'

'Men's business.'

'Oh, now, men's business, is it? And was it men's business in Ireland when I was loading guns for you, and fighting beside you?'

'My, and it's a temper you've got on you. That's what I like, fighting talk.'

He pulled her into his arms and kissed her so hard she was unable to utter another word.

17

Sally

Sally's heart thumped in her chest, and her palms were sticky with sweat. She had arrived at a railway station in a strange town far away from home. Her suitcase bumped against her leg as she scurried up the platform anxiously looking for Miss Brown.

What if she couldn't find the person supposed to meet her? What would she do? The letter said she would be met in front of the ticket office. But where was the ticket office? Was it inside or outside the station? And there were so many people here. Her mind whirled and her anxiety grew.

Relief surged through her when she spotted a woman holding aloft a piece of cardboard with the inscription, Miss Brown. Several girls stood beside her, some clutching bags or valises and some with suitcases. They were mostly young, and they all looked scared. She scurried along the platform to join them.

'Come along,' the woman said. 'What's your name?'

'Sally Scott.'

The woman consulted her list and crossed her name off. 'We're nearly all here, and once the stragglers arrive we will be on our way.'

Sally tucked herself in at the back of the group, still holding her suitcase in a tight grip despite the weight pulling on her shoulder muscles. If she lost it she would have nothing.

'That's the last one arrived now, so we'll be on our way. Follow me.' Miss Brown strode off in the direction of the exit.

The assorted bunch of girls straggled behind the woman in an untidy line, like a mother cat leading her kittens. Sally wondered where they were going and how they would get to Gretna.

The mystery was soon solved when Miss Brown stopped beside a charabanc. 'Get on board, girls.' She opened the door and stood back.

The journey was bumpy, the wooden seats dug into Sally's legs, and the charabanc engine wheezed so much Sally was sure they would never arrive at their destination.

'Out you get and line up, girls,' Miss Brown said when they arrived, 'and matron will book you into the hostel.'

Sally staggered when she stepped down from the charabanc. She grabbed the side of the door for fear she would fall. Despite the numbness in her feet and calves she climbed the two steps into the hostel and joined the queue in the long narrow hall. While she waited in the line, the feeling in her legs returned, to be replaced with excruciating pins and needles. She bit her lip and stared ahead until the stabbing needles abated. But her legs still shook and she couldn't be sure if that was due to the journey, or fear of the unknown.

Eventually, she reached the table at the end of the hall where the matron entered all her details into a log book. 'You will be in cubicle fifteen. All the girls in this hostel work the early shift, six o'clock to two o'clock. You get your breakfast here before you start, your dinner in the canteen at the mixing station where you will be working, and your tea here in the hostel at half-past five. If you go out in the evening come back before ten o'clock, after that the doors are locked, and latecomers are put on a report. Anything you're not sure about you can ask me, or one of the housekeepers. Next?'

Summarily dismissed, Sally made way for the next girl.

'Cubicle fifteen? Follow me.' Miss Brown, led her to a door at the rear. 'The dormitories are through here. The dining room is the first door when you come into the hostel. There are also recreational facilities; a games room, a library, and a room you can use to do sewing or knitting. You can explore these tomorrow.'

By the time she stopped speaking they had arrived at Sally's cubicle.

Miss Brown pulled the curtain aside to reveal a bed, a chest of drawers and one chair. 'I will leave you here.'

Left on her own, Sally surveyed her cubicle with dismay. She was accustomed to sharing a room, but only with her mother and sister, never with strangers. There were so many cubicles in this dormitory, so many strangers who would see and hear everything she did. Fear gnawed the pit of her stomach. How would she cope?

Tears gathered in her eyes, and she threw herself on the bed. Why had she come here? She wanted her mother, her little sister, and her home. But she didn't have a home any longer. The Silvertown explosion had taken care of that.

18

Aidan

'Last drinks.' The pub landlord's voice soared above the clatter of voices.

Aidan pulled out his pocket watch. 'A bit early for calling time?'

Cormac grinned. 'You'll get used to it, mate. All the pubs around here are operated by the Ministry of Munitions, and after half-past-nine, they close.' He gulped his drink. 'Barbaric system, but then, what else can you expect from the English.'

Shannon tugged at his arm. 'Walk me to the train, Aidan.'

'Can't you stay longer?'

She giggled. 'Chance would be a fine thing, but the hostel locks its doors at ten o'clock, and there's hell to pay if we're late.'

Aidan grabbed her around the waist and pulled her to face him. 'Since when did you pay any attention to rules?'

Her eyes sparkled with mischief. 'I would if someone was inside to open the window for me, but we're all here, and I don't much fancy spending the night outside.'

'Stay here with me then.'

'What, bunk in with all you boys? Haven't they told you about the sleeping arrangements here?'

'Dermot said he'd arrange a bed for me.'

'Sure, he'll have done that. He'll have squeezed another trestle bed in the room they all share.'

'Is that right, Dermot? Do we all share a room?'

Dermot slapped him on the back. 'Sure, we do. What else did you expect? Gretna and Carlisle are bursting at the seams with all the munitions workers needing a place to stay. The girls have been looking for lodgings in Carlisle ever since they got here, but until they find somewhere else, they're stuck in a hostel at Gretna Township.'

Shannon dug her fingers into his ribs. 'Come on, walk me to the station. If I miss the train I'll be locked out.'

'We'll all walk the girls to the station.' Finn Donovan slung his arm around Vera King's shoulders. 'Maybe I'll get a kiss from Vera on the way.'

Vera giggled and linked her arm through Shannon's. 'Best to keep them guessing.' Both girls turned their backs on the men and walked to the door.

Aidan scowled and walked behind them, closely followed by the rest of the girls and the navvies.

Dietger leaned against the bar and watched Aidan and his friends leave. His dealings, with Irish groups in the past, meant he was familiar with their propensity for stirring up trouble due to their ingrained resentment of the English. He was sure he could use this group to his advantage, but so far he had not figured out a plan that would enhance his surveillance objective.

'Sorry, sir, but you will have to drink up and leave. Licensing laws.'

Dietger turned to face the landlord. 'I am sorry, I am newly arrived in Carlisle, and was not aware you closed so early.'

The landlord shrugged. 'Not my doing, bloody government's doing. It doesn't stop the men drinking, they just drink faster.' He cleared some empty glasses from the counter depositing them in a small sink behind him.

Dietger gulped the rest of his beer. The time had come for him to find his accommodation.

He did not need to consult a map, nor did he need to ask directions. The map of Carlisle imprinted itself in his brain after he memorized the instructions passed to him in the barber's shop.

The room was in a crumbling building at the end of an

alley. He removed a brick adjacent to the door. Behind it was the key to the room on the top floor. The stairs creaked under his footsteps but the other doors remained firmly closed. Inside the room was a bed, a chair, a table, and a gas ring instead of a cooker. The sink was black and did not look too clean, but it would do for the time being.

He would use the room as a base while he charted the geography of Gretna Munitions Factory.

Aidan was taken aback. It didn't seem possible that six men could live in such a confined space, but there were three sets of bunk beds lining each wall leaving only a tiny area in the middle of the room.

'Damn it to hell, this is worse than Frongoch. At least we had room to move between our beds.'

'Sure, it's diabolical, I know,' Dermot said. 'But you'd be hard pushed to find lodgings in Carlisle any better than this. Looking on the bright side, there are no English soldiers ready to put a bullet up your backside when you want to go out.'

'Just a crabby old landlady with her hand held out every Saturday for the digs money. She's making a fortune.' Finn slumped on the bottom bunk at the right of the door. 'This is my bed.' He stretched his legs out. 'Your one's the top bunk over there.'

Aidan shrugged. 'I suppose anything is better than sleeping on the street.' He looked around. 'What do I do with my case?'

'Up to you. Under your pillow, at the foot of the bed, or under the bed.'

Aidan surveyed the narrow space underneath the bunks. 'You must be joking.'

'Bit of a tight squeeze but you can do it with the use of some muscle.' Dermot joined him and took up position beside him. 'I'll lift the edge of the bed and you shove your case underneath. Mind you, it isn't easy when you want to change your clothes.'

'I thought the smell was high in here.'

'No worse than your ma's piggery back home.' Dermot grinned.

'Bloody English must be making a fortune,' Aidan said. 'A bullet up their backsides is what's needed.'

Dermot turned to the rest of the men in the room. 'I told you Aidan would have a plan.'

'If I do, are you in?'

'Damned right, I am. What say you lads? If Aidan plans to thwart the English are you in?'

It was as Aidan thought. These men would be easily convinced, although he would need to keep an eye on Fergus who seemed less certain than the others. However, he didn't doubt his ability to talk Fergus around, and if that didn't succeed there were other ways to deal with the man.

19

Kirsty

The army truck jolted to a stop in front of a long, low wooden building shrouded in darkness.

Kirsty struggled to rise from the wooden bench that lined one side of the truck. Ethel, on the opposite bench, held out a hand to Martha, perched on a box in the middle, which Kirsty suspected held ammunition.

'I think I may have bruises in places I've never had them before.' Martha grabbed Ethel's hand and scrambled to her feet.

Kirsty grinned. 'Me too.' The tent-like fabric covering the top of the lorry meant she couldn't stand upright.

A thud outside signalled the driver jumping from the cab, and within seconds, she was beaming at them while she unpinned the backboard and let it fall. 'Everybody out,' she said. 'We've arrived.'

Kirsty lowered herself from the lorry and waited for Martha and Ethel to join her, but Lydia jumped down next.

The young policewoman brushed her skirt with her hands. 'It was not very clean,' she complained when she saw Kirsty looking.

'Not what you're used to?' Kirsty couldn't resist the dig. Lydia had been lording it over them for most of the journey, making it clear the travel arrangements were unsatisfactory.

'Oh, put a sock in it, Lydia,' Martha said. 'You're not in Mayfair now.'

Lydia blinked and turned away from them, but not quick enough to stop Kirsty spotting a tear. She felt an unexpected twinge of sympathy for the girl who seemed to be having difficulty fitting in, and was obviously out of her depth. It didn't bode well for her future in the women's police force.

The door of the wooden hut opened and a large woman, wearing a uniform with sergeant's stripes on the sleeve, strode out. 'Hurry along ladies,' she said in a booming voice. 'We don't have all night, and you're on duty at six o'clock tomorrow morning.'

She marched the small contingent into the hostel which was surprisingly spacious inside, and after taking a role call and ticking their names off on a list, she allocated them to their rooms. 'Breakfast is at five,' she said, before vanishing further up the corridor.

'Well, at least we've got a room rather than a cubicle,' Kirsty said to Martha who was in the room next door.

She thrust the door open and stared in dismay at the compact space, not much bigger than a closet. A bed took up all the space on one side of the box-room, and a clothes rail and chest of drawers with a basin and large jug on top, filled the space along the other side.

The bed was iron-framed with bars at the head and the bottom, and when she sat on it the springs underneath squealed in protest. Kirsty reckoned it was going to be an uncomfortable and noisy night, but she was so tired she didn't care, and quickly replacing her clothes with her night attire, she huddled under the blankets. At least they seemed clean.

Troubled thoughts, about her duties the next day, kept her awake until, eventually, she lapsed into a restless sleep.

'Breakfast in fifteen minutes.'

The knock on the door followed by the unfamiliar voice woke Kirsty. She groaned. It hardly seemed more than a few minutes since sleep claimed her. A blanket had her in a stranglehold, her pillow teetered on the edge of the bed, and her bones ached from the jarring journey in the army truck last night. She struggled to sit up and when she finally managed she viewed her surroundings with a jaundiced eye.

Her quarters in London's section house had been more comfortable than this tiny room which was not much bigger than a cubicle. Still, comfort wasn't an issue when there was a job to do, particularly such an important one for the Women's Police Service. It signified acceptance by the establishment.

Kirsty slid her feet from under the blanket and emerged from her warm cocoon into the freezing cold of a January morning. She dressed as fast as her numb fingers would allow and pulled a brush through her auburn hair. Thank goodness she had it cut short several months ago, it was more manageable now than the unruly curls that used to spill over her shoulders and down her back.

The sound of feet and muted voices signalled the hostel coming to life. Kirsty opened her door to join the others as they searched for the dining room.

Martha and Ethel, further up the corridor beckoned to her. Muttering apologies she pushed past several women.

'I didn't expect so many policewomen to be here already.'

'Apparently they've been drafted in from various towns over the past three weeks,' Martha said. 'We're the first contingent to be sent from London.'

'Jildy, jildy!' The sergeant's voice boomed, echoing throughout the building.

'What on earth does she mean?' Kirsty had never heard that expression before.

'She spent time in India with her husband,' the woman behind them said. 'I think it means hurry up.'

The dining room was basic. Wooden tables and benches to sit on and, at the end of the room, a longer table where a large, red-faced woman doled out porridge into plates set out in rows.

The friendly woman standing behind her said, 'Grab a plate, and you will find tea in the urn.'

'Be quick, girls.' The sergeant's voice resounded over the clatter. 'We can't miss the train.'

'Train? What's she talking about?' Kirsty started to feel like Alice in Wonderland in danger of vanishing down the rabbit hole.

'You must be part of the new batch.' The woman at her left sounded amused. 'The description of Gretna as a factory often has folk mystified, because instead of being one great big building, there are loads of separate buildings. The site stretches for nine miles, from Mossband in the south to Dornock in the north. You will soon become used to it.'

Kirsty grabbed a bowl of grey looking porridge and filled her cup with tea from the urn.

'Over here, there's space at this table.' The woman dumped her plate and cup down and straddled the bench. 'My name's Sandra by the way, and she's Clara.' She indicated the woman who had been behind Kirsty. 'And don't worry, we will keep you right.'

Ethel and Martha were already sitting at a table at the other side of the room. Martha waved for her to join them, but Kirsty didn't want to be rude to Sandra and Clara, so she shrugged and sat down.

Reluctantly, Kirsty lifted her spoon and dipped it in the porridge, pleasantly surprised to find it better than it appeared. She couldn't remember when she last tasted genuine Scottish porridge and had become more accustomed to the English way of making it which did not include salt and left it tasteless.

'New arrivals to me,' the sergeant commanded.

Kirsty, Martha, Ethel, and Lydia, stood to attention in front of her.

'Each of you will be teamed up with experienced policewomen.'

Kirsty bit her lip to prevent her responding they were all experienced policewomen.

'WPC Campbell, you will be with Forbes and Collins.' She continued speaking until they had all been allocated policewomen to act as their mentors.

'Dismissed,' the sergeant said.

The policewomen were already forming up in the hallway. 'Who are Forbes and Collins,' Kirsty hissed to Martha.

'That's me and Clara,' Sandra said. 'I'm Forbes and she's

Collins.'

The sergeant opened the front door and the squad of policewomen marched out into the chilly January air.

Early morning frost, glistening on the moonlit road, crunched under their boots while they marched in military formation to Gretna Township's railway station. Workers, muffled in shawls, scarves and coats, hurried along in a less orderly manner, making for the same destination where the train sat waiting for them. Kirsty was amazed at the throng starting to board. It hardly seemed possible it could hold them all.

'Be ready to hop on if you want a seat,' Clara said.

'Are they all munitions workers?' Kirsty couldn't keep the amazement out of her voice, although seeing the hordes of women on the station platform helped her to understand why so many policewomen were needed. Keeping order among the girls, nicknamed 'munitionettes' by the newspapers, would be a gigantic task.

'Yes, most of them are all right and don't give us any problems, but there are some troublemakers. You will soon recognize them.'

Ten minutes after boarding the train at Gretna Township it arrived at the Wylies, the station where the munitionettes disembarked to start their work in this section of the munitions factory.

Several guards manned a gate in a heavy duty wire fence, Sandra waved to them. 'We have four new lady police to keep the workers on their toes.' She pointed to Kirsty and her friends.

The guards waved them through.

'They'll know you the next time,' she said, marching through the gate.

Kirsty followed anticipating an industrial compound with buildings and machinery. But all she could see in the moonlight was hilly, open countryside. Where were the buildings? Where was the factory?

The sound of laughter made her turn. 'Your face,' Clara spluttered unable to contain herself.

'Don't be mean,' Sandra said. 'It was the same for us when we first got here. D'you see those grassy hillocks, well they have a joint purpose. The mounds form a barrier encircling a set of factory buildings situated in the hollow at the other side. This masks them from view, as well as isolating and safeguarding all the other buildings on the site in the event of an explosion.'

Clara was already walking in the direction of one of the hillocks. Kirsty and Sandra hurried to catch up with her.

'How do we get into the factory?'

'Through openings, like small tunnels. Here we are at our one.'

Leading the way through the small hill, Clara pointed at one of the long low buildings on the other side. 'Now we're here, our job is to stand guard at the entrance to the workspace, to ensure the workers aren't taking anything in they shouldn't. No cigarettes, no matches, no hair grips, no rings, no buttons on their clothes, nothing metallic. In fact nothing at all. You see, if anything falls into the mixture then it could go up with a big bang.'

Clara pushed the door of the building open. In the inner hall, there were three doors, and she took up a position at the door facing them. 'The factory area is in here. That door,' she pointed to the one on the right, 'is where the girls change into their work clothes, and the other door is the canteen where they take their meal breaks.'

'What do they actually do?' Kirsty wished someone had explained more about her duties and the work the munitionettes were doing.

'You haven't been briefed?'

Kirsty shook her head. 'We arrived too late last night, and they expected us on duty first thing this morning, so I suppose there was no time.'

'The girls won't be long, so I will make this quick. This is the mixing station. Workers in this part of the factory mix the guncotton and nitroglycerine. They knead it together until it looks a bit like the porridge you ate for your breakfast. A writer came here to see the factory a few months ago and he called the mixture devil's porridge. The name stuck.'

'When you say they knead the nitroglycerine and guncotton together, they don't do that with their hands, do they?'

'Yes, I am afraid they do, which is one of the reasons it is important they don't take anything in with them. The least bit of contamination with an outside object could cause an explosion.'

Kirsty shuddered. She couldn't imagine putting her hands into such a mixture.

'Here they come. Be ready to search if you think they might be taking something in.'

The girls, now dressed in khaki tunics and trousers, surged out of the changing room. Kirsty braced herself for the task ahead.

20

Beatrice

Beatrice shivered in the chill air of the ancient bathroom. Her face stung where she had scrubbed it with cold water, and she did not feel clean after drying it with the thin towel that smelled of damp and mould. However, it was the best she could do with what was available. Perhaps there would be better facilities at Gretna.

According to the information supplied to her by Melville, the government had built a brand new township for the munitions factory workers. Even though she did not know where she would be accommodated it could not be worse than this dilapidated hotel, where the floorboards creaked underfoot, the bed sheets were grey, and the windows so dirty nothing outside could be seen. She had expected more from a station hotel, but she supposed the war had led to deteriorating standards.

She fastened the buttons on her blouse, straightened her skirt, slid the bolt on the bathroom door, and exited into the corridor.

'About time too, darling.' The man standing outside pushed past her. 'Some of us work for a living.'

'I am sorry, I did not know,' Beatrice said, but she was addressing the closed door which he had slammed behind him.

Keeping her eyes averted, she sidled past the line of half-clothed men which had formed outside the bathroom.

'You all right, love?'

'You should have given a shout, we'd have come in to help you.'

Laughter rippled down the row of men.

'Don't pay them no heed, miss.' The man at the end of

the line smirked at her.

Heat rose up from her neck to her face, and she scurried along the corridor to her room to get away from their ogling eyes.

The door was ajar. Strange, she could swear she closed it. Her breathing quickened and she paused with her hand on the doorknob. She had closed it, she was certain, it could only mean one thing. Someone was inside the room.

She turned and took two steps along the corridor before halting. The stairs were beyond the bathroom, which meant pushing past the line of men.

No, she decided, she did not want to run that gauntlet again. She had no option other than face whoever was in the room.

Her heart beat faster, and she walked back to the door, and pushed it open.

Alice kept a wary eye on the receptionist and cupped her hand over the telephone mouthpiece. She was tired after tossing and turning all night in the hotel bed which was so hard it was like sleeping on the floor.

'What number please?' It had taken ages before the switchboard responded and the woman who answered sounded as if she were yawning.

Alice's tone was clipped as she read out the London number.

'Putting you through,' the voice said. The phone clicked and hummed before ringing at the other end.

Alice cast an anxious glance at the clock above the reception desk. The minute hand had moved from the hour and now pointed at one minute past six. Melville's instructions had been to telephone him at 6 am, and he was a stickler for time. She tapped her fingers on the directory attached by a length of string to a hook on the wall. Patience was not one of her strong points.

'Yes?' The voice on the other end of the line was guarded.

'It's Alice.' She knew better than call him sir, or boss on the telephone. You never knew whether the switchboard might be listening.

'Ah, yes, Alice. You arrived safely, I trust? How was your journey?'

'Uneventful, but the train was crowded. I had hoped to see a friend but there was no sign of him.'

'I see. Your other friend, the lady you travelled with? She is well, I trust?'

'As far as I can tell. But I'd hardly call her my friend, more of an acquaintance. I had thought I might reintroduce myself to her over breakfast. She might have news of the friend I am anxious to trace, as I fear he may not know of my interest.'

'Tut, tut, Alice. You and your men friends.'

Alice giggled, for the benefit of the switchboard. She waited for Melville's response to her guarded request to make contact with Beatrice, knowing he would be thinking about it while he chatted.

'Is that wise if the lady has an interest in the gentleman as well?'

Alice laughed. 'I have my doubts about that, and if she doesn't know of my interest I fail to see how she can help me.'

'I will never understand you modern women,' Melville said. 'In my young day, the gentleman made the advances.'

'Life's too short, uncle, and you're not such an old fogey as you make yourself out to be.'

'Well, if you are sure that is the best way I suppose you have nothing to lose. But if you take my advice you will not be too hasty in mentioning your mutual friend until you have established some common ground.'

Alice smiled, she'd wanted to make contact with Beatrice from the beginning. Shadowing her had not been one of Melville's best ideas.

'Oh, I forgot to tell you, but your cousin Tommy has been taken sick and an arrangement has been made for you to fill in for him at Gretna Township Post Office. It will save him losing his job, and you already know all the arrangements for your friend's arrival.'

'I don't know anything about Post Office work,' Alice said.

'You are a clever girl, Alice, you will soon pick things up, and you will keep me informed, of course.'

'Yes, uncle.' She was speaking to a silent phone line. Melville had hung up.

No wonder he had agreed so readily to her revealing herself to Beatrice, because in Tommy's absence, Alice would be the contact between Beatrice and Melville.

'Damn,' she said, and replaced the phone on its wall cradle.

The fair-haired woman sitting on the end of Beatrice's bed was a stranger.

'How did you get into my room? And who are you?'

The woman rose. She was smaller and older than Beatrice who guessed she must be in her thirties.

'Your door was open. I knocked but there was no answer so I came in to wait for you,' the woman said. 'I am Alice Blake, your contact at Gretna.' She held out her hand for Beatrice to shake.

Beatrice ignored the hand. Melville had said her contact was named Tommy, he'd said nothing about a contact named Alice.

'That was not the name he gave me.'

The woman smiled. 'I am afraid Tommy is no longer available. I am his replacement.'

Beatrice's suspicions subsided. The woman knew the name of her contact, so perhaps she was genuine.

'If you are, as you say, my contact at Gretna, what happens now? Melville only told me to check in here and someone would be in touch.'

'You will take up a position as assistant matron at the Mary Queen of Scots Hostel on Dominion Road. Everything is arranged and they are expecting you to arrive this morning. This hostel is where the Irish girls are billeted. I understand your brief is to keep watch on them.'

Beatrice nodded. 'How do I get there?'

'I've drawn you a pencil map from Gretna Township Station to the hostel.'

'Gretna Township Station?'

'Yes, you take a train there. It only takes ten minutes. As your contact, I will keep a low profile, so I won't accompany you.'

'I see.'

'If you find out anything which necessitates a report I will be based at the Post Office. But be careful not to arouse suspicion. The other postal workers are not involved.'

Alice walked to the door. Hesitating, with her hand on the knob, she said, 'I know this is your first time, but you will be fine.' And with that final remark she left.

Beatrice sank down on the bed. What had she got herself into? All this cloak and dagger stuff tied her in knots, and she had no idea what she was supposed to do. She wished she had never agreed to Melville's plan.

21

Beatrice

The winter sun glimmered through the clouds when Beatrice stepped off the train at Gretna Township. She walked along a street lined with stone buildings and shops at one side, while a fence shielded the railway line running up the other side.

At first glance, it resembled any other small town in Britain or Belgium, until the houses came into view. Long lines and rows of wooden huts and houses laid out in a grid system, with no resemblance to the normal haphazard arrangement of housing in a town or city.

She followed the directions on her map until she stood in front of a long low wooden building, the hostel allocated as her work base.

Tightening her grip on the handle of her suitcase she mounted the steps and opened the door. Weak daylight penetrated the empty corridor, but she could hear voices and laughter from one of the rooms on her right. The door to the room stood partly open. She pushed it and peered into a large kitchen where a red-faced woman kneaded dough on a floury table, and a girl washed pots in one of the sinks that lined the wall under the windows.

The woman brushed the flour off her hands and wiped them on her apron. 'You must be the new assistant matron. We've been expecting you.'

Beatrice nodded. 'I was not sure where to go.'

'Matron is busy in her office. Wee Maisie will show you the way.' She stuck her head out of the door and yelled, 'Maisie!'

A young girl rushed out of a door further up the corridor. 'I was just finishing off the beds.'

'About time too.' She turned to Beatrice. 'You have to

keep chasing these young uns, or they'd never do anything.'

'I does my best,' Maisie muttered.

'And I'll have less of your cheek, young Maisie. Now this here's our new assistant matron, and I want you to take her to matron's office.' The cook turned back to her kitchen table. 'I'd take you myself, but this baking has to be finished before the shift ends.'

Beatrice followed the girl up the corridor. She had not been expecting domestic staff in the hostel, thinking it simply a place where the workers slept. But already she had met two kitchen staff and a maid. She wondered how many more of them there were, and what her job would entail, because she did not know what an assistant matron was supposed to do.

Maisie tapped at a door and pushed it open. 'Matron,' she said, 'our new assistant matron is here.'

The woman behind the desk smiled and said, 'Come in.'

The maid turned to leave, but matron called her back. 'Take Miss Jacobs' suitcase to her room, Maisie.'

The girl grabbed the case and left.

Beatrice stood, waiting, until the woman stopped writing in the ledger before her. It seemed an age before she looked up. A smile softened her severe expression. 'Pull over a chair from behind the door,' she said.

Beatrice pulled the chair in front of the desk and sat down.

Matron sorted through a pile of papers. 'Ah, here we are. Beatrice Jacobs. I understand you have no experience.'

'That is correct.'

Matron sighed. 'Well, I don't suppose you're any different from the majority of the workers here, but I can't help feeling it would be nice if you had some experience.'

Beatrice nodded.

'The job isn't too difficult. You just make sure the girls are looked after, help the new ones settle in, address any problems, and look after their welfare. We have a full staff, cooks, maids, and so on. Plus most of the facilities a girl might want. There are recreation rooms, clubs they can join, a library, and a sewing room with access to sewing machines. We like to encourage them to take advantage of the activities in the hostel rather than going out to the cinema or the dance hall.'

'How many girls does the hostel accommodate?'

'This hostel is for the early shift workers and houses sixty-five. The bigger two storey hostels on Victory Avenue can take between ninety to one hundred and twenty. A new batch of girls came in last night, so we are full at the moment.'

Matron picked up and shook a small hand bell. 'You will require an assistant matron's dress. Maisie will take you to the storeroom where you can select the correct size, and then she will show you around. After that, she can take you to your room.'

Beatrice's head swam by the time she reached her room, but she waited until she heard Maisie's footsteps fade into the distance. She slung the drab brown dress over the back of the only chair and lay down on the bed. Closing her eyes, she wondered what she was doing here. No one else, apart from Alice, knew of her spying mission. But she was damned if she knew how to tackle it, and wished Melville had been more explicit with his instructions. She reckoned she must be the worst spy England had ever employed.

But at least she had a room with a door which she could close, unlike the workers' cubicles with only a curtain they could pull if they wanted privacy.

Beatrice woke with a start. She had not meant to sleep, but must have dozed off. Chattering voices, laughter, and the banging of the front door echoed through the building. That must be what woke her.

Sitting up, she swung her legs over the side of the bed, knocking her knee on the suitcase which lay where Maisie had left it. She rubbed the sore spot and contemplated unpacking, but she was curious about the girls living in the hostel and keen to identify the Irish ones as soon as possible.

A lock of hair flopped over her face. She pushed it back, and tucked it into the coil at the nape of her neck, before feeling for any other loose strands. There was no time to let her hair down to recoil, so she hoped she was tidy.

The noise increased when she opened her door and stepped into the corridor to face an onslaught of girls. What now? Should she introduce herself? A strong urge to retreat to her room swamped her and her hand tightened on the doorknob, but she gritted her teeth and smiled. Some of them smiled back, but several others ignored her. To them she did not seem to exist. How on earth was she going to do this impossible job?

'Don't hang about girls.' Matron's voice soared above the laughter and chatter. 'Your meal will be in an hour, and we have a special treat for you today. Cook managed to find some dried fruit and she's made a batch of fruit cakes.' Matron pushed past the girls to Beatrice's side. 'Ah, I wondered where you got to.'

Beatrice nodded because she was not sure how to respond. 'Is this the full complement of girls in the hostel?' It was the only thing she could think to say.

'Yes, they've just come off shift and they will be tired and irritable. Be prepared for arguments. They often arise over whose turn it is to wash, there are never enough sinks to cater for them all.'

'Do we sort it out if there is trouble between them?'

'If it's serious, yes. But otherwise, you're better staying out of the way to let them resolve things themselves.'

Matron looked her up and down making Beatrice feel like a child. 'The teatime meal is in an hour, that will give you time to freshen up.'

Beatrice raised her hand to the coil of hair, evidently she was not as tidy as she thought.

'Yes, Matron.' She turned the doorknob and escaped into her room.

22

Kirsty

The door leading into the mixing room clanged open, and the munitionettes streamed out, rushing to the changing rooms to take off their foul smelling tunics and put on their own clothes. One of them barged into Kirsty without a word of apology.

The girl tore her mob cap from her head and flicked it so that it whizzed past Kirsty's nose, leaving a tangy chemical odour in its wake. The action seemed deliberate and Kirsty glared at her, but she was already gone, pushing into the crush of girls all keen to get changed as fast as they could.

Sandra grabbed Kirsty's elbow. 'Time to go. If we move quickly we will get a head start on the workers, that way we stand a better chance of getting a seat on the train.'

Kirsty nodded. It had been a long exhausting day, and her feet encased in hard leather boots weighed her down. They felt like lumps of lead and were now so numb she no longer felt the aches and pains that tormented her earlier.

'It's good to be in the fresh air again after being cooped up all day,' Kirsty said.

The mixing station door clanged shut behind her, stifling the noxious smells, and muffling the excited chatter of the munitionettes. She ran a few steps to catch up with Sandra. Clara was out of sight, in the tunnel, between the mounds.

'You won't say that when the ether plant discharges its fumes and the wind blows them this way. When that happens you need to hold your breath because you will never smell anything fouler than that. Besides, if you breathe it in, you might find yourself in the infirmary having a wee sleep, because the fumes go to your head and they make you woozy.'

Emerging from the tunnel they found Clara chatting to Martha and Ethel. 'I told them you were behind me,' she said, 'so we waited. But we need to hurry now. Once the girls finish changing their clothes they will make a dash for the train, and if we don't beat them to it we will be standing all the way to Gretna.'

A belch of steam and smoke heralded the arrival of the train when they still had several yards to go to reach the station.

The thud of running feet, and the exuberant voices of munitionettes freed from their place of toil, sounded behind the policewomen.

'Time to put a spurt on.'

Clara rammed one of her hands on top of her hat and ran towards the station.

They had almost reached the platform when the new shift of workers erupted from the carriages, forcing them to stand at the side of the road to allow the mass of girls to pass.

When the last of the new batch of workers alighted, Clara said, 'Hop on and grab a seat while we can.'

The policewomen hardly had time to draw breath before the platform became jammed with a horde of munitionettes, pushing and jostling to get aboard. Kirsty tucked her feet as far under the seat as she could for fear of being trampled in the crush. At last, everyone was on and the train steamed off.

Ten minutes later they disembarked at Gretna Township. Kirsty, along with Ethel, Martha and Lydia, waited on the platform in the expectation they would march back in military formation in the same way they did in the morning.

Sandra was the last one to pile out of the carriage. She'd been jammed at the back, hemmed in by munitionettes. 'Let's go.' She linked arms with Kirsty. 'No sense hanging around here.'

'I thought we'd have to march back.' Kirsty walked alongside Sandra to the street outside.

'Now the shift is finished, we're on our own time.'

Kirsty considered herself to be on duty all the time, and the concept of time of her own was foreign to her. However, this was not London, but a strange new world of independent-minded, working girls, comfortable with the freedom their new lives provided.

Earlier in the day when the policewomen marched to the station Kirsty paid little attention to the quiet streets. But now, the shops lining the avenue were open, their windows bright with goods on sale. Many of the wares were things she thought unobtainable due to the war.

Sandra laughed at Kirsty's expression when a mauve silk scarf caught her eye and she turned her head to peer into the shop window. 'You look like a child in a sweet shop,' she said.

'I haven't seen a silk scarf since the war started.'

'We can go inside if you like.' Sandra pulled her towards the door.

Kirsty shook her head. 'I am afraid I have no money with me.'

'Well, we can come back later.'

'I don't understand,' Kirsty said. 'I thought they built Gretna to house the munitions workers and didn't expect a complete town.'

Sandra started to walk along the road again. 'When the government decided to build a munitions factory here they soon realized the thousands of workers required to operate it needed to be housed. So they built the houses, and then expanded into a town to supply everything the workers would need, and that included shops. The township has a Post Office, a laundry, a bakery, and lots of recreational things.'

She gestured towards a building, 'That's the cinema, and the dance hall is further up. And there are libraries, bowling greens, billiard rooms, and sports grounds, as well as various clubs and a couple of hotels. You will find plenty of things to do in your spare time.'

'Is there anything Gretna doesn't provide?'

'The only thing we lack are pubs, but the workers go into Carlisle for those. Some of the girls go a bit daft here because they earn so much money, and because so much is on offer, we have to keep an eye out so they don't land themselves in trouble.'

Kirsty was silent for a moment while she digested the information. Eventually, she spoke. 'Does that mean the government owns everything here?'

'Yes. The Ministry of Munitions took over all the pubs and hotels in Carlisle as well, to prevent a lot of the carousing that used to go on. Alcohol is strictly controlled in this area. Thank goodness for that.'

'I see.'

By this time they had reached the top of the avenue, and they turned left in the direction of the policewomen's hostel.

'The sports fields are further along this road on the edge of the township,' Sandra said. 'I am in the hockey team, but there are lots of other sports. How do you fancy joining the women's football team?'

'Women's football? I thought only men played that.'

'Not here. Women can do anything they have a mind to.'

Martha, who was walking behind them, said, 'I wouldn't mind joining the football team.'

'Really!'

Kirsty strode towards the hostel, her mind turning over everything talked about on their journey from the station. More and more, she was coming to the conclusion that Gretna was a most unusual and exhilarating place, where women had more freedom than anywhere else in the British Isles.

As they drew nearer to the hostel, Kirsty got her first view of it in the daylight. When they arrived last night and left for work this morning, it had been dark.

The wooden hostel was not an attractive building, appearing bleak and ugly in the rays of the winter sun, with its black painted boards and iron framed windows.

Kirsty climbed the two steps and pushed the door open.

'Oh, sorry, I didn't hear you coming.' The girl in the overall, at the other side of the door, dumped her scrubbing brush into a bucket of water and stood back to let them in.

'I forgot to tell you,' Sandra said, 'the ministry employs

maids, cooks and housekeepers to take care of us. So, our free time really is free time.'

Kirsty turned to Martha and Ethel. 'This is the strangest place I've ever worked. It's nothing like London.'

23

Kirsty and Dance Hall Duty

Martha had left the hostel half an hour earlier. 'Dance hall duty tonight,' she said when she passed Kirsty in the corridor. 'I'll see you there.'

'Blast, I'd forgotten.'

'Better not let Sarge catch you.'

After scurrying to her room in a mad dash to get ready Kirsty was out of breath and running late. Finally, her ablutions completed, she pulled her belt tight, lifted her hat from the locker beside her bed and rammed it on her head. A quick look around the room established nothing was forgotten. She hurried down the stairs to the hall to double-check the duty roster on the wall. The rota confirmed she was listed for duty, to patrol the dance hall, to ensure the munitionettes remained safe and did not succumb to temptation. It was so easy for young girls to be led astray, particularly when so many navvies remained working on the factory site.

Perils abounded for them in the dark streets. Wartime measures enforced a blackout, even though Gretna Township was in a secluded part of the country and the Zeppelins never came so far west.

Unlike the area where the work was carried out, the township had paved roads, and the sound of Kirsty's boots on the hard surface provided the reassurance she was alone. She rounded the corner into the avenue and everything changed. Groups of young women, walking arm-in-arm, giggled and chatted, a crowd of noisy navvies burst into song as they ogled them, and another group further down the street did a jig in the middle of the road.

Kirsty spurted along the road to catch up with the first

group. She glared at the men, before saying to the girls, 'Move along. No loitering.'

One of the girls turned. 'What's it to do with you?'

She stiffened. 'Do what you're told and move along.'

'Or what?' The girl's defiant voice echoed along the street, but she turned to the others and said, 'Come on, let's get out of here, or the Lady Police,' her voice was full of sarcasm, 'might arrest us.'

The girls skipped and ran down the road, giggling and laughing. The Irish ones were always the worst. Defiance seemed to be part of their nature. If only they knew the trouble they were courting.

Kirsty wished someone had been there to look out for her when she was their age, then maybe her life might not have been wrecked, and she would still have her parents' support. It was only through her own attempts she'd been able to pick up the pieces and formulate a new life for herself. But a niggle of self-doubt never left her, worrying away at the core of her being, drawing her into a career where she could help other girls before it was too late for them.

The sound of music, faint at first, and then louder the further she walked down the street, indicated her arrival at the dance hall. She halted at the door, reluctant to enter. It had been the lure of dancing that changed her life.

Women, girls, and young men, elbowed and jostled their way into the dance hall. She pushed thoughts of the past out of her mind and followed them in. The music was louder now, and from her position in the doorway, she could see the dance floor.

Immediately the memory of that awful time, eight years ago, returned. She remembered exactly where it all happened. At the other end of the lawn, music played in the ballroom and girls chatted and laughed, waiting for their dance cards to be filled by eligible young men wishing to dance with them. The older women sat close by and kept watch to make sure no undesirables approached their charges. Her chaperone, so near and yet so far away, would be gossiping with the others. The safety of her charge would not cross her chaperone's mind because she was accompanied by a young man of honour, a family friend. She closed her eyes and the smell of whisky laden breath filled her nostrils. In vain she tried to stop the fumbling hands tearing at her dress, and no matter how she tried to twist away, those cruel lips bruised hers with an unimaginable violence, leading up to the final outrage.

She snapped her eyes open, suppressed a shudder along with the memory and, bracing herself, walked into the dance hall.

The music continued to play and the dancers gyrated in time. The modern dances were so intimate, not like the formal balls that had been part of her youth, she pushed the thought away before the past resurrected itself. The foxtrots and waltzes were bad enough, allowing dancers to embrace on the dance floor, but even worse was the most indecent dance of all, the tango, which had become so popular among young people.

These young girls, the munitionettes, had no idea of the dangers they attracted.

Sally pushed her arms into the sleeves and pulled the dress over her head. She wriggled until the silk material slid down her body. A dress like this was something she never thought she would own, and she would never have bought it if Maggie hadn't been with her. When they saw it, in the shop window in Central Avenue, Maggie said it would look good on her. 'Go on, try it on.' Sally didn't need much persuasion.

After her arrival in Gretna, Sally had taken a few weeks to settle in. Some of the girls in the hostel were rough and raucous, the type of girl she always stayed clear of in Silvertown. The Irish girls, in particular, frightened her. Maggie, a Glasgow girl, was the one who had befriended her, shown her where everything was, and helped her fit into the working schedule which was completely different to her Silvertown munitions work.

'You should go out more, have some fun,' Maggie said

earlier this evening. 'Did you ever go dancing in London?'

Sally shook her head. Her mum would never give permission. But her mum wasn't here and would never know, so she gave in to Maggie's entreatments. 'Just this once,' she said.

'Are you ready yet?' Maggie opened the cubicle curtain. 'Aw, you're looking awfully bonny. A little touch of lip gloss, and all the boys will be after you.'

'Decent girls don't use lip gloss.' Sally wondered what her mother would think.

'Don't be daft. All us modern girls wear it nowadays.'

'I'd rather not.'

'Oh well, suit yourself. But we'd better hurry, all the others have left, and we're last out.'

Sally would have preferred her bed, but she followed Maggie out into the dark street.

24

Dietger Joins the Irish Navvies

The Irish navvies clustered in a group to the left of the stage where the lights were dimmer. Aidan turned his back to the dance floor, raised the bottle to his mouth and gulped the fiery liquid. Wiping his lips with the back of his hand he passed it back to Dermot.

His friend winked at him. 'A taste of the good stuff. Poteen brought all the way from Ireland.'

Aidan grinned. 'First good drink since I got here.' His eyes surveyed the dancers, looking for Shannon.

He frowned when he saw her talking and laughing with the fellow she'd met in the Carlisle bar a few weeks ago. Grabbing the bottle from Dermot, he took another swig. No girl made a fool of him. He'd teach the little scrubber.

He rammed the bottle back into Dermot's hand and clenched his fists.

Dermot clutched his arm. 'Ca canny, laddo.'

'I'll lamp him, that I will.' Aidan flexed his hands.

'Don't be an eejit, that will only draw attention. If ye're in the clink what good will that do the cause.'

Aidan inhaled several times until his pulse calmed. He could see the sense of what Dermot was getting at. The cause was more important than any scrubber, even Shannon.

'Come on, let's dance,' he said, grabbing Vera around the waist and swinging her onto the dance floor. However, his eyes never left Shannon.

It was Dietger's first visit to the dance hall where the young munitions workers let their hair down. When people relaxed, they were off guard, and the chances of acquiring information increased.

He wandered around the edge of the floor, surveying the dancers. He compared it with the structured, elegant balls and dances in his homeland, and found this one a rabble. The music, loud and discordant to his ears, matched the lack of inhibitions in those dancing. The war was to blame, he was certain.

'Sure, and I didn't expect to see you here.' The voice sounded low and melodic, and decidedly Irish.

Dietger turned, a smile on his lips. He had already worked out a use for the Irish girl, and been frustrated at his inability to find her during his search of Carlisle's public houses. But now, he had found her. She and Aidan were his entry ticket to Gretna Township, and ultimately the factory areas.

'I thought I might meet you here. You seem to be a girl who appreciates a good time.'

'And what would you be meaning by that?'

'I mean no offence. I simply made a statement. I hoped to find you here and asked around because think I might be of use to your friends.'

'And here am I thinking you were interested in my charms.'

'There is that as well,' he said. 'But I do not even know your name.'

'Ah, now, my name is it you're wanting?'

'It would help me to know what to call you.'

She stared across to the corner where the navvies clustered. No doubt sharing an illicit bottle of the hard stuff while plotting something subversive.

'You want to meet my friends?'

'Yes.'

'Follow me then, but don't expect a welcome from Aidan. He thinks you're after me. Oh, and my name's Shannon.'

He followed her around the edge of the dance floor until they reached the group of navvies.

She grabbed the arm of one of them. 'Cormac, this is

Derek Clark, he says he can be of use to us although I can't imagine how.'

Dietger sensed the animosity of the men towards him and straightened his posture from the slouch he developed for his Derek Clark persona, to his more usual erect bearing. He needed his height and physical strength to make an impression on this group.

'What makes you think you would be of benefit to us?' The deceptively soft tone of Cormac's voice masked something more aggressive.

'I share your sympathies. I was in Ireland at the time of the troubles, and I helped with the supply of guns for the conflict. So, if you are planning anything, I am sure I could be of assistance.'

'Why would you be thinking we were planning something? And why should we trust you?'

Animosity radiated from Aidan, who obviously did not recognize Dietger as the man he met in London.

'I have no love for the English.' Dietger kept his voice low. 'But I cannot do much on my own, although my contacts can supply anything you might need. That is why I thought that together we might hit back at them when they least expect it.'

'You're making a lot of assumptions.' Aidan turned to face the navvies. 'I say don't trust him, he might be an English spy.'

Dietger shrugged. 'I am no spy, just a fellow sympathizer. But ...' he shrugged again, 'if you do not want to avail yourself of what I can offer, then that is up to you.'

One of the navvies pulled the others aside. They whispered feverishly among themselves, and Dietger could see Aidan arguing with them. After a few minutes of further argument, the men came out of their huddle, although the scowl on Aidan's face indicated his displeasure with their decision.

Cormac held out his hand. 'I'm Cormac Doyle, this here's my brother Dermot, and you've already met my sister.' He gestured towards Shannon.

'Finn Donovan.' The squat man with the dark moustache and beard grabbed Dietger's hand in a firm shake.

'Declan Adair.' He grinned. A charmer with a roguish twinkle in his eye, although his receding hairline detracted from the boyish appearance.

'Fergus Murphy.' Unmistakable with his ginger hair and beard.

Dietger had met him before in a Carlisle ale house, although the man gave no indication he remembered their encounter. But Fergus had been so drunk that night his memory would not have retained anything, which was just as well because he provided him with a lot of information about the group.

'You must be Aidan Maguire.' Dietger faced the scowling man who had not yet introduced himself.

'And how would you be knowing that.'

Aidan was smaller than him but Dietger sensed it would be a mistake to underestimate this man.

'I was a friend of James Connolly, and I am aware you spent time at Frongoch.'

'A friend?'

'Yes, I wept when the British executed him. They did it in such a vile way, tied to a chair for the firing squad because his injuries prevented him from standing.'

A wave of revulsion swept through the navvies, and Dietger held his breath. Would they accept him?

Dermot turned and held out his hand again. 'Welcome to the group.'

25

Sally

Sally found a seat at the edge of the dance floor. The girls sat here while they waited for a dancing partner. The men clustered in groups around the hall, most of them beside the entry doors, and some at either side of the stage. Even to Sally's untrained eye, it was evident girls far outnumbered men.

Maggie was already dancing but Sally, scared someone would ask her to dance, hoped no one would notice her. She shrank as far back in her chair as possible, studying each man as he approached, terrified he might be coming for her.

'Would you like to dance?'

A young man she recognized as being one of the lab technicians stood before her. He looked at her expectantly and held out his hand.

Blood pounded in her ears, and the music faded. She rose out of the chair, as if in a trance. 'I don't actually know how to dance.'

'Don't worry, I will show you,' he said.

He placed one arm around her and grasped her hand with the other. 'This is a foxtrot,' he said. 'You walk two steps, then take a step to the side, and then put your feet together. That's all there is to it. We do it in time to the music and repeat the same steps over and over again.'

Sally followed his lead, concentrating so much on the steps, she forgot she was in a man's arms.

'You're a natural,' he said, whirling her around the dance floor.

Intoxicated with the music and her partner's praise she abandoned herself to the dance, but in her exhilaration, she stumbled and bumped into the group of men standing to the left of the stage.

Hot with embarrassment she turned to apologize to the men and met the eyes of someone she thought she would never see again. Rosie's boyfriend. The one she intended to meet on the night of the Silvertown explosion. The man with her when she died. But how could that be? Rosie was dead, and he was here, full of life.

Kirsty, hands clasped behind her back, stood to the right of the entrance door watching for any trouble among the dancers swirling around the floor in time to the music. Apart from intervening earlier on, when she spotted a girl attempting to escape a man's attentions, the evening had been trouble-free. She recognized many of the girls from her inspection duties on the early shift at the mixing station, the place where the girls hand-mixed the nitroglycerine and guncotton.

Kirsty did not envy the girls, and she supposed they were entitled to some fun after doing such a dangerous job. But she did have a duty to protect them, because their desire for a good time exposed them to different kinds of danger.

The Irish girls, in particular, were prone to flirt with the navvies, but they seemed more worldly wise than some of the others. Sally, whom she spotted earlier sitting at the side of the dance floor, was now dancing with one of the lab technicians. He looked a nice enough young man, but Kirsty knew from experience how the nicest young men change when the desires of the flesh overcame them. And Sally was vulnerable, that had been obvious when they'd travelled to Gretna in the same railway carriage. She determined to keep a close eye on the sixteen-year-old girl.

When Sally stumbled and bumped into the men standing beside the stage, Kirsty tensed, ready for action if things got nasty. The navvies in the group were a rough lot, and unpredictable, however, they appeared to be in good humour and they laughed and waved her away. Kirsty relaxed, tangling with navvies was not something she looked forward to, and she was thankful it wouldn't be necessary.

Sally's response, though, was unexpected. She froze, then she broke away from her dance partner to run for the door, leaving him standing with a bewildered look on his face. She barged past Kirsty and ran down the stairs.

Kirsty ran after her, catching up as they reached the street. She grabbed the girl's arm. 'Sally, what's wrong?'

Sally whirled to face her. 'It's him,' she spluttered.

'Who, Sally?' Kirsty tightened her grip to prevent the girl running off.

'He recognized me.' Sally stared at the entrance to the dance hall. 'I'm afraid he'll come after me.' She struggled to break free.

'I will walk with you. He won't touch you while I am here, and once you're in the hostel you will be safe.'

Sally nodded, but lapsed into silence as they walked, and every few steps she cast anxious glances over her shoulder.

'What are you afraid of?' Kirsty broke the silence.

'I can't tell you here. He might be listening.'

'But nobody else is here. The street is empty, everyone is still at the dance.'

However, no matter how much prodding Kirsty did, Sally remained silent.

The hostel loomed in front of them, a long, one storey wooden building. Kirsty escorted Sally up the steps and into the entrance hall.

A young woman walked forward to meet them. She looked familiar, and Kirsty guessed she must either be the matron in charge or one of the housekeepers.

'What's wrong, Sally? You are back early from the dance.' The woman's eyes flickered over Kirsty. 'Why are the lady police involved?'

'Someone at the dance hall frightened her, but she won't say who or why. She's terrified he will follow her.' Kirsty released her grip on Sally's arm now they were safely inside the hostel.

'Oh, Beatrice, I was so scared.' Sally's voice quivered.

Beatrice put her arm around the girl's shoulder. 'You will

be safe here. I will not let any harm come to you. But you must tell us what is troubling you.' She turned to face Kirsty. 'My room is at the end of the hall. I have a kettle and can make a cup of tea. If we go there maybe Sally will feel able to confide in us.'

Kirsty followed her into the small room and sat on the only chair. Sally perched on the edge of the bed where Beatrice joined her after she made the tea.

'Here, drink this. I have made it sweet to counteract the shock.'

Sally swallowed a mouthful.

'Feeling better now?' Beatrice said. 'So perhaps you can tell me and the lady police what the problem is.'

'It was something that happened at Silvertown.' Sally hesitated. 'There was this big explosion. It killed my best friend.' She gulped some more tea. 'The thing is, she shouldn't have been in the factory when it exploded, she had a date that night with her boyfriend. She told me he asked her to take him inside the factory because he was a newspaper reporter and wanted to write about it. But they never found his body, and now he's here. I think he had something to do with Rosie's death.' She buried her face in her hands. 'And I'm so scared he'll come after me.'

Kirsty leaned forward. 'I am not going to let that happen. But I need you to describe him to me, and when I find this man you will need to identify him, and if he did have anything to do with your friend's death I will make sure he's locked up.'

Her name escaped him. He wasn't even sure he ever knew it, she was just Rosie's friend. She might not even remember him or associate him with the explosion. But when their eyes met it left him in no doubt she recognized him.

The sight of this girl brought back memories of Rosie, whom he courted and killed. Lovely Rosie, who trusted him and gave him her love. He would have preferred not to kill her, but she knew too much about him and he couldn't risk her identifying him. Now, this girl, her friend, was here, although it was likely she didn't know much. But judging by the shocked look on her face she recognized him, and by doing so, she presented him with an unforeseen danger which he would have to do something about.

One of the men pushed a bottle into his hand. 'Drink up mate, there's more where that came from.'

He nodded, and put it to his lips, but his eyes followed the fleeing form of the girl who had bumped into them.

26

Sally

Doubts flooded Sally's mind. The lack of proof that Rosie's boyfriend caused the explosion that led to her friend's death, undermined her certainty of his guilt. Maybe it was all a horrible coincidence. Maybe she was worrying for nothing.

Her tea cooled while she talked to Kirsty and Beatrice. She drank the rest of it until only tea leaves remained in the bottom of the cup.

'What will you do?'

Kirsty tapped the piece of paper containing her written notes of Sally's description of the man who had frightened her. 'I will go back to the dance hall. If this man's still there, I will question him.'

Sally cringed. If she was wrong, she'd be creating trouble for him. 'I don't really know if he caused the explosion. I just got such a shock when I saw him.'

She watched Kirsty's face cloud over.

'I still have to check him out, Sally. I can't ignore what you told me.'

'I suppose.' Sally shrugged her shoulders. It was all a muddle, and she couldn't think straight.

'Of course, and if he knows we're keeping an eye on him you should be safe enough.'

Sally turned to Beatrice after Kirsty left. 'It will be all right, won't it?'

'I am sure there is nothing for you to worry about, and the best place for you now is bed. So off you go.'

The dormitory was quiet. Sally wriggled out of her dress and dived into bed, pulling the blanket over her head, and wishing her cubicle had a door rather than a curtain. However, sleep did not come. She tossed and turned, listened to the clatter of the girls when they returned, tossed and turned some more, and worried about her accusation against Rosie's boyfriend. Was he innocent or guilty? She had been convinced of his guilt, now she wasn't so sure.

Kirsty quickened her pace. Sally's story had been confusing. At first, she was sure the man she had seen in the dance hall had been responsible for her friend's death, and then she expressed doubts. Uncertain where the truth lay, but convinced of her duty to check the story out, Kirsty hastened to get back before they played the last dance and everyone dispersed.

Although out of breath by the time she reached the dance hall she didn't stop until she was inside. The band played *If You Were the Only Girl in the World*, and several couples swayed around the floor in time with the music, but there was no sign of the men who had frightened Sally. From where she stood she could see Martha tapping a couple on the shoulder for dancing too close, but as soon as the policewoman turned her back they resumed their hold on each other.

Kirsty beckoned to Martha, who walked across to her when the music stopped.

'The navvies,' Kirsty gasped, she hadn't got her breath back.

'What about them?'

'Have they gone?'

She ignored the curiosity in Martha's eyes.

'They left ages ago. I think this place is too tame for them. Why do you want to know?'

Before Kirsty could answer the band struck up *God Save the King* and everyone stood to attention.

'It's a long story,' Kirsty whispered. 'I will tell you all about it once we finish our shift.'

Some of the dancers seemed in no hurry to leave, while others struggled into their coats before leaving the warmth of the dance hall for the chilly air outside. Kirsty and Martha kept careful watch, ready to break up any couple who seemed too amorous.

'That seems to be everyone,' Kirsty said. 'We'd best go outside and make sure no one is still hanging around or getting up to anything they shouldn't.' However, when the policewomen left the hall, no one remained on the street except for the last of the revellers turning the corner at the top of the avenue.

Kirsty took the opportunity to brief Martha about Sally's story as they walked slowly up the road.

'It has to be checked out.'

'Do you know what the navvies look like?'

Kirsty sighed. 'Not really. My attention was focused on Sally. But I am determined to find them.'

Martha laughed. 'How many navvies do you think work here at Gretna? It will be like looking for a needle in a haystack.'

Kirsty stopped in the middle of the road. 'You're right. I didn't think about that. I'm going to need Sally to identify the man who frightened her.'

She started walking again, her shoulders no longer erect, and her posture reflecting the drop in her spirits. She had set herself an impossible task.

27

Sally

He waited for her in the street outside Gretna Station. She worked on the early shift, therefore, she should be on the next train, the one bringing the workers home.

While he waited, he practised what he would say. It was imperative to win her over and prove to her that he was not responsible for what happened to Rosie. His mother always said he possessed a silver tongue, and that if he had a mind to, he could charm the birds out of the trees.

Judging by the fear Sally showed when she saw him at the dance hall, he realized he would need to use all the charm he could muster to convince her, and if that didn't work his only option was to silence her.

However, that final choice would disrupt all the plans he had so carefully laid for his time in Gretna.

The train arrived and the doors clanged open. Workers, mainly women, and girls, spilled out in a chattering horde, pushing and jostling in an attempt to be the first to reach the exit.

How on earth would he find her in this crowd? He focused on the gate leading out of the station where the crowd thinned to allow them to pass through, and there she was. He manoeuvred through the hurrying workers until he reached her side.

'Sally!'

She turned, but when she saw him she shrank back, the fear evident in her eyes.

'I could tell you were afraid of me, but I only want to talk to you,' he said. 'I wanted to visit Rosie's friends after what happened, but I couldn't. It was such a tragedy, and I miss her so much.'

He didn't need to fake tears because he did miss her, and now they rolled down his cheek and dripped off his chin. Not a day passed he didn't regret Rosie's death, although it had been necessary at the time. He dashed the tears away with the back of his hand.

'Just hear me out,' he said.

'I don't understand. If you miss her so much why did you run away?'

'It was impossible for me to stay because the authorities arrest conscientious objectors. I am on their apprehension list.'

Sally's expression didn't change. 'You were supposed to be with her that night.'

'I know. But I couldn't find an omnibus. They've sent so many of them to the front, it's difficult to find one.' He dashed a tear away with the back of his hand. 'It torments me to think I could have saved her.'

'Another thing I don't understand is the reason you were meeting Rosie. Why did you want to go inside the factory?'

He thought quickly. Rosie must have told Sally why they were meeting.

'I intended to write an article for the newspapers on Silvertown. I would have written from the viewpoint that the explosives being manufactured kill people. I am against violence and killing, that is why I'm a conscientious objector. And I suppose the explosion that night illustrates how destructive they are. But after the factory blew up, I had to leave in a hurry to avoid arrest.'

Sally frowned. Her expression conveyed doubt.

'I am here because I want to do a follow up to the article Conan Doyle published last year, but if you would rather I leave, I will understand.'

'No, stay and do your article.'

He smiled at her, the smile he used when he wanted to charm a woman. 'Thank you. I am most grateful. And after I obtain the information I need, I will leave.'

Sally's expression softened.

'One last thing,' he said, 'I am still wanted for being a

conscientious objector. Promise you won't give me away.'

'I promise,' she said.

Sally ignored her sore feet and sped up the avenue. 'Why didn't you wait for me?' she said when she caught up with Maggie.

'I didn't want to get in the way of you and your sweetheart.' Maggie grinned at her. 'Oh, now you're blushing.' Maggie skipped a few steps and her grin widened.

'I am not, and he isn't.'

'Isn't what?'

'My sweetheart.'

'He looked mighty interested, and he's nicer than that lab chap who's been mooning after you.'

'He used to be the boyfriend of one of my friends.'

'Well, he seems interested in you now.'

'I'm not interested in him,' Sally snapped.

'If you don't want him I'll maybe try my luck. I fancy him.' Maggie looked back. 'Blast, he's disappeared.'

'Please yourself.' Sally focused on the road ahead and walked faster. 'I'm tired and desperate for a rest before our meal at the hostel.'

Sally admitted to herself Maggie was right, Rosie's ex-boyfriend was nice, and it was clear he missed her. She bit her lip when she remembered how tears rolled down his face when he spoke of Rosie, and wished she had been able to comfort him. But she didn't know how to do that. Besides, he might not welcome her sympathy, particularly when he seemed to want to present a stiff upper lip to his friends, although this was in direct opposition to the underlying vulnerability she sensed. Heat suffused her neck, spreading to her face, as shame engulfed her at the thought of how she misjudged him.

'I wonder what's on the menu tonight?' she said to break the silence, and take her mind off Rosie. And the man she now found attractive.

28

Kirsty

Kirsty sat on the edge of the bed. Her feet ached and she wanted to pull her boots off and lie down until the bell rang to herald dinner. But Sally's story about the Silvertown explosion had been eating away at her mind all day, and her own failure to find the man involved, weighed heavy. Her preoccupation with the implications of this man being at Gretna filled her thoughts, making her immune to the taunts of some of the more outspoken munitionettes, and she welcomed the end of her shift at the mixing station.

'You're worrying about that girl, aren't you?'

Kirsty hadn't heard Martha approach. It was as if her friend had second sight and knew she needed some reassurance.

'I feel useless. I am supposed to be a policewoman, and I can't even do something simple like finding the man who frightened her.'

'You are a policewoman,' Martha said, 'and a good one. Just because the man you were looking for wasn't at the dance hall when you got back doesn't mean you won't be able to trace him. Interview Sally again, make her give you a complete description of him, and instruct her to let you know if she sees him again.'

'You're right, of course.' Kirsty rose from her seated position. 'Sally did give me a description last night, but she was upset. She will have had time to think and maybe she can give me something new that would help to identify him.'

'Would you like me to come with you?'

'Thanks for the offer but she's young and nervous and a new face might inhibit her, so it would be best if I went alone.'

The minute Kirsty stepped outside her confidence left her, despite her experience of policing. She understood how to patrol, how to safeguard foolish girls, even how to send opportunistic young men on their way with a flea in their ear. But nothing in her training prepared her for investigating deaths and sabotage. And she was sure the Silvertown explosion had been sabotage, and the death of Sally's friend was connected to that. If she was right, then Sally could be the key to the whole thing.

She quickened her pace, the sooner she spoke to Sally, the better.

'One of the lady police is at the door, miss.'

Beatrice glanced up from the report she was writing. 'Did she say what she wanted?'

The maid looked worried. 'I didn't ask her, miss. She asked for someone in authority, and I couldn't find matron.'

'Matron has gone to Carlisle. Show the policewoman in. I will attend to the matter.'

'Ah!' she said when Kirsty entered the office. 'I expect you are here to talk to Sally again.'

Kirsty nodded. 'I have concerns in respect of her story.'

Beatrice fingered her pen. 'She is one of our newer arrivals, young and vulnerable, never been away from home before, and I do not think she has had many encounters with boys or men.'

'Yes, but I gave a lot of thought to what Sally told us last night, and I think there's more to it than a scary encounter. I think someone dangerous may be in our midst.'

'What makes you think that?'

'The Silvertown connection. It was a massive explosion, and there were rumours of sabotage at the time. That, plus the death of Sally's friend, suggests the appearance of this man here, at Gretna, may be more than a coincidence. If he was involved in the explosion, then he might be planning something similar here. Whether or not that is the case it needs to be investigated. We can't ignore what Sally told us.'

'And if it is the case?'

Beatrice knew the information must be sent to Melville through her contact Alice, and Melville would expect to be informed about Kirsty's intentions.

'Firstly, I need to interview Sally again. She might remember something new and provide a better description. We need as much information as possible to identify this man.'

'What then? This is not something we can do on our own.'

Kirsty leaned back in her chair, and it was clear to Beatrice the policewoman had not thought that far ahead.

After a few moments, Kirsty said, 'I'll report back to my superior officer, of course. But I will also keep looking for this man.'

'If you are right and you find him that could prove dangerous.'

'Danger is nothing new to me.' Kirsty's voice bristled with indignation.

'I am only trying to say you should not tackle this on your own. This is too big not to be shared.' She had not meant to annoy Kirsty, but it was too late. 'Perhaps we should find Sally now, and if you do not mind I will sit in on the interview.'

Kirsty nodded, although the frown on her face indicated her displeasure.

Beatrice rang a little brass handbell and within a few moments Maisie appeared.

'Would you ask Sally to join us?'

'Yes, miss.' Maisie scuttled down the corridor and returned several minutes later with Sally.

'Come in and sit down, Sally.' Beatrice pointed to a chair. 'The lady policewoman wanted to ask you a few questions about your experience last night.'

'But I told you everything.' Sally wriggled in her seat.

'You were upset. You'd had a scare and needed time to think,' Kirsty said. 'I thought you might now remember other details that would help us identify the man.'

'It was all a mistake.' Sally mumbled.

'Pardon?'

'A mistake, my imagination ran away with me, and I'm sorry if I caused trouble.'

'But you said the man was at Silvertown at the time of the explosion.'

'So were lots of other folks, it don't mean they had anything to do with it.'

'But your friend, Rosie, was killed.'

'Any of us could have been killed, that's what happens when something explodes.'

'You need to understand, Sally, it requires to be checked out. If the man had nothing to do with the explosion or Rosie's death, then that is to his benefit.'

'I told you I'm sorry if I made trouble, but I've been thinking about it and I'm sure he had nothing to do with it. It was all just a big coincidence.'

'Sally ...'

'I told you everything.' Tears dripped down Sally's face. 'It's all a big mistake. Can I go now?'

Beatrice nodded, and Sally left the room.

'What now?' Beatrice stared at the closed door. Sally's response had not been what she expected, and she wondered why the girl was so adamant that her scare last night was a mistake.

Kirsty shrugged. 'It doesn't look like Sally plans to help us find this man, so all I can do is work with what I have, and report back.'

Beatrice nodded. As soon as Kirsty left she would seek Alice out and give her the information to send to Melville.

Kirsty burst through the door of the women's police hostel as the dinner gong sounded. Doors slammed, and the babble of voices echoed along the corridor.

The sergeant's voice soared above the noise. 'Hurry along, ladies. No time for idle chatter.'

She headed in the direction of the voice, she wanted to make her report as soon as possible.

'Excuse me, ma'am. Can I have a word?'

Sergeant Agnes Duncan turned to face her. 'What is so important it can't wait until after dinner?'

'It is important, ma'am, and I don't think it can wait.'

'All right, then,' Sergeant Duncan sighed. 'If you must.' She turned and led the way to her office.

Kirsty followed, and as soon as the door closed she detailed her contact with Sally, the interviews, and her suspicions.

'You think there might be a saboteur at Gretna.' The sergeant's voice was thoughtful.

'It seems to be too much of a coincidence, ma'am. First the explosion at Silvertown and now a report the same man is here.'

Sergeant Duncan tapped her fingers on the desk. 'You say this girl is not being co-operative.'

'Yes, ma'am. She was willing to talk yesterday, but not today. I think he may have contacted her.'

'That would mean she is in danger.'

'Yes, ma'am.'

'But she does not think she is in danger.'

'No, ma'am. She keeps repeating she made a mistake.'

The sergeant lapsed into silence. Kirsty remained standing to attention and watched her.

At last, the sergeant looked up. 'I need to take this to a higher level. This is not something we can cope with on our own. In the meantime, try to keep a watch on this girl in case he makes contact. But, if your supposition is correct, this is a dangerous man, and on no account are you to do anything on your own. You will note any details and report back to me. Understood.'

'Yes, ma'am.'

29

Dietger

Dietger leaned on the handrail of the bridge separating the platforms at Gretna Township's station. It was the best vantage point for the Solway Firth he could find, although being exposed like this made it risky. He sketched quickly, shielding the small sketchbook with his arm while remaining alert for approaching footsteps.

His sketchbook was filling up nicely after a day spent exploring the geography of the area. Tomorrow, he would concentrate on Eastriggs, the township adjacent to the acid and mixing plants.

'You wouldn't be waiting for Shannon, now, would you?'

He rammed the sketchbook in his pocket and turned towards the voice. Aidan's face was impassive, but his eyes flared with aggression. Dietger had not heard the man come up behind him and was not sure how much he had seen.

'That was not my intention, but I did notice Shannon and her friends leave the train after their shift. As far as I am aware they went to their hostel.'

Aidan leaned on the handrail beside him. 'I can't figure you out.' His voice lost the soft Irish lilt and became harsher. 'You're here on your own, but you're not seeking work. You wriggle your way into our group, charm our girls, drop hints about your Irish sympathies, and scribble in that notebook you stuffed in your pocket. Just who the hell are you?'

Dietger's eyes focused on the receding tide of the Solway Firth. 'They say the Solway is not to be trusted,' he murmured. 'Apparently it is all too easy to drown there, the tide comes in so fast.'

'Damn the Solway.' Anger roughened Aidan's voice.

'You didn't answer my question.'

'I do not intend to answer. We have met before and you are already aware of who I am. You do not need to know anything else. All you need know is that our aims are the same.'

A flicker of recognition appeared briefly in Aidan's eyes.

'What aims would those be?'

'The downfall of the English.' Dietger held his breath. Had he gone too far? Had he revealed too much? He remembered sensing this man's distrust at the London meeting and his own reservations. But the Brotherhood had insisted he was a man to trust.

'How would you be knowing that was my aim?'

'I make it my business to learn about the people I meet. I am aware you fought at the Easter Rising in Dublin and that out of all your friends, you were the one incarcerated at Frongoch. You are close to Michael Collins and you have no love for the English.'

'You know a helluva lot.'

'As I said, I make it my business.'

The two men stared out over the Solway.

'Something you may not be aware of is my friendship with Roger Casement, and my involvement when the *Asgard* brought guns to Howth harbour, although that turned out to be a disaster. I also met James Connolly several times, a fine man. It was shameful of the British to execute him the way they did, tied to a chair. He was dying in any case, but they did not allow him the decency of an honourable death.'

'They executed Casement as well.'

'Yes, August last year. Another fine man gone.'

'The English have a lot to answer for.'

'And you think you are the one to make them answer?' Dietger turned to face Aiden. 'I can help. I can access information you might never hear about, and when you do find out it would be too late to make use of it.'

'What kind of information?'

'Probably something that will make you delay what you are currently planning.'

Aidan remained silent but a look of discomfiture passed over his face.

Dietger had not been wrong when he guessed the Irish revolutionary planned to sabotage the munitions factory, although the factory was so vast and so spread out that any sabotage could only affect a small part of it.

'There is to be a royal visit.'

He searched Aidan's face for a reaction but the man's expression did not change.

'King George and Queen Mary are to visit Gretna Township in May.'

'Why would that be of interest to me?'

'I am sure you can work out this visit will provide more of an opportunity to hit back at the English than any paltry act of sabotage. I will leave you to plan the details.'

Dietger held out his hand. 'It is not necessary for us to be friends, but let us shake on a working relationship which will be of mutual benefit to both of us.'

Aidan grasped the proffered hand. 'As long as you remember to stay away from Shannon.'

'Your lady friend does not interest me. However, she could prove useful to our cause.'

30

Sally

Sally's heart skipped a beat when she saw him standing outside the station gates the next day. If anyone asked her she would deny looking for him, but her eyes let her down as they searched the crowd for his familiar face.

'You go on,' she said to Maggie. 'I'll catch you up in a minute.'

Maggie grinned at her. 'I thought you weren't interested.'

'I'm not, but I can't be rude.'

'Is that so.'

Maggie's tone indicated she didn't believe her, but Sally didn't care and turned away, waiting until her friend moved out of sight before turning to smile at him.

He reached a hand out to her, but drew it back again, as if he were afraid she would rebuff him. 'I couldn't get you out of my mind, even though you blame me for your friend's death. I should leave, but I had to see you again.'

Sally found it difficult to breathe, and she tried hard to suppress the fluttering inside her chest. 'I don't blame you.'

'You don't?'

'No.'

'Then I can hope?'

Uncertain what he meant, or what he hoped for, Sally tried to ignore the strange sensations coursing through her body. Was he interested in her in the way Maggie kept referring to? She suppressed the thought before it took hold and made her say something she might regret.

He turned his back to the swarming crowd leaving the station. 'I shouldn't have come here, it's risky.'

Sally frowned. 'Why is it risky?'

'Someone who used to be a friend spotted me yesterday,

and I'm afraid he will tell the authorities I am here.'

'Surely he wouldn't do that if he's a friend.'

'He's no longer a friend, and he hates conscientious objectors.'

Sally's breath caught at the back of her throat. Was that the reason the lady policewoman had questioned her? She thought it was connected to her running scared from the dance hall, but what if it had been something different? That would mean he was in danger and it was all her fault.

'One of the lady police asked me questions about you yesterday.' She studied the crowds hurrying up the avenue, expecting to see a policewoman on every corner. If they saw her talking to him it would be disastrous.

'What did she want? What did you tell her?' His voice deepened with anxiety.

'She wanted me to tell her what you looked like, and asked me to identify you.'

His eyes widened with alarm. Sally's heart thudded and she concealed her concern with difficulty.

'I didn't tell her anything. I don't even know your name.'

He grasped her hands and peered into her eyes. 'My name's Daniel.' His hands tightened on hers. 'I must go, but I risked everything to come here today, and I can't bear not to see you again.'

He stared at the ground, his eyes following the movement of his foot tracing a pattern in the dust. His grip on her hands was now so tight her fingers were numb, but she did not pull away.

'Will you meet me in Carlisle?' He shook his head. 'No, I have no right to ask you to do that. Forget I ever said anything.'

'Yes,' she whispered. 'Tell me when and where, and I'll come.'

31

Aidan

'Where were you today? I had to make an excuse to the gaffer that you were sick.' Cormac slapped Aidan on the shoulder. 'Good job he's not here or you'd be down the road.'

Aidan shrugged. His funds came from the Irish Republican Brotherhood, so keeping the job was unimportant, although it did give him access to areas of the factory that otherwise might be problematic.

'I scouted around,' he said. 'Planning where we can strike.'

Cormac looked over his shoulder at the horde of navvies crowding the station platform. At the end of their working shift everyone was anxious to return to Carlisle before the pubs closed for the night.

'Watch what you say. Not all the navvies are Irish.'

Aidan's mind had been so occupied with thinking about the stranger who said his name was Derek, although Aidan doubted that was his real name, he'd been oblivious to the arrival of the other navvies.

'There are things we need to discuss,' he muttered, 'but we'll talk about them when we get to our lodgings.'

The noise of the train pulling into the station ensured no further conversation took place. Aidan pushed his way on, followed by Cormac and his gang. They crammed into a carriage where the heat and smell of the men already there, plus the lack of fresh air made Aidan's head spin. The ten-minute journey felt like an eternity and his lungs were at bursting point when he staggered from the train to the platform at Carlisle. However, the air he gulped was so full of soot and smoke that he was glad when they left the station to be met with an icy gale.

The wind whipped around the men and rain stung their faces.

'Bejeezus,' Finn said, 'give me Irish rain any day, this stuff would slice your skin open.'

'Race you to the pub,' Declan said, 'I feel a mighty thirst coming on.'

'No.' Cormac's voice halted them in their tracks. 'Aidan has things he wants to discuss.'

'Bejeezus, what's more important than the pub after a hard day's graft?'

'Ireland, of course. We all said we'd be in on Aidan's plans. If he reckons there are things to discuss, then that'll be what we do.'

'What can we do that will make any difference? We've got good jobs with good money that we send back home. A prison cell doesn't appeal to me. So you do what you want. I'm off to the pub.' Fergus pulled his collar up and stamped off.

Aidan watched him go. If Fergus became a threat, he would have to do something about him. He couldn't risk him jeopardizing their plans.

'Never you mind him,' Cormac said. 'We'll pick up fish and chips on our way back to the digs, and we still have some of that poteen left.'

32

Dietger

Dietger kept his head down to ensure Aidan did not see him when he boarded the train at Gretna Township, not that it would make a great deal of difference, but he was not yet sure he could trust the Irish revolutionary. The man was too unpredictable and seemed to operate from an emotional base rather than a logical one.

Arriving in Carlisle, he waited until the navvies alighted before he stepped out of the end carriage. Tagging on behind a group of chattering workmen, he used them as a shield to stay out of sight until they reached the street outside, then searched for a hiding place where he could eavesdrop on the Irishmen. He spotted an empty alcove next to the station entrance and slipped into its shadows.

Clearly, the men planned something but their decision to discuss these plans at their lodging-house prevented him from finding out the details. But Fergus was the weak link, so he waited for the navvies to move off, and then followed him.

By the time he reached the pub Dietger's ears stung with the cold, and rain dripped from the peak of his cap down his face and off the point of his chin. He pushed through the door into the smoky warmth of the room beyond, took off his cap and slapped it against his arm to remove the worst of the wet, before ramming it back on his head and joining the throng waiting to be served at the bar. Within a short time, he spotted Fergus.

'Hello mate, where are your friends?' Dietger knew exactly where the other navvies were, but Fergus would not be aware of that.

The man turned. 'What business would that be of yours?'

Fergus towered over Dietger.

'I was just being friendly, mate. No offence meant.'

'Ah!' The Irishman's shoulders slumped. 'They went back to the digs. Didn't want to come to the pub.'

'You did not go with them?'

'Naw. I'm not interested in their shenanigans. A glass of ale is better.'

'Let me buy you one.' Dietger raised his arm to summon the barman.

Fergus laughed. 'Obvious you haven't been here for long.'

Dietger frowned.

'We're not allowed to buy anyone else a drink? Daft English law says we can't treat anyone.'

'That's right. It would be more than my license is worth,' the barman said. 'Now what can I fetch you?'

'A glass of beer will do for me,' Dietger said.

'And ...?'

'And what?'

'What are you eating?'

'Just the beer, thank you.'

'No grub, no beer. It's the law.' The barman mopped the top of the bar with a cloth.

Fergus struggled to contain his laughter. 'Stop taking the piss,' he said to the barman. 'He's new here. He doesn't know about the barmy regulations the government has brought in. Give him the usual plate of biscuits.'

He turned towards Dietger. 'All the pubs in Gretna and Carlisle are owned by the government, and they've got all these daft regulations, no treating, early closing, and no drink without a meal. The pub landlords get around that one with a plate of biscuits, you don't have to eat them if you don't want to, but you do have to buy them.'

'I did wonder why they always gave me biscuits with my beer,' Dietger said. 'Thanks for setting me straight. I appreciate it.'

'Quick, there's a couple of seats at the back of the room, let's grab them before anyone else does.' Fergus picked up his glass and plate of biscuits and hurried across the room.

Dietger followed. He did not know it yet, but Fergus would be his informant alerting him to the activities of his fellow navvies. The big Irishman would never know he was doing it.

Dietger lifted his glass. 'Cheers. I think we are going to be good friends.'

33

Aidan

'Best hide that until we're in our digs,' Cormac said. 'Old crabby,' his nickname for the landlady, 'objects to us taking our own food in.'

Aidan extracted a chunk of fish and a chip from the newspaper-wrapped parcel and shoved them in his mouth before cramming the parcel inside his jacket where it lay, hot and greasy, against his chest.

The rain still tipped down, but it didn't seem to affect Declan and Finn, dancing and swaying on the wet road, as they shadow boxed each other.

'Shh,' Cormac said when they reached the door of the lodging-house. 'Quietly does it.' He eased the door open, and the men, now silent, followed him inside and up the stairs.

Aidan removed the hot parcel from his chest, shrugged off his dripping jacket and slumped on his bunk tearing at the paper to reach the fish and chips inside. He was starving, not having eaten anything since breakfast.

'What did you want to discuss?' Cormac's eyes glinted with curiosity.

'We've all talked a lot about getting back at the English for what they did to us at the rising.' Aidan licked his greasy fingers.

'Yes, but how are we to do that?'

Aidan thought he detected an element of doubt in Finn's voice.

'I wasn't sure until today.'

Dermot was quick to chip in. 'I told you Aidan would have a plan.'

'But how risky will it be? My ma depends on the money I

send her every week.'

'Not as risky as blowing the factory up. And you'll still have jobs afterwards.'

Dermot leaned forward. 'So, what's the plan?'

'I'm still working on it, but I received information today that a visit by King George is planned for Gretna.' Aidan grinned. 'I am sure we can arrange a warm welcome for him.'

'How did you come by this information?'

'That chap, Derek, the one who's always latching on to us, told me.'

Dermot frowned. 'How can we tell whether the information is sound?'

'I wondered that. But he has Irish connections and sympathy for the cause. He was friends with Roger Casement and James Connolly. And he was mixed up with the gun-running at Howth Harbour. Maybe he's a spy.' He avoided informing them about the Brotherhood's instructions to help this man.

'What do you think, boys?' Dermot turned to the other men.

Aidan tensed, waiting for their decision.

The men muttered between themselves before nodding their agreement.

'We'll need to plan what to do then.'

Aidan relaxed. It was going to work out. 'We may need to bring one of the girls in on this. If we're planning to get anywhere near King Geordie, we'll need one of them to create a diversion.'

34

Dietger

Dietger lay on his stomach at the top of the grassy hillock where he had a clear view of the nitroglycerine section. A massive building over to the left was probably the glycerine distillery which housed boilers and machinery. The hydraulic plant and refrigerating plant also lay in the hollow. The railway line linking the buildings snaked on a gentle slope in the direction of the mixing stations.

Dermot and Cormac hadn't needed much persuasion to smuggle him into the construction site behind the security fences. They supplied him with cement stained trousers and jacket, and he sat between them in the truck.

'Hundreds of us navvies go in every day,' Dermot said, 'and the soldiers on guard can't check us all, so keep your head down and you'll be fine. We just have to make sure we're not in one of the first trucks to go through the gates. By the time they've checked fifty of them their attention is dwindling.'

The Irishman tipped him a wink when the trucks pulled up. 'I told you it would work.'

The engine stopped with a shudder, and the men nearest the back of the truck lowered the tailboard and leapt to the ground. Dietger followed Dermot, staying close to the Irish navvy.

'When we reach the work area grab a barrow,' Dermot said, 'and follow me.'

The navvies surged towards the site, grabbing shovels and pickaxes from the pile of tools stacked to one side. Dietger grabbed a wheelbarrow and trundled it along, trying to look knowledgeable about what he was doing.

Dermot stopped at the edge of a half-built structure. He

bent over and threw some bricks and rubble into the wheelbarrow. 'Keep hold of it and no one will question you. They'll think you're either taking rubble away or bringing more bricks. I'll be working here when you've finished what you have to do.'

Dietger nodded. He grabbed the handles of the barrow and wheeled it to the rear of the construction site. Depositing it in a place it would not be seen, he climbed the hillock separating the building site from the factory.

His viewpoint from the top of the mound meant the risk he ran coming here was well worth taking because what lay before him had been concealed from view until now. The nitroglycerine section nestled in the hollow which was larger than he had imagined. In the middle sat various substantial buildings with smaller structures dotted in between, and behind them the massive glycerine distillery. A railway line emerged from inside each building to connect up and lead to all the others and, as he lay watching, a wagon emerged from one of them with three girls pushing. They laughed and joked together oblivious of his watching eyes.

He withdrew the notepad and pencil from his pocket and quickly sketched the buildings below making notes and adding geographic pointers at each side of the paper. The Solway Firth over to his left and the main road to his right. With a quick look over his shoulder, he wriggled back down the slope, collected his wheelbarrow and headed back to where the navvies were working.

The phone call came as Dietger prepared for another day at Gretna.

'Telephone.' The shout came from the bottom of the stairs.

Dietger hurried from his room and leaped down the stairs, two steps at a time.

'Bloody telephone,' the crone holding it said. 'Just because my room's next to the blasted thing doesn't mean I have to chase folks up.'

He flashed her a smile and grabbed the handset from her hand. The only person aware of how to get in touch with him was his contact in London. He would not phone if it was not important.

'Thanks,' he said to the crone, who shuffled off down the hall. He knew she got her room at a special rate because of the telephone.

He waited until she closed her door before cupping his hand over the mouthpiece and saying, 'Yes?'

'I wondered how you were enjoying your holiday,' the tinny voice replied.

'The holiday is quite enjoyable. I may stay for longer. The scenery here is lovely, ideal for sketching.'

'That is good. I talked with your cousin the other day, and he said his brother, George, is planning to visit you on the 18th May.'

'I look forward to that, and I will ensure he gets a warm welcome.'

'Oh, and before I forget, one of your friends, Michael Williams, is on his way north. He left this morning.'

'Thanks, I will make sure to look out for him.'

The phone clicked and the caller was no longer on the line. Dietger hung the handset on its cradle on the wall and returned to his room. He wrote nothing down. He did not need to do that to decipher the message. The royal visit was scheduled for the 18th May, and William Melville was on his way to Gretna.

35

Meeting with Melville

Kirsty paced back and forth on the station platform in an attempt to lessen the penetration of the cold wind from the firth. The train was taking forever to arrive. She stared out over the Solway, a dangerous place when the tide rushed upstream, the water surging in fast to trap the unwary. Today, the mudflats stretched for miles and the beach was deserted.

The blast of a whistle alerted her to the train's arrival. She raised her hand to acknowledge the driver, standing in the engine beside his furnace of flaming coals. He returned a smile to her from his soot-streaked face.

Melville wasn't hard to spot. Tall, grey-haired and with a bushy moustache, just as he'd been described to her.

'Sir,' she said, 'I am WPC Campbell, here to escort you to the women's police hostel.'

The man laid his briefcase on the platform while he buttoned his coat and turned his collar up. 'Is Gretna always as chilly as this?'

Kirsty lifted the briefcase. 'The cold air comes from the wind blowing in from the firth. Once we leave the station it will be more sheltered.'

Melville thrust his hands into his pockets. 'Let's go then. The sooner we get this business out of the way the better it will be.'

He lapsed into silence as they walked up the avenue, and Kirsty wondered whether she should say something. Perhaps tell him about Gretna and the factory. She sneaked a sideways glance at him, but his eyes seemed to be fixed on something in the far distance that only he could see, and he was so preoccupied she decided not to speak. Better to leave him to his thoughts.

Sergeant Duncan was waiting at the hostel door when they arrived. Melville surfaced from his trance when Kirsty introduced them, and after shaking hands, the sergeant led them to the dining room.

'I am sorry we don't have a formal meeting room,' she said opening the door, 'but most of my policewomen are on duty this morning so it's unlikely we will be disturbed here.' She guided him to a table in the corner. 'I've asked cook to bring tea and sandwiches for you. I am sure you need some sustenance before our meeting starts.'

'That is most kind of you,' Melville said, the severity of his expression softening. 'The journey from London is a long one.'

Kirsty laid his briefcase on the table in front of him, but when cook arrived with a loaded tray he moved it to the floor.

'Miss Jacobs is on her way,' the sergeant said. 'Once she arrives we can discuss our problem.'

Kirsty walked to the door to await Beatrice's arrival.

Dietger had kept Melville under surveillance since his arrival last night, and once he ascertained the spymaster had booked into the Station Hotel it was simply a matter of watching and waiting.

Rather than following him from the hotel the next morning, Dietger waited at the railway station. Two deep alcoves flanked each side of the main entrance and he tucked himself out of sight in one of them. The alcove had not been the warmest place to wait. A chilly draft searched out every corner, teasing the edges of his jacket, slipping icy tentacles between his collar and neck, and circling his feet until they froze. By the time Melville appeared, striding out in his confident way with his pipe clamped tightly in his mouth, Dietger was so chilled he found it an effort to move.

Once the train arrived at Gretna Township, Dietger waited until Melville and the policewoman had walked more than half-way up the avenue before he emerged from the last carriage to follow them. He hovered at the corner of the street after Melville vanished inside the women's police hostel, and that was when he saw Beatrice, hurrying along with her head down.

Now, what was that all about? Some kind of meeting, he guessed. But what were they discussing? Maybe the time had come to meet Beatrice again.

All the girls were at work and silence cloaked the hostel when Beatrice left to attend the meeting. Kirsty had arrived earlier that morning to inform her that her senior officer thought Sally's situation warranted the involvement of a higher authority, and in response a London official had been dispatched.

A cold wind blew in from the Solway Firth, whipping the ends of her hair, and forcing Beatrice to turn up the collar of her coat and push her hands into the pockets. She should have brought a scarf, but in her hurry left it dangling from a hook on the back of her room door.

Kirsty was waiting for her at the entrance to the women's police hostel. 'He's here,' she said. 'I am not sure who he is and he didn't give much away when I escorted him from the station.'

'Am I late?'

'No, the meeting hasn't started. Cook's plying him with tea and sandwiches.' Kirsty held the door open for her. 'How is Sally? Is she saying anything yet?'

'She is avoiding me.' Beatrice frowned. 'I cannot help worrying about her.'

'The meeting is in the dining room.' Kirsty led the way along the corridor but stood aside to allow Beatrice to enter first.

The man had his back to her when she entered the room, but when he turned her heart thumped, and she stopped so suddenly that the policewoman rammed into her back.

'Sorry,' Kirsty said. 'I didn't expect you to stop.'

Beatrice struggled for breath. The last person she expected to see here was William Melville. Given the nature of the job he had tasked her with she was uncertain whether or not to acknowledge him.

'Ah! I take it you are Miss Jacobs.' He held out his hand.

She shook hands with him. That solved her dilemma. 'My pleasure, sir,' she said.

'Sit, sit.' He pointed to one of the chairs. 'You too, Miss Campbell. I believe you have a story to tell me that relates to one of the munitionettes.'

Kirsty and Beatrice, taking turns to speak, explained everything that had happened.

Beatrice finished by saying, 'I am worried about Sally. I think this man has made contact with her and convinced her she is mistaken about him. I think her first instinct was the correct one.'

'I agree,' Kirsty added. 'I think we may have a murderer in our midst, and that Sally is in danger.'

'I see.' Melville tapped his empty pipe on the table. 'Whether or not the man is a murderer is the lesser part of the problem for me. The fact that this man was present at the Silvertown explosion, and he is now in Gretna, is the most important part of this story. Intelligence received by the department indicates there is a German spy operating in this area, and he has been here for some time. Sally knows who this man is and it is imperative we use her to trace him.'

'Sally refuses to divulge anything,' Kirsty said.

'In that case, she must be kept under observation to find out who she is seeing in order to prevent a similar situation to Silvertown occurring here.'

'Is there any indication who this spy is?' Sergeant Duncan's voice sounded more strident than usual.

'Oh, yes. We know who he is.' Melville sucked at the stem of his pipe. 'The problem is he's a wily character and changes his appearance at will. He's also a charmer. The ladies like him.' He turned to look at Beatrice. 'His name is Dietger Leclercq, and we've been trying to catch him for some considerable time.'

The room became fuzzy, voices faded into the distance, and Beatrice's heart thumped so violently she feared it might burst from her chest. How could Dietger be a German spy? He was Belgian, not German.

'Are you all right, Miss Jacobs?'

Melville's voice came from far away, and she struggled to regain her composure.

'Yes, sir. I am just warm after hurrying here.'

He turned away from her and addressed Sergeant Duncan. 'You can see how important it is for this man to be identified, and any help you can provide would be of immense value to the country.'

'We will do everything we can to assist you,' the sergeant said. 'You can rely on us.'

'I will remain in Carlisle for the time being. You can find me at the Station Hotel, should there be anything to report.'

Beatrice's pulse slowed and her heart stopped thumping. Melville must be mistaken. If Dietger was in Gretna, she would surely know.

36

Dietger and Beatrice

Dietger remained hidden behind the policewomen's hostel until after Melville left. Once the man was safely out of sight he emerged and walked along the road. It would not do to follow Beatrice from the hostel; suspicions might be raised which would jeopardize his mission. The hedge at the corner provided sufficient concealment, and he stopped there to light a cigarette and wait.

While he waited, he rehearsed what to say. He was not sure what Melville would have told her about him, or if she knew anything, so his first task would be to find out and allay any suspicions she might entertain. It was essential to retain her trust in him.

Footsteps approaching forewarned him of her arrival. He took several deep breaths in an attempt to calm his thoughts and prepare himself. The first few minutes would be crucial.

'Beatrice,' he said, placing a hand on her arm.

She gasped, and a flicker of alarm showed in her eyes, enough to tell him that Melville must have informed her he was a spy.

'When I saw Melville here, I had to speak to you. I cannot bear for you to think badly of me.'

'It is true then. You are a German spy.' Beatrice shook his hand off her arm.

'No! No! I am no more a German spy than you are. I am Belgian. If I am a spy do you think I would reveal myself to you and risk the hangman's noose?'

'Then why does Melville think you are?'

'Melville is a suspicious man who sees spies everywhere. He probably thinks you are a spy as well.'

'Me? Why would he employ me if he thought that?'

'He is a devious man who is perfectly capable of using a spy to catch a spy.'

Beatrice lapsed into silence.

Dietger sensed her wavering. She was probably comparing Melville's information with what she knew about him.

'If you are not a German spy you must have given Melville reason to believe you are.'

'Not knowingly, although I often travel between Belgium and England.'

Beatrice's eyes narrowed. 'Why do you do that?'

'I work in the Belgian underground, helping people get out where possible, and I bring messages to Belgian refugees in England about their relatives. If you recall, I have been trying to find out what happened to your parents and brother.' He paused. 'So, I suppose I am a spy of sorts, but not a German one.'

Beatrice's expression softened. 'I remember. But each time we talked you had no news.'

'That is why I came to Gretna. I found your family and wanted to tell you, but I could not get near you because you were being followed.'

'Followed?'

'Yes. One of Melville's operatives has had you under surveillance since you left London.'

'What?' She stared at him. 'Why would Melville have me followed?'

Dietger shrugged.

Beatrice seemed to regain her composure. 'You said there is information about my family.' She sounded subdued, her voice little more than a whisper.

'They are in one of the of the refugee camps in the Netherlands. To begin with they were interned at Hontenisse, but they transferred to Camp Uden a year ago. Your family is safe which is the main thing, and once the war is over it is hoped they can return to Belgium.'

Tears trickled down Beatrice's cheeks. 'I thought them dead.'

Dietger grasped her hands. 'No, not dead. Safe. When I go back to Belgium I will do my best to get them to England, and you can be a family again.'

'Thank you, Dietger. That would please me greatly.'

Convinced he had won Beatrice over, Dietger said, 'I must go now. It is risky for me to be here. But, I need to know whether you will tell Melville I contacted you.'

Beatrice hesitated so long before she answered that Dietger thought himself unsuccessful in convincing her he was not a spy. If that was the case he would have to change his plans.

At last, she said, 'I will not give you away Dietger, not unless you give me cause to.'

He kissed her on the cheek before he left and hoped he was right to trust her.

37

Sally

The street was deserted and Sally shivered with anticipation when Daniel slid his arm around her waist. A sudden awareness of her body and the nearness of him, made her breathing quicken. Strange sensations swept through her, scary but delicious at the same time.

This was the third night she'd met him in Carlisle and she was certain she was falling in love with him.

'Are you cold?' His arm tightened around her waist.

She shook her head and leaned closer to him.

He bent his head and kissed her on the lips. She had never been kissed by a man before and the intensity of her desire for him took her by surprise. Her lips responded and she clung to him, never wanting it to end. When it did, and he drew back to gaze into her eyes, her stomach flipped and she wondered whether he sensed the raw emotions coursing through her body in a crashing wave of desire.

He looked into her eyes and she knew he sensed what she was experiencing.

They walked further down the street until they came level with an arched entry. He drew her into the alley beyond, his lips seeking hers. At first, they were chaste kisses, but they became more and more frenzied and passionate. It was as if an electrical charge between them sparked a fire deep within her.

When their passion subsided, she adjusted her clothing and wrapped her coat around her body. What had she done? What had she been thinking about? Her mother's warnings of the dangers young men posed flashed through her mind, and she drew back from him.

'What's wrong?' He pulled her close again.

'I shouldn't have ... we shouldn't have ...' Her voice tailed off.

'You're right. It was wrong of me to take advantage of you. But I couldn't help it. I love you so much.'

'You love me?' No one, except her mother, had ever told Sally they loved her, and she was amazed at the warmth and longing that swept through her.

'Yes, and I am sorry I lost control and let my passion for you get the better of me. Will you forgive me?'

'Of course, I forgive you. But,' she hesitated, 'what if something happens ...' Sally thought of the shame of an unwanted baby, and how she would explain it to her mother.

'Nothing will happen. I took precautions. And even if it did, I would stand by you. How could I leave you after we succumbed to our love for each other.'

Sally didn't know what he meant by precautions, but she trusted him and relaxed into his arms. She had never been happier.

Daniel kissed Sally lightly on the mouth when he left her a few streets away from the station.

'Come with me, just this once.' Sally clung to him. After what had happened surely he would accompany her to the train.

'I can't. I do not want to be seen, it's too risky.'

Sally leaned back and looked into his eyes. 'I don't want to leave you.'

'I feel the same way,' he said. 'But you must go now, or you will miss your train.'

Sally nodded and turned her face away from him to hide the tears welling up. She blinked hard to prevent them spilling down her cheeks. 'Will I see you again?' Her voice wavered, despite her efforts to control it.

'Of course.' He kissed her again.

Reluctantly she let go of him, stood for a moment, then walked away. When she reached the end of the street she stopped and looked back, but he was no longer there.

Her reluctance to leave him meant she was late for the train. It was already moving when she arrived at the station. Without stopping to think, she bolted up the platform, grabbed a carriage door handle, and jumped aboard before it picked up speed.

Gasping for breath, she collapsed on a seat in the empty carriage. Conflicting thoughts tormented her during the ten-minute journey. Love for Daniel consumed her, but guilt fought with pleasure over what they had done.

Fear gripped her. What if he did not want her now? She had heard tales of men who deserted women after they got what they wanted. She shivered. But she was convinced that Daniel was more honourable than that, and he had said he loved her.

Several girls alighted at Gretna, but Sally stayed behind them when they walked up Central Avenue, afraid her guilt would give her away.

She reached the hostel with a minute to spare. She pushed the door open expecting to see Beatrice waiting to lock up, but it was Matron who stood there with a pocket watch in her hand.

'You are just in time,' she said, 'another minute later and you would have been put on report.'

'Yes, Matron,' Sally said, keeping her head lowered so she would not have to meet Matron's eyes.

She only felt safe when she reached her cubicle and pulled the curtain shut behind her. Now, she was alone with her thoughts and fears, and a guilt that tormented her mind.

38

Shannon

Shannon wriggled out of her bed and thrust her feet into her shoes. She pulled the curtain aside and peered into the gloom of the dormitory. Once certain the dark areas contained nothing but shadows she sidled out of her cubicle, closing the curtain behind her.

She froze when a floorboard squeaked under her foot. When nothing stirred, she tiptoed past the curtained cubicles, left the dormitory, and crept along the corridor until she reached the bathroom at the end. The door opened silently, and she slipped inside.

Avoiding the iron bath sitting in the middle of the floor, she slid the window catches open, pushed the sash upwards until the gap became large enough for her to climb through. Once outside she lowered the window, leaving just enough room for her to open it again.

A hand reached out to her in the darkness and grasped her wrist. He drew her into a shadowy area and pulled her into his arms.

Excitement gripped her, the rush of blood, the catch of her breath, the desire a living thing inside her. She would do anything for him.

He pressed his mouth to hers, at first tender and loving, and then bruising, rough and passionate. His hands explored her body, and she clung to him, drowning in a sea of emotions.

Her head swam and she panted for breath. Never had she experienced anything as exquisite as his lovemaking. And when the ecstasy subsided, she shivered. Strange sensations pulsed through her body and, although the shiver might be due to the cold, she thought it more likely to be the after effects of her passion.

Leaning back against the wall he reached into his pocket for a cigarette, lit it and stared up into the dark sky.

She couldn't tell what he was thinking.

'You do love me,' she said, uncertain of him now it was over. Doubts filled her mind. Would he still want her?

'Of course, I do,' he said. 'But I wondered what you would do when I am no longer here.'

'You're going away?' Dismay swept through her and the chilly night air grew keener. She pulled her shawl closer around her shoulders, to shut out the cold and mask the sudden pain that squeezed the breath out of her body.

'Not in that way.' He drew smoke into his lungs before expelling it in a misty cloud. 'I would never want to leave you. You mean too much to me.'

'If I mean so much to you then you would stay.' She grasped his arm. 'Or take me with you.'

'I can't take you with me because there's no coming back from where I am going.'

Shannon shivered. There was something here she didn't understand, and a pang of fear, cold and raw, trembled through her.

'Tell me,' she said.

'It's my duty.' He put his arms around her. 'I intend to die for what I believe in.'

She couldn't take in what he was saying. Surely he didn't mean it. But many men were willing to die for a cause, she only had to think of the troubles in Ireland to know that.

'Become a martyr?' She was unable to put any enthusiasm into her voice. 'Why?'

'You are Irish so you will understand that it is for the same reason James Connolly did, and all those others on Ireland's barricades. I sometimes wish I'd been one of them. Because what is Ireland as a nation if it is not free? What am I if I do not fulfil my destiny?'

'But now we're together, I couldn't bear to lose you.'

His arms tightened around her. 'You will soon forget me and find someone else.'

'Never,' she said. The thought horrified her. She lapsed into silence for a moment. 'If you're going I want to go as well.'

'You don't mean that.'

'I do. If you intend to be a martyr, then I will be one as well.'

39

Beatrice

Unaware of the passing of time, Beatrice sat in the office going over and over the events of the day. It was apparent Sally might be in danger from the mystery man she refused to identify. But the information Melville dropped into the mix about Dietger affected her more than she liked to admit.

It was impossible. Melville must be wrong. Dietger could not possibly be a German spy. All Belgians hated the Germans and he was Belgian.

Her feelings for Dietger were mixed. He helped her escape to England when she fled Belgium at the start of the war and, twice after that, he came to tell her of his attempts to find her parents. Initially he thought they might be in hiding, or in one of the refugee camps. She had always been glad to see him, and was grateful for his help in the past.

Now, he was here in Gretna and had confirmed her parents were interned in The Netherlands, and he had promised to help them come to England.

Conflicting thoughts whirled through her mind, but she could not, would not, give credence to Melville's belief that Dietger was a German spy.

When she came into the office she meant to make notes about the meeting, but the sheet of paper in front of her remained blank. Sighing, she placed her pencil in the drawer. She would write her notes in the morning when her head should be clearer. She slid the drawer closed, rose out of the chair and stretched her legs, massaging them to get some sensation back. She had no idea of the time, and the heavy blackout curtains hid the darkness of the night.

Clicking the light off, she opened the door and crept along the corridors to her room. Her bedroom door was almost closed when she became aware of movement from one of the dormitories. She paused and held her breath. Through the chink of the door, she watched the shadowy figure of a girl creep up the corridor and vanish into the bathroom.

Once the bathroom door clicked shut, she tiptoed along the corridor and knelt to listen at the keyhole. She heard the window slide up, and the slight thud as the girl landed on the ground outside. Pushing the door open, she crossed the room to listen to the muffled voices. Her duty as an assistant matron was clear, it was her responsibility to confront the girl and march her back inside the hostel. But the girl's voice had an Irish accent, and Melville had tasked her with spying on the Irish girls, so she knelt and listened.

Heat rose through Beatrice's neck to her face when she realized what she was hearing. She wanted to close her ears, blot it out but was unable to do so.

She had led a sheltered life in Belgium and had never experienced the throes of love, although there were occasions when she had strange yearnings which she found difficult to explain or understand. Now, kneeling on the floor below the window, there was no mistaking the sound of lovemaking. Her breath caught in the back of her throat. What they were doing was immoral. She should stop it immediately, but that would mean confronting the couple, and admitting she was spying on them. The thought of what she would have to witness was abhorrent.

The collar of her blouse seemed to have tightened, and she undid the button at her neck. What was she thinking of, kneeling here listening to something that should be private? She should leave the bathroom and return to her room at once. But she could not, because Melville had ordered her to spy on the Irish girls, although she was sure this was not the kind of activity he had in mind.

At last, the sounds stopped, and her breathing returned to normal. She stood, flexing her cramped legs, preparing to leave the bathroom before the girl returned. When they resumed talking she continued to listen, once again feeling like an eavesdropper. At first, their talk focused on the girl's fears about whether or not he loved her, but when it turned to whispers about being martyrs to a cause, Beatrice held her breath, listening in horrified silence. She bit her lip. The pair of them were plotting something, and she did not like the sound of it. Melville would have to be informed.

Sleep did not come easily to Beatrice. After she stumbled into bed she spent a disturbed night peppered with nightmares. In her dreams she was back in Belgium, struggling to escape from something horrendous, although it had no shape or face. 'Beatrice!' The voice echoed through her head, and she reached out to grasp her mother's hands. No matter how far she stretched, she could not quite reach. 'Mama,' she screamed, 'wait for me,' but the face had morphed into that of Dietger. 'I will always wait for you,' he said, his accent more Irish than that of the navvies. She woke up to the sound of 'martyrs for a cause,' echoing in her brain.

She rolled over in her bed in an attempt to ease the ache in her back, the result of her restless night. It was early but sleep had deserted her, and the munitionettes would soon be getting up. The building would resonate with the noise of them making their ablutions and breakfasting, before leaving for another day's toil in the biggest munitions factory in Britain.

The ice-cold floor chilled the soles of her feet and shot a shiver up her spine. She rummaged below the bed for her shoes, but they were just as cold and did nothing to relieve the heaviness of her limbs. She closed her eyes, trying to remember her dreams. Disjointed fragments flitted through her mind, including her mother coming to her in the night, but all she recollected was the echoing sound of 'martyrs for a cause.' A reminder of what she heard prior to retiring to bed a few hours ago.

She washed and dressed in a daze before joining the munitionettes in the dining room for breakfast, and going through the motions of eating. But everything she put in her mouth tasted like ash, and it was a relief when she had to separate two of the Irish girls after a fight broke out.

Later, on the train to Carlisle, she wondered what she would say to Melville, and how she would explain her decision to report directly to him rather than her Gretna contact, Alice. The real reason, of course, her need to know why he thought Dietger a spy. It was rubbish. It had to be. Dietger could no more be a spy than she was. They were both Belgian, after all.

40

The Trap is Set

He waited for her in his usual place at the side of the fence, outside Gretna Township's railway station. The cigarette he smoked gave him the excuse to partially shade his face with his hand. Shannon was one of the first through the station gates, and he turned away so she wouldn't recognize him. Sally, not as pushy as Shannon, would be one of the last to exit. This suited him because he did not want Shannon and Sally to collide.

Once Shannon was some distance away he swung around to watch for Sally. At last, he spotted her, but she was talking to one of the policewomen. He frowned. Sally was becoming too much of a risk. Two nights ago she had told him that one of the lady police wished to talk to him about Silvertown.

'I can't,' he'd said.

'But it would stop her pestering me.'

'Yes, and how long before she found out I am a conscientious objector? It would be prison for me then.'

He managed to convince her. However, it left him under no illusion Sally posed a threat to him, and he would have to resolve this problem.

The same difficulty had occurred with Rosie. He never wanted to lose her, but she gave him no choice. Even now, he often dreamed of her, and regretted her death.

When he saw Sally coming out of the station he nipped the glowing end of the cigarette between his finger and thumb and walked to her side. 'You were talking to the policewoman.'

'I didn't tell her about you,' Sally said.

Grabbing her arm he pulled her around a corner into a

side street. 'Do you remember I told you about the man who recognized me? Well, he's reported me to the authorities and they're looking for me. I cannot remain here any longer. I must leave. I have no other option.'

'But where will you go?' Her eyes widened with fear.

'I don't know. I bought my ticket and almost boarded the train to Glasgow this morning, but I couldn't go without seeing you.'

'Can I come with you?'

'Would you?'

'I would follow you anywhere.'

'That's settled then. We leave tomorrow, but I can't go back to my lodgings so I need somewhere to hide tonight and I know just the place.'

'Tell me where to meet you tomorrow.'

'Too risky,' he said, shaking his head, 'in case they're watching for me. I may need to change my plans, and we could miss each other. You must come with me tonight, but you have to be careful so no one will suspect. That means no suitcase, just you.'

And so the plan was laid. Sally would leave the hostel without anyone seeing her. She would join the night shift in a pretence of coming to work and they would meet outside the Wylies station.

Lydia was worse than useless so Martha left her at the guard house.

'I am wet and cold and I do not feel well,' the young constable complained.

'Stay here then,' she snapped, and then felt guilty because her patience had run out. 'I will finish the patrol and collect you on the way back,' she said, more gently. The girl was young and munitions factory duty was not the best way to break in a new recruit.

'Are you sure you do not mind,' Lydia murmured, already pulling her chair closer to the fire.

The wind and rain battered Martha when she started her

patrol. Did the rain never stop here? It seemed more like winter than early May. What she wouldn't give for a night of London fog. She turned up the collar of her serge jacket, but it was so wet it only made her neck colder. Where were those promised greatcoats? All that had arrived were the new boots; horrible heavy things rumoured to be Land Army rejects. Although if deemed unsuitable for the Land Army girls she was damned if she could figure out why they foisted them on the Women Police.

The factory was a massive place, stretching for miles. The sections, housing the different processes, were well spaced out, built in such a way that humps of ground separated them to reduce the effect of any explosions which might occur. But, to see the girls laughing and chatting as they worked, it was hard to believe that this daily risk was at the forefront of their minds.

There was no moon tonight, although the rain and puddles on the paths between the various buildings glistened faintly. However, the dark did not worry her. She had patrolled here so often she believed that even if she were blindfolded she would be able to negotiate her way to the buildings she had to check.

The midnight patrol was always the worst one when the night was at its darkest, and it was easy to imagine spies lurking in the shadows. Maybe Lydia wasn't as daft as she appeared. Martha pushed the uncharitable thought away, this damned place was changing her.

No lights showed from the buildings, although they hummed with activity. The blackout was in force with doors and windows kept closed and covered, and lights vetoed outside. Those in charge claimed the German Zeppelins were unable to reach the Gretna factory. Not entirely convinced of this she used her lamp sparingly.

She stamped her time-clock as she inspected each building where the girls were hard at work. She did not envy them their job, particularly the workers who kneaded guncotton and nitroglycerine together into something resembling dough. Rather like making a massive loaf of bread.

The rain had stopped by the time she ended her patrol and she turned to go back to the comfort of the guard house, where Lydia would be toasting herself at the fire. But it was a long way back, four miles or more. If she took a short cut, through the part of the factory still under construction, it would halve the distance.

That area of the site lacked paved paths, but the navvies had laid boardwalks, and she had her bullseye lantern. In any case, if she stepped off the boardwalk she would no longer hear the clatter of her boots.

41

A Complication

He watched the girls leaving the train at the Wylies. They chatted and laughed, as if they hadn't a care in the world, while they walked to the buildings where they mixed their devil's porridge. Was Sally in their midst? Would she come? If she didn't, he would have to think of another way to deal with her.

Rain pattered down in increasingly large drops and an icy wind whipped around his body. Pulling his coat collar up in an attempt to stop the wind and rain encroaching, did not help, and he resigned himself to the effects of the weather. The munitionettes passed close by but he tucked himself further into the shadow of a hedge and they moved on along the road, unaware of his presence.

His thoughts turned to Sally. Persuading her had been easy, even though, as a creature of habit, she didn't like to flout authority. He knew how to play on her emotions, her love for him, and her fear she would never see him again. In a way, he regretted what he intended doing.

But where was she? Had she changed her mind?

The crowd of girls thinned until only a few stragglers remained. He had almost given up hope when Sally slipped out of the station behind them.

Reaching out a hand he pulled her into the shadow of the hedge. 'I thought you weren't coming.'

'I waited until last,' she said. 'I thought it might be safer.'

'Clever thinking.' He brushed his lips against hers.

Her arms went around him, and she held her face up for a proper kiss.

'Not here,' he said. 'We will have plenty of time soon.' He glanced around to ensure no munitionettes lingered on the road to the factory. 'Follow me.'

He guided her along a road which led in the opposite direction to the guard house.

'Where are we going?'

'You'll see.' A few seconds later they reached the wire fence protecting the site.

Grasping her hand he ushered her further along the fence. 'This spot will do fine.' He glanced around to make sure no one was nearby.

The wire cutters were cumbersome and bruising to his skin, so it was a relief to pull them from underneath his jacket to snip a hole in the fence. 'You go through first.' He guided her towards the entry. 'And I will follow.'

Once both of them squeezed through to the other side he hid the cutters in the grass and pushed the wire back into place.

'This way.'

'Won't we be seen?'

He squeezed her hand. 'This section of the site is still being built and the navvies do not work during the night. But some of the buildings are nearly finished and I've found a cosy little nest for us that will do until morning.'

Their footsteps clattered on the wooden boardwalk as he led her deeper into the construction site. Wind battered against them, and he felt her shiver, although she didn't complain. He put his arm around her and drew her closer.

'We will soon be there,' he said.

She stopped walking, pulling him to a halt.

Her face was barely visible in the dark but he sensed her alarm. 'What's wrong?'

'A light,' she gasped, 'flickering up ahead.'

'You're imagining it, there's no one here but us.'

'But it's there. It's getting nearer.'

'Impossible, this part of the site is deserted at night.'

Then he saw it, a swinging light spilling from a lantern being held by someone walking towards them.

'Quick, behind here and stay quiet.'

Mud sucked at his feet when he pulled her off the

boardwalk and pushed her into the shadows of the building that loomed in front of them. He hugged her close, trying to calm the shivers that racked her body, while the staccato sound of footsteps drew nearer.

The earlier rain made the boardwalk slippery, slowing Martha down. Her feet ached and she craved a hot cup of tea, but she was still some distance from the guard house. She trudged on. The faster she walked, the sooner she would get there.

She had been at the munitions factory long enough to become accustomed to the eerie atmosphere of the place. A huge area of spartan buildings separated by mounds and hillocks, although usually you could hear activity within the darkened buildings, and occasionally a door would open, spilling light outside until someone pulled it shut. In the parts still under construction, the silence increased the eerie ambience, and Martha couldn't rid herself of a feeling of foreboding which made her wish she'd taken the longer way back.

Lights were frowned on by those in charge, although the Solway Firth area had never been bombed. However, she didn't want to miss her step and land up in the mud at either side of the boardwalk, so she swung her lantern back and forth to illuminate the way ahead.

She continued walking, the reassuring sound of her footsteps magnified in the stillness of the night. Buildings, in various stages of construction loomed up out of the darkness, contributing to the ominous atmosphere, making her uneasy.

Martha had been walking for about thirty minutes, which meant she had passed the halfway mark, when she thought she saw movement up ahead and the squelch of someone stepping off the boardwalk into the mud.

Her grasp on the lantern tightened, and she increased her pace. Rumours of spies abounded in the area, and her job was to challenge any unauthorized person found inside the factory grounds. Her heart thumped, and her pulse quickened. Damn Lydia, she should have been here with her. However, as a trained policewoman, Martha understood her duty.

'Who is there?'

Martha held the bullseye lantern up. Was that a shadow at the side of the building?

She looked at the boardwalk, and at the glutinous morass alongside, but she had no option. She stepped off. Mud sucked at her feet and she swayed to regain her footing.

The shadow moved. She swung her lantern in his direction, but she was too slow, and too off balance. He punched her and slammed her to the ground, pressing her face into the mud until it filled her nostrils and eyes and mouth. She struggled. He rammed his foot on her head, pushing her face further into the mud. Dollops of choking sludge filled her throat when she opened her mouth to gasp for breath, and in a few moments, it was all over.

The lantern spun out of the policewoman's hand when the man punched her. It landed a short distance away, where it guttered for a moment, before reviving to allow enough light for Sally to see Daniel push the policewoman to the ground and stamp her head into the mud.

Sally's eyes widened in disbelief. Her chest heaved against the band of steel compressing it, and her body became rigid. She slumped against the wall of the building, desperate to close her eyes to the horrific scene being played out in front of her, but the paralysis affecting her body prevented it from obeying commands from her brain.

This couldn't be happening. This was not the Daniel she knew. But, despite her horror, she could not stop watching as he pressed the policewoman's face even further into the mud. Sally struggled to breathe, fighting the hypnotic effect his actions invoked in her. Time slowed, and it took forever before the breath rasped back into her lungs in a searing rush.

Her voice rose in a scream. 'You'll kill her.'

Daniel looked up and smiled, an unholy smile. Dancing shadows, combined with the flickering light from the lantern, illuminated the demonic expression on his face.

Sally shrank back into the protective darkness of the building, unable to take her eyes off the scene in front of her. She knew now, that she had been right in the first place. Daniel killed Rosie. How could she have been so foolish to let him persuade her otherwise?

Panic bubbled inside her. She had to escape. She must run, or she would be next.

She took a few steps backwards, sidling around the building until she reached the opposite side. Then she ran. If she was lucky and fast enough – if he didn't catch her – she might reach the factory buildings at the other side of the construction site.

42

Sally Runs

He breathed heavily. The arrival of the policewoman had been a surprise, and it disrupted his plans.

Her body lay before him, no longer moving, no longer a threat. He picked up the bullseye lantern, and turned to look for Sally, but she was gone. Vanished into the night.

He swung the lantern in an arc searching for where she might be hiding, but there was no sign of her. His lips tightened. He couldn't let her escape. If she managed to reach the authorities all his preparations and work would be over. He had to find her.

'Sally! Sally!' His voice soared, floating off into the night.

There was no response.

'Sally, come back. You have nothing to fear.'

Swinging the lantern in front of him, he searched for her footprints, but the mud had oozed back to fill them in.

He scowled. She couldn't have run far, and the mud would slow her down. It wouldn't take long to find her.

The glutinous mud sucked at Sally's feet. Her attempt to run turned into a stumble as she pulled each foot from the morass with every step she took. She glanced over her shoulder, peering into the dark which cloaked the building she had so recently left. Daniel must be there, hidden in the shadows. Even though she couldn't see him, she didn't doubt he would be tracking her.

'Sally! Sally!' His voice resonated in her ears, much too near for comfort.

She put her head down and continued on her laborious

way. If she made it as far as the working part of the factory before Daniel caught her, she would be safe. The distant rumble of wagons negotiating the rails between the ether plant and the mixing station guided her through the darkness. 'Sally, come back. You have nothing to fear.' He sounded further away, over to her left.

Closing her eyes she sent up a silent prayer. 'Please, don't let him find me.'

As if in answer to her prayer, she stepped out of the mud, and onto firmer ground.

Sally ran until she came to the base of a grassy mound, and then she climbed. Her legs ached, her breath whistled into her lungs in painful gasps, but she must get to the top and within reach of the factory buildings at the other side. Once she reached one of them, she would be safe.

Reaching the summit of the hillock she stared down into the hollow. Below, in the moonlight, three munitionettes chatted and laughed, their voices echoing in the still night air, while they pushed a wagon loaded with guncotton. Behind them loomed the dark shape of one of the factory buildings.

He circled, swinging the lantern backwards and forwards, trying to penetrate the darkness all around. Where would she go? Would she find a corner to hide? Or would she make a dash for freedom, back to the gap in the fence? That would be easy to check and he could get there quicker than her if he used the boardwalk. But as he turned, a flicker of movement caught his eye. She was running to the factory buildings. He couldn't allow her to reach them.

Mud sucked at his shoes, slowing his progress, and he could no longer see her. But he could tell he was going in the right direction when the rumble of a wagon's wheels sounded in the night air. She would also have heard it.

His mind was so preoccupied with the need to find Sally it was a few moments before he realized the ground beneath his feet was solid and he now walked on grass. One of the mounds which protected the factory buildings at the other side rose up before him. Gritting his teeth he started to climb the hillock, he must reach her before she started her descent. The rain had stopped, and the moon slipped out from behind the clouds bathing the scene in front of him in its rays. He looked up to the summit of the mound.

She stood on top with the moon shining on her, bathing her in an ethereal light and silvering her hair. Like an angel reaching to heaven. He would have liked to pull her to him, make love to her for one last time, but she was too far away and he would never reach the top of the mound before she started her descent.

He didn't want to kill her, but she was a danger to him, and his mission was more important than one girl's life no matter how fond of her he had become. Her death was unavoidable. It was for the greater good.

He pulled up the leg of his trousers and slipped the knife out from the scabbard tucked into the top of his sock. 'I am sorry,' he whispered as the knife winged through the air. 'I didn't want it to be like this.'

He was crying as he turned to retrace his steps back to the fence. So many girls, so many last chances. Would it always end this way?

The clouds shifted, allowing the moon to shine through, illuminating her in its rays as she stood on top of the hillock. At the bottom, in the hollow, the munitionettes pushed their wagon, and the outline of the mixing station beckoned to her.

Smiling, she stepped forward to slither down the side of the mound. She never heard the sound of the knife whistling through the air towards her. All she felt was a thump in her back as if someone had punched her. Then she toppled forward, and slithered down the hillock, to a safety she would never know.

43

A Shock for Kirsty

Kirsty yawned, the night was dragging, and it would be a good half hour before the first of the girls left the mixing room for their meal. She would be glad when her week of night shifts ended and she was back on days again.

'I think I will go out for a breath of fresh air,' she said. 'It's stifling in here.'

Clara nodded. 'That's all right, I'll hold the fort here. Sandra will soon be back in any case.'

They drew straws at the start of the shift to find out who would eat in the canteen first, and Sandra had been lucky. Kirsty's turn would come after the first wave of munitionettes had eaten, which meant dirty tables, although there would still be plenty of food. Clara drew the short straw. Her turn to eat would come after everyone else finished, and only the leavings remained.

The rain had stopped and chilly air embraced Kirsty when she stepped outside. Shivering, she pulled her collar up and wrapped her arms around her body, but she didn't mind the cold, which she found more invigorating than the heat and smell inside the mixing station.

A clatter of wheels on iron rails and the chatter of voices heralded the approach of a wagon. That would be the workers, coming back with another load of guncotton for the munitionettes to mix into their devil's porridge.

The moon broke through the clouds illuminating the munitionettes and the wagon, and on the top of the hillock behind them, another figure was silhouetted against the night sky.

Kirsty frowned. It was a strange place for one of the girls to be. What on earth was she doing up there?

The figure crumpled and slid down the side of the mound. The wagon stopped. The munitionettes froze. And Kirsty ran.

A whiff of foul-smelling fumes from the Ether Plant drifted on the breeze. Mindful of the effects of the noxious fumes, she clamped a hand over her nose and mouth while continuing to run. She didn't stop until she reached the bottom of the hillock.

Kirsty looked up to where the body had come to rest, and grasping a handful of grass she pulled herself up the slope. The girl lay, face down, her long hair spread out, circling her head like a halo. Pushing the hair aside she placed her fingers on the girl's neck to check for signs of life.

Turning, she shouted to the girls who were still standing immobile beside their wagon. 'Don't just stand there. Fetch some help.'

The munitionettes gave her a scared look and ran in the direction of the mixing station.

The moon slipped behind the clouds and Kirsty was alone with the body. Her fingers kept searching for a pulse, even though she was sure the girl was dead.

Nothing in Kirsty's training had prepared her for this, and she doubted her ability to handle the situation.

What was she supposed to do?

Thoughts swirled through her brain in confused disorder, and she drew in a deep breath in an attempt to calm them. She was a policewoman, not a flighty young girl afraid of her own shadow, it was time to act professionally.

Doing her best not to dislodge the knife in the girl's back, she turned her over and brushed the hair away from her face. An involuntary gasp escaped her when she recognized Sally. She remembered the girl's fearful flight from the dance hall, and Sally's subsequent belief she had been wrong to be afraid of the man she recognized. However, her original fear had been justified, and she had paid the price for not identifying him.

'I am so sorry, Sally,' she said, wrapping her arms around the body. 'We should have protected you better.'

But what could they have done? She and Beatrice had done their best. They couldn't be held responsible for Sally's lack of co-operation and, without knowing the identity of the man, they were helpless to prevent what happened.

A shaft of light pierced the darkness. A door slammed and the light vanished. Someone was coming at last.

Kirsty released her hold on the body and stood up so that the new arrival would see her.

At that moment, an icy finger of fear gripped her heart. What if it wasn't reinforcements. What if it was the killer returning?

The clatter of iron wheels on iron rails stopped to be replaced by a woman's voice shouting for help. For a moment he thought it was Sally's voice and he was on the point of turning back to finish the job, but the accent and tone of voice were different. Besides, his aim had been sure. The knife had not missed its mark.

A tear slipped down his face when he thought of Sally, but her death couldn't be avoided, his mission had to come before any personal feelings he might have. Now, he must leave this place, as quickly as possible because the alarm had already been raised.

The lantern he carried flickered over the ground in front of him. He swung it one last time to get his bearings before tossing it into the darkness. It landed with a thump, but the flame inside continued to burn. Hopefully, the flickering light would draw any pursuers away from him.

A quagmire separated him from the boardwalk which he needed to reach, so he searched for the shadowy shapes of buildings in the gloom. Mud sucked at his feet slowing him down but he continued to head for the buildings. Eventually, he would come to the boardwalk.

He cursed under his breath. The guards would soon be alerted and his escape blocked. His mind whirled, planning what he would do if the hole cut in the wire fence had been discovered. How would he defend himself? His knife was buried in Sally's back. And he had no other weapon. To protect himself he would need to use force and his bare hands. He clenched them in anticipation.

A faint beam of light flickered in the hollow in front of her followed by a muttered curse. The light flitted over the wagon which had been deserted by the girls. Whoever was advancing must have walked into it or tripped over the rails.

Kirsty slid to the ground and put her arms around Sally's cold body.

The flickering, accompanied by the faint sound of footsteps, drew closer.

Hypnotized by the light, unable to stop watching, she offered up a silent prayer.

'Are you all right, miss?'

Standing over her was a tall soldier, although in the darkness she couldn't determine his rank.

She scrambled to her feet. 'Yes,' she muttered, wiping grass from her skirt. 'But she's not.' Kirsty gestured to the body. 'I felt for a pulse, but couldn't find one. I think she might be dead.'

The soldier bent over Sally's body. 'I think you may be right, miss. We will take her to the infirmary for the doctor to check.'

Kirsty nodded, although the darkness cloaked her action.

'Do you know what happened?'

She shook her head. 'All I know is that I noticed her at the top of this mound, and then she seemed to crumple and fall. I thought she might be unwell, and might have injured herself, so I ran to help.' Kirsty shivered. 'I found her like this with the knife in her back.'

'I see.' He rose from his crouching position and looked to the summit. 'We will take over from here, miss,' he said without looking at her. 'I will arrange for someone to take you back to the mixing station.' He stared into the darkness. 'Private Jones, will you escort Miss ...' He turned to Kirsty. 'I am sorry, I didn't catch your name.'

'WPC Kirsty Campbell.' She suppressed an urge to address him as sir.

Another soldier joined them beside Sally's body.

'Ah, there you are Private Jones. Escort Miss Campbell to the mixing station.'

'Yes, sir.' Jones grinned at Kirsty. 'Follow me, miss. You'll be safe with me.'

Stung by the officer's dismissive attitude Kirsty clamped her lips shut, to prevent her annoyance spilling over into something she would later regret saying. Still seething, she followed the soldier striding out in front of her. Behind her, she could hear the officer snapping orders to other shapes emerging from the gloom.

'You'll be all right now, miss,' Jones said, holding the door of the mixing station open for her.

Kirsty turned with a sharp retort on her lips, but he looked so young and eager to please, she changed her mind and thanked him.

The door slammed behind her. She stood for a moment to allow her eyes to become accustomed to the light. Familiar sounds and smells enveloped her with a stifling warmth, and the shock of what had happened consumed her body with a paroxysm of shivering she was unable to control.

She leaned against the wall and closed her eyes, trying to shake off the horror of what she had seen. But she couldn't erase the vision of Sally's body from her mind.

44

A Killer on the Run

Mud clung to his shoes and every step he took sucked his feet deeper into the mire. So, when he reached the boardwalk and pulled his feet from the morass, he almost cried with relief. He would reach the perimeter of the site faster now the mud did not slow him down. A few steps later, his relief changed to alarm as the staccato sound of his footsteps broke the silence of the night. Bending down, he slipped his mud-caked shoes off. His feet would make less noise in his socks.

He stopped running when the earth at the side of the wooden boardwalk changed from mud to solid ground. It signalled the proximity of the wire fence.

Lumps of sludge plopped from his shoes when he wiped them on the grass. Once the worst of the muck was removed, he replaced them on his feet. He hesitated for a moment to listen for sounds of any pursuers, then he inched forward, ready to drop to the ground if he spotted a guard.

The road in front of the fence was empty and, judging from the clamour behind him, the soldiers were hunting for him on the site. They wouldn't take long to find the gap and hunt him down in the streets of Eastriggs.

After finding his entry point without too much trouble, he pulled the wire up and slipped through the opening. Once through to the other side he pushed the wire back into place.

The sound of an engine caused a quiver of alarm to shoot up his spine. It was time to move fast. He headed in the direction of the town, and crossed his fingers, hoping he would reach the houses before the vehicle appeared.

Luck was with him and he vaulted over the garden fence of the first house, as the truck clattered past on the road.

Keeping to the rear of the buildings, he hurdled over the

fences moving from garden to garden until he reached an overgrown hedge separating the gardens from the main thoroughfare. Leafy branches, which had never seen pruning shears, formed a perfect barrier and he crouched, parting them, to get a clearer view. The road was silent and deserted, but there was no time to lose because as soon as the guards found his exit from the site they would converge on all the roads leading out of Eastriggs. He ran to the end of the hedge and scaled the boundary fence. Balancing precariously on the top he leapt over the hedge. A piercing yowl startled him and he remained where he landed until he identified the origin. Green eyes glared at him, and a cat, its tail swishing from side to side, stalked off into the darkness.

He pushed himself up from his knees. His senses remained on high alert but the only sound, faint and far off, came from the munitions factory. A smile twitched the corner of his mouth. The searchers were looking in the wrong place, but he was under no illusion he was safe yet. They wouldn't take long to figure out his escape route. With a final glance along the road, he rose to his feet and sprinted across.

Houses on this side of the street were smaller, probably built for farm labourers before the war. The endless row of cottages, with doors opening directly onto the pavement and no access to the rear of the buildings, presented an impenetrable barrier with nowhere to hide. The rumble of an engine sounded in the distance. He must get off the road, he was too exposed here.

He thought about retracing his steps, to seek more cover, but he was too late. The sound had increased and the faint glimmer of sidelights showed in the distance.

His hand grasped the knob of the door nearest to him, and to his surprise it opened. He slid inside. The house was in darkness. The occupants, probably farm folks the only ones who would leave doors unlocked, must be sleeping. Holding his breath, he pressed himself against the wall behind the door. His elbow caught on the side of the hall stand. He reached out to silence the clatter and his hand closed over a walking stick.

The truck stopped outside the house and the engine cut off.

Had he been seen?

In the distance, another engine sounded, although this one didn't have the heavy rumble of a truck.

Reinforcements must be arriving.

The engine puttered to a stop followed by a metallic clatter and a voice.

'What have you stopped here for?'

'Thought I saw something.'

'There's nothing here.'

'I'm not sure, I could have sworn something moved.'

'Well, if you're sure,' the voice sounded doubtful, 'maybe we should search this area.'

'Can't do it with only two of us.'

'But if anyone is here and we go for reinforcements, they'll get away. And you know what the sarge will say. He'll skin us for breakfast.'

'You're right. Tell you what, you stay here on guard, and I'll drive to the guardhouse to collect some more men to help with the search.'

An engine growled into life, and the truck rumbled off.

A match was scratched on the brickwork at the other side of the door. The man must be lighting a pipe or cigarette.

It was now or never.

His hand tightened on the walking stick and, letting his breath out in a long sigh, he eased the door open.

The soldier stood, with his back to him, leaning over the handlebars of a motorcycle with his hand cupped around the lit end of his cigarette.

He grasped the walking stick with both hands and whacked the soldier on the head. The man fell forward with his head resting on the petrol tank and his arms dangling at either side, while the cigarette landed on the road in a flurry of sparks.

Raising the stick, he brought the heavy knob down on the man's head again. That would make sure the soldier didn't revive before he escaped.

The motorbike rocked when he dragged the body off, and for a moment he thought the machine would topple. Panicked, he grabbed the handlebars and let the body slump to the road; he sighed with relief when the bike steadied.

There was no time to waste, he had to flee before the other soldier arrived with reinforcements.

The motorcycle, an army issue Douglas model, was a blessing because of his familiarity with the machine. Gripping the handlebars tighter, he swung his leg over the petrol tank and placed his foot on the kickstarter. Past experience indicated it would require a robust kick to start, so it did not surprise him when the first kick failed to start the engine, but several kicks later it ignited with a roar. Settling into the seat and gripping the petrol tank with both knees, he aimed the bike at the road and was well on his way before the first of the trucks arrived at the row of cottages.

45

Kirsty

'Are you all right?'

Kirsty made a vain attempt to suppress the shivers engulfing her body and forced a smile. 'I will be fine. I just needed a minute.'

Sandra slung an arm around Kirsty's shoulders. 'Clara's getting you a hot cup of tea.'

Kirsty allowed herself to be steered to the canteen.

Several munitionettes, finishing their meals, whispered among themselves. Normally she would acknowledge and share a few words with them, but she was unable to meet their eyes and questioning looks.

Keeping her head down she followed Sandra to the rear of the room.

'Over here, we've bagged a table in the corner.' Sandra pushed Kirsty into a chair and thrust a cup into her hand. She beckoned to Clara. 'Have you added plenty of sugar? She will need it for the shock.'

Kirsty's hand closed around it. Her first sip of the hot liquid burned her tongue and tasted too sweet, and her shaking hands found it difficult to retain a grasp on the cup. Some of the liquid slopped out and pooled on the table in front of her. She gazed in fascination at the widening puddle, unwilling to look up and meet curious and sympathetic stares.

After more than two years as a policewoman, Kirsty thought she had hardened and become immune to the misfortunes and disasters that dogged many of the women, who belonged to what was commonly referred to as the underclasses, but nothing in her training prepared her for the death of a vulnerable girl whom she knew.

She gulped the tea.

Sandra and Clara sat, one on each side of her, and as soon as the cup emptied Clara refilled it. Gradually her shivering abated. She raised her eyes to acknowledge her gratitude and was surprised to see the canteen empty apart from themselves.

'I am sorry,' Kirsty said. 'I don't want to be a burden.'

'Nonsense, you've had a shock. Clara and I are amazed you coped so well.'

Kirsty smiled ruefully. 'I am not so sure I've coped well.' She lapsed into silence thinking about the strange atmosphere in the canteen when Sandra ushered her in. 'Does everyone know?'

'The girls you sent to get help made sure of that. Once they got over their shock they soon spread the news. I suppose it made them feel special.'

Kirsty shuddered at the thought of Sally's death making someone feel special.

'Where are they now?'

Sandra sighed. 'After their brief moment of glory, the supervisor sent them back to their job pushing the guncotton wagon. She told them production must continue.'

'Isn't that dangerous? The killer might still be out there.'

'Oh, I'm sure they don't mind, they've got a couple of soldiers protecting them. Mind you, I suspect, they might be the ones who need the protection.'

Despite herself, Kirsty laughed, and then found she couldn't stop. Shocked at her response when Sally's body lay outside, but unable to suppress the hysteria that threatened to swamp her, she wrapped her arms around her middle and let out a cry of despair.

Clara laid her hand on Kirsty's. 'Let it out of your system. Laugh, cry, whatever you want to do, we're here for you.'

'I'm fine,' Kirsty said, 'just a wee bit emotional.'

'That's understandable.'

'Stay here,' Sandra said. 'One of us will stay with you. Clara and I will take turns at covering the doors.'

'No. I am here to do a job,' Kirsty said, 'not sitting moping in the canteen.'

At regular intervals during the night, Sandra and Clara tried to persuade Kirsty to return to the canteen, but she maintained her refusal.

The night seemed endless, and Kirsty couldn't stop remembering every detail nor suppress the images. She kept seeing Sally at the top of the mound, toppling forward and sliding down, and the knife sticking out of the girl's back. The desire to do something overwhelmed her. Sally must be avenged, she owed it to her.

With that in mind, she marched to the door but the guard on duty insisted she stay inside. During the night, she looked outside several more times, but the guard remained until the end of the shift when they were all ushered to the train with a military escort.

Determination replaced her lethargy, and she vowed to find Sally's killer, and the army and all the officials in the kingdom would not prevent her from doing this.

The wind whipped through his hair and the throb of the engine vibrated through his body.

He whooped with delight at the sensation. The power of the machine below him matched the power he felt after his two kills. Sympathy for his victims disappeared, leaving exhilaration in its place.

Carlisle was quiet. The early closing times of the public houses and hotels had sent the revellers home, and only a few hardy souls and night workers frequented the streets. However, he avoided the main part of the town and drove the motorbike to the river's edge. He brought it to a stop, swinging his leg over the petrol tank until he stood beside it. The handlebars throbbed beneath his hands, and it only took a moment to aim the bike into the river. The force of its engine ensuring its fate, only cutting out when it submerged into the depths.

The military would never find the motorbike here. He

was safe for the time being.

Smiling to himself he walked through the darkened streets. His preparations were complete. Now it was time for action.

Exhaustion hit her as soon as Kirsty finished her shift, and she wanted to collapse into bed. But the vision of Sally lying sprawled on the ground and the feel of the girl's body in her arms, haunted her.

Flashbacks to the scene continued, even on the train and the walk up the avenue. The chatter of the policewomen who accompanied her, a far-off buzz of sound, hardly penetrated her consciousness.

'Are you all right?' Sandra grasped her elbow.

She blinked, conscious someone was shaking her arm. 'What?'

'I asked if you were all right.'

'Yes, I am fine, but I can't stop seeing Sally's face.' Tears pushed against her eyelids and she shut her eyes to prevent them escaping.

Sandra placed her arms around Kirsty's shoulders and hugged her. 'We're home,' she said. 'You need to sleep, you're worn out.'

Never had so few steps seemed so mountainous as Kirsty entered the women's police hostel. She longed for sleep. But first, she needed to report to her commanding officer.

Sergeant Duncan sat at her desk in the office attacking a pile of papers from her in-tray. Kirsty wondered if the woman ever slept.

'Ma'am,' Kirsty said hesitantly.

'Yes, Constable Campbell? What can I do for you?'

'I need to make a report.' Kirsty's confidence deserted her. Why was she so unsure of herself? It wasn't like her.

'Well?'

'We had a murder on the site last night.' The words toppled out of Kirsty in a rush. 'Sally, the girl we discussed at the conference, was killed.'

The sergeant shuffled the mess of papers in front of her into a neat pile and replaced them in the in-tray. 'You'd better tell me about it then,' she said, leaning forward and placing her elbows on the desk.

Kirsty described the events of the night as clearly as she could, although she felt her report lacked clarity.

'I see,' the sergeant said when she finished. 'And the military now have the investigation in hand.'

'Yes,' Kirsty said. 'But surely we have a responsibility to investigate Sally's death as well. Particularly as we were supposed to be protecting her.'

'Is that so.' Sergeant Duncan picked up a pencil and twirled it between her fingers. She seemed to think for a moment before looking up and fixing Kirsty with a stare.

'You do know that is not what we are employed for. We are here to supervise the munitionettes and to ensure their moral safety and wellbeing. It is no part of our duties to investigate a murder. That is the responsibility of the military in this area.'

'But surely we have a duty to Sally because we failed to protect her ...'

'I will hear no further argument about this matter, Constable Campbell. You are out of order. Dismissed.'

The sergeant rose to her feet. 'You may leave now Constable Campbell, and I suggest you concentrate on the duties for which you are employed.'

'But ...'

'I said, dismissed.' Sergeant Duncan glared at her. 'Unless you want to be put on report.' She waved her hand dismissively and pulled more papers from her in-tray.

Kirsty clamped her teeth on the inside of her lip to stop her fury from spilling over. Unable to suppress the anger, surging through her body, she glared back at the sergeant, who was already too focused on the papers in front of her to notice.

It needed every ounce of Kirsty's discipline to prevent her from slamming the door when she left the office, but when she returned to her room she lay on the bed and pummelled the pillow, until it was in danger of spilling its feathers.

Anger quickly turned to tears, and the horror of Sally's death mutated to sorrow and recrimination. She felt she should have done more to protect the girl by concentrating on finding the mystery man. But now, the unimaginable had happened, the best she could do would be to provide justice for Sally, find her killer and make sure he got his just deserts. The vow she made to investigate the girl's death was unbreakable, and she intended to keep her promise, despite her sergeant's instructions.

46

Beatrice

It was later than the time she normally rose when Beatrice left her cubbyhole of a room to stride down the corridor to the dining room. The girls were already out of bed and preparing for their working day. The hostel seemed alive with sounds. Pots and dishes clattered in the kitchen signalling the preparation of breakfast, while the splashing of water, shouts, and laughter, echoing from the bathrooms and washing areas indicated they would soon emerge, damp and hungry. Beatrice smiled to herself. The munitionettes were a cheery lot, and in a few minutes, they would be jostling each other as they hurried to the canteen, anxious to be the first served. She increased her pace from a walk to a run wanting to arrive before the crush.

The problem this morning had been her hair which had been more unruly than usual, resisting her efforts to contain it in a bun on the nape of her neck. Perhaps she should cut it in the shorter style the girls favoured, but she liked her long hair and would have let it flow loosely around her shoulders if she could. But certain standards required to be upheld, and she was expected to dress formally and maintain an appearance in accordance with her position.

Maisie was piling plates and bowls on a table at the end of the room when she entered. The cutlery was already in place and a heap of toasted bread filled an ashet next to a massive bowl of boiled eggs. 'We're nearly ready, miss,' she said, 'it's always a rush so early in the morning.'

'You've forgotten to put out the ladle.' Cook bustled in the door carrying a large iron cauldron.

'Sorry, cook. I'll get it.' Maisie hurried out of the room.

'She's a good enough worker, miss. But she has to be

178

told everything. Not much use at thinking for herself.' Cook placed the cauldron on the table. 'I think we're almost ready for them, miss.'

Beatrice, suppressing a shudder, peered into the pot at the grey mixture which British people called porridge. How could anyone bear to eat the stuff? In this country, there were no buttery croissants, steaming bread, and the thin slices of cheese she was accustomed to in her native Belgium. But, she had to admit the munitions workers were much better fed than the general population. She just wished the food was not so stodgy. Her life now was so different to what it had been before the war, and she wondered if she would ever return to that life which seemed so out of reach.

A clamour of voices drawing nearer heralded the arrival of the munitionettes. Maisie scooted in the door brandishing a ladle a few seconds before the first of them arrived. Cook grabbed it from her and stirred the porridge while Beatrice stood back to give them room to work.

'Blimey, ain't there no sausages?'

'Bloody porridge again.'

'I don't like eggs.'

Cook slapped ladles full of porridge into the plates lined up in front of her. 'You're bleeding lucky to be getting porridge, young lady. And it's eggs today, like it or not. If you're in luck you'll maybe get sausages tomorrow.' Without looking up, she muttered, 'There's no pleasing some of these girls. They don't know how lucky they are that extra rations are provided so they can keep production up.'

Beatrice knew the comment was meant for her and she murmured her agreement.

At last, everyone was served and the porridge pot nearly empty. The eggs had all gone and the mountain of toast was no more.

Something had been niggling Beatrice ever since she entered the dining room. She had not been able to identify the source of her unease, but now, as she surveyed the room, she realized, with a jolt, that Sally was absent. The girl must have slept in, although how she could do that with all the racket going on was beyond her. On the other hand, maybe she was not well.

'One of the munitionettes is missing, I will go check on her,' Beatrice said.

Nothing stirred in the silent dormitory. Some of the girls had closed their curtains, some left them open to display unmade beds and their possessions in disarray. Maisie would have her work cut out to ensure everything was clean and orderly by the end of the morning.

Beatrice checked the cubicle numbers. Cubicle fifteen's curtains remained closed. 'Sally,' she said, 'are you awake?'

There was no response, so Beatrice pulled the curtain aside. The cubicle was empty, and the bed had not been slept in.

The breath caught in her throat and a premonition of something she could not explain overcame her. Where was Sally? She was not the type of girl to stay out all night, and she would not go home without telling someone. All sorts of thoughts and fears invaded her mind. Beatrice had been convinced the girl was at risk after her recognition of the man from Silvertown, although Sally did not think so.

When did she last see Sally? Beatrice thought hard. The girl had been present at the evening meal, and she remembered saying goodnight to her in the corridor, mistakenly presuming Sally was on her way to bed. Where had she gone?

She hurried back to the dining room. Some of the munitionettes had not finished eating. Cook and Maisie were tidying up, but the cauldron remained on the table.

Beatrice picked up the ladle and banged it on the cauldron. Remnants of porridge splattered everywhere, but she did not care.

'Attention, girls,' she shouted.

Heads turned and some of them sniggered.

'Does anyone know where Sally Scott is, her bed has not been slept in and she is not here.'

'Probably out on the randan, miss.'

'What, that wee mouse? She wouldn't know a good time if she saw it.'

'She's probably gone home to her mammy.'

Several ribald comments echoed around the room, accompanied by sniggers and laughter, but most of the girls shook their heads.

Beatrice's anxiety and sense of foreboding increased. Where was Sally? Why had she gone? And what on earth could she do to find her?

47

Kirsty

The rumble of an engine followed by the squeal of brakes woke Kirsty from a restless doze. She had not meant to fall asleep, and now she jerked her head off the pillow, momentarily disoriented. The noise outside indicated something out of the ordinary was happening and curiosity overcame her desire to sink back into sleep.

When she sat up the events of the night came crashing back. She dashed away a tear before swinging her legs over the side of the bed and standing on tiptoe to peer out of the tiny window. An army truck, its engine still shuddering, had drawn up outside the hostel. A private rushed to open the passenger door and a tall officer jumped out. His appearance triggered a flashback, and Kirsty was back kneeling on the grass beside Sally's body, with the officer looming over her. She shook her head to clear the image, smoothed her uniform skirt, tugged the jacket into some semblance of order, grabbed her hat from the floor where it had fallen and rammed it on her uncombed hair. He must be here to report Sally's death to Sergeant Duncan and she wanted to be present. Perhaps the sergeant would change her mind and accept some responsibility for the investigation.

'If ye wait here, sir, I'll let the sergeant know.'

'That's all right, Jessie,' Kirsty said to the maid. 'Sergeant Duncan is in the office, I will escort the officer there.'

She did not want to give the sergeant time to prepare – far better to take her by surprise. Perhaps it would make her more amenable to Kirsty's suggestions.

'If you will follow me, sir.'

The officer marched behind her, showing no signs of

recognition, and Kirsty wondered if he had even registered her presence at the murder scene last night.

Kirsty threw the office door open.

Sergeant Duncan looked up, her brows arched in surprise. 'I thought we were finished, Kirsty.'

'Yes, ma'am, but an army officer wishes to see you. He might be here about Sally.'

'Lieutenant Allen, ma'am. I am afraid I am the bearer of some disturbing news.'

'WPC Campbell has already informed me of the munitionette's death. Am I right in thinking the military are in charge of the investigation?'

The officer's eyes flicked over Kirsty before focusing on the sergeant.

'I am afraid the situation is much more serious than that,' he said. 'We found a second body which we have reason to believe may be one of your staff.' He held out a small leather wallet. 'I found this in her pocket.' He handed it to the sergeant.

Sergeant Duncan drew in a swift gasp of air when she inspected the contents. She sat back in her chair, a stunned expression on her face.

'Where ... How ...?'

'We found her in a part of the factory site which is still under construction. It appears our killer forced her face into the mud and she suffocated.' His voice gentled. 'I am so sorry.'

Kirsty's mind whirled. A second body?

'The investigation.' The sergeant struggled to regain her equilibrium. 'Is there anything we can do?'

'Everything is in hand, ma'am. As this is a death on military ground the responsibility for the investigation rests with the army. However, we will advise you of any progress we make.'

'Are you the person in charge of the investigation?'

'Yes, ma'am. We will require access to her room. And her family will need to be informed.'

'Of course.' Sergeant Duncan considered for a moment

before she spoke again. 'Kirsty, perhaps you can show Lieutenant Allen to Martha's room.'

Martha? It wasn't possible. Nausea churned in her stomach. They must be wrong. Her mind struggled to grasp the implications, but she realized Sally's death had occupied her mind so much everything else had been blotted out, and she hadn't seen either Martha or Lydia returning to the hostel. The room spun, a mist descended and filled her mind, everything seemed so far away and she barely noticed the arm reaching out to catch her.

She came to in time to hear the sergeant saying, 'Martha and Kirsty were friends, they both came to us from the Metropolitan force.'

The arm around her was strong and comforting, but she struggled to free herself. 'I am sorry, ma'am. I am not usually so unprofessional.'

'Your reaction is understandable, Kirsty. I will ring for Jessie to take the lieutenant to the room.'

'No, ma'am, I would prefer to do it. Martha is ... was, my friend after all.'

They left the office and marched in silence to Martha's room. When they arrived, Kirsty turned to him. 'I know I shouldn't ask,' she said, 'but can you tell me anything about what happened to Martha.' The word death stuck in her throat.

'Not much, I'm afraid.' His voice expressed sympathy. 'We think she came across the killer with the girl, and her intervention facilitated the girl's escape attempt. A few minutes more and she might have made it.'

'And Lydia? She patrolled with Martha. Is she all right?'

'We found her in the guard house, apparently she was too unwell to accompany your friend, so Martha patrolled alone. Lydia collapsed with shock when I informed her and she was taken to the infirmary.'

A rush of anger consumed Kirsty. Lydia should have been with Martha. If she had been, neither Martha nor Sally would be dead. She breathed deeply, anger would not solve anything, and it wouldn't help in her quest to find the killer.

'Last night,' Kirsty said, 'you didn't ask for the identity of the girl.'

He removed his hand from the doorknob of Martha's room and turned to face her. 'You know who she is?'

'Yes, she's Sally Scott. Her billet is the Mary Queen of Scots Hostel on Dominion Road.'

'Thank you,' he said. 'Once I am finished here I will go to the hostel. They must be wondering what happened to her. And now, if you don't mind, I will attend to things here.'

Kirsty realized he didn't require her help and, slightly miffed, walked to her room. She had her hand on the door when he called out to her.

'Perhaps we will meet again, Miss Campbell.' For a moment, the expression on his face seemed that of a diffident boy, rather than a starchy army officer.

Kirsty shivered. A chill crept through her body and a curious feeling of numbness overwhelmed her. Frequent rustles and knocks emanating from Martha's room next door indicated the thoroughness of Lieutenant Allen's search. She shivered again. Was this what happened when someone died? Strange hands rummaging through your most private possessions? Martha would hate this invasion of her privacy.

The first time she met Martha was in Dundee, outside the Kinnaird Hall, when she had been trying to pluck up the courage to go inside to hear Winston Churchill speak. Martha had introduced herself and accompanied her into the hall. A mental picture of the small, dainty woman with the most amazing dark gold hair formed in her mind. Her hat, perched on her curls at a jaunty angle, was much more fashionable than Kirsty's own bonnet. Similarly, her dress was the latest model and she carried an exquisite frilly parasol. But she had a gleam in her eyes that Kirsty couldn't quite identify and an air of excitement that seemed inappropriate for a political meeting. She recalled her surprise when Martha stood up and challenged Churchill by asking what he meant to do about the franchise for women, and what a coward she had been when Martha was forcibly ejected from the hall. But it had been the start of a friendship, and her introduction to the suffrage cause. And now Martha was dead.

She pushed her tears away with angry fingers. What right did anyone have for ending Martha's life? Bending over she covered her face with her hands and sobbed.

At last, her grief spent for the time being, she turned her thoughts to what she could do to find Martha's killer, and that was when the realization struck that she'd given no thought to Sally since she learned about Martha's death. She remembered her vow to avenge Sally, and now that was doubled because she had to avenge Martha as well.

The sounds of movement in Martha's room had ceased. Had Lieutenant Allen completed his search and left for Sally's hostel? Or was he still there?

Kirsty rose, poured some cold water from the pitcher into the basin, and splashed her face to remove the remnants of her tears. Opening her door she peered into the corridor before emerging to check Martha's room. It was empty.

Returning to her own room, she brushed her hair, straightened her clothes and donned her hat. She wanted to discuss things with Beatrice.

48

Beatrice

'Hurry up Shannon, if you miss the train you'll be quartered again,' Vera shouted as she shot out the door.

It was one of the conditions of the munitions workers' employment. They lost some of their wages if they were late, and they hated that, because if they were even five minutes late it meant the loss of a quarter of an hour's pay.

'Wait for me, I'm coming.' Shannon bolted past Beatrice without a glance in her direction, but that was nothing out of the ordinary because Shannon only associated with her Irish friends, She had no time for any other nationality.

The early morning sun on the horizon painted the sky red and cast an eerie glow on the munitionettes running down the street. Beatrice remained on the doorstep until she could no longer see them. They would be hard at work at the mixing station at Eastriggs before the sun rose higher. She stood a few minutes longer wondering where Sally spent the night, and her anxiety, suppressed until the girls left the hostel, increased to envelop her in a crippling wave of emotion.

Beatrice closed the door, shutting out the chilly morning air, while she tried hard to quell the fearful thoughts rampaging through her mind. Matron would need to be informed and the authorities notified. But the hour was too early because she did not come on duty until nine o'clock, neither would any of the other authorities be available until then, and it was only half-past-five.

She paced the hall, back and forth. Wandered the corridors. Visited the kitchen, but cook shooed her out because she was busy clearing up after breakfast. She went back to her room but could not settle. Even trying to do some paperwork in the office did not work. Blank paper sat in front of her, but the pencil gripped between her fingers remained motionless.

Sally would not leave her thoughts. Beatrice buried her head in her hands, she felt so helpless. A sudden thought struck her, maybe she would find a clue to Sally's whereabouts in her cubicle. Rising, she hurried to the dormitory area.

A quick search of the girl's cubicle revealed nothing out of the ordinary. However, her clothes and personal belongings were still there, so Beatrice surmised she had not planned to leave the hostel. So where was she?

Questions continued to circulate in Beatrice's mind when she returned to the office, increasing her concerns for the missing girl. At eight o'clock, Maisie brought her a cup of tea. 'Cook says to tell you she knows you like coffee better, but she doesn't have any, and the tea will perk you up. She also said you should stop worrying about Sally, she'll turn up when she's good and ready.'

Less sure than cook that the tea would perk her up, but not wanting to offend her, Beatrice smiled and said, 'How kind of her.'

Half an hour later the maid reappeared.

'Yes, Maisie?' She laid her pencil on the desk.

'An army officer is asking for Matron, and I don't know if I should disturb her. But he says it's important.'

'That is all right. I will see him before deciding whether to disturb Matron.'

'Yes, miss.'

Beatrice rose to shake hands with the officer when Maisie ushered him into the office. He was tall, with striking blue eyes, and a serious expression.

'Please sit.' She gestured towards a chair. 'That will be all, Maisie,' she said, as the maid showed no signs of leaving.

'Yes, miss.' Maisie closed the door behind her, but Beatrice guessed she would be listening at the keyhole.

'I am Beatrice Jacobs. What can I do to help you?' An

irrational fear built within her and her anxiety escalated. It was unusual for a member of the military to visit the hostel, and she had a premonition it might be something to do with Sally's disappearance.

'Lieutenant Allen, ma'am. I am afraid I bring some sad news.'

Beatrice's stomach churned, and an icy hand squeezed her heart.

'A body was discovered in the factory grounds last night, and the policewoman who found her tells me she lived in this hostel.'

'Sally,' Beatrice gasped.

'You knew?' He sounded puzzled.

'A guess. Sally has been missing since last night and she is not the type of girl who would stay out late. I worried about her.'

Beatrice struggled to remain composed. 'Tell me what happened.'

'The young lady was stabbed. We found her with a knife in her back. But the unexplained thing is no one has any idea of why she was at the factory. From what I can gather, her name is not on the list of night shift workers.'

'That is correct, her shift is the early one which works from 6 o'clock in the morning until two in the afternoon.'

'So, there would be no reason for her to be inside the factory grounds last night.'

'That is correct.'

'We will require to ascertain her movements, therefore, arrangements will be made for everyone in the hostel to be questioned. And now, I need to inspect her room.'

'I searched her room this morning when we became aware she was missing, and I found nothing to explain her absence.'

'Nevertheless, I will require to see it for myself.'

'Of course.'

Beatrice rose. 'Follow me,' she said.

'When is the best time to interview the other residents?'

'They usually arrive back here about half-past-two.

Anytime after that.'

They halted at the entrance to Sally's cubicle.

'Is this it?'

'Yes. Inform me when you finish your inspection.' Beatrice turned away, anxious to regain the sanctuary of the office.

A few minutes later he rejoined her. 'You were right, I found nothing to indicate why she went to the factory site, so I shall take my leave. I will return at two-thirty, please ensure all the residents are available at that time.'

'Before you go ... You mentioned a policewoman found the body but you did not mention her name.'

'I believe her name is Miss Campbell.'

'Thank you.'

Beatrice scribbled the details of his visit on a sheet of paper and placed it on Matron's desk before she left the office.

Sounds of activity and voices infiltrated from the kitchen into the corridor. No doubt Maisie would be imparting everything she overheard to the rest of the staff, and Sally's death would be the main topic of conversation for many days to come.

Beatrice had no desire to be cross-examined by cook or anyone else, so she hurried to her room, grabbed her coat, and without stopping to fasten the buttons, she scurried to the front door. She must find Kirsty.

49

Kirsty

The sound of birdsong floated in the air like the birds themselves. Was this what people described as the dawn chorus? Kirsty closed the door behind her and ventured outside. A slight breeze rustled the leaves in the trees bordering the road, but apart from that, nothing moved. It was too early for many people to be on the streets. The girls on the morning shift would be hard at work by this time, and the night shift workers would have sunk into a restless sleep, while the sun rose high in the sky with the promise of a glorious spring day.

Kirsty was oblivious to everything around her. She didn't spot the fox, foraging at the side of the building beside an upturned rubbish bin, nor did she notice the cat crouched at the bottom of a tree, getting ready to leap into the branches. Her mind churned with thoughts of Martha and Sally, and her footsteps quickened as she hurried to seek out Beatrice.

She hesitated at the corner of the street when she saw the army truck outside the munitionettes' hostel. The army officer had been nice, but it was Beatrice she wanted to compare notes with, and he would get in the way. As she dithered, trying to decide whether or not to continue walking to the hostel, he came out and climbed into the truck, and with a cloud of exhaust, it roared down the street in the opposite direction.

On Kirsty's approach to the hostel, the front door opened and Beatrice emerged. The young woman, her fingers struggling to fasten her coat buttons, appeared flustered.

'You've heard,' Kirsty said.

Beatrice looked up and nodded.

'Do you want to go back inside, or shall we walk?'

'I do not want to talk here,' she said, 'too many ears.'

Neither of them spoke as they walked to the edge of the town. Straight ahead lay open countryside, and the road to Eastriggs. To the left were the town's sports areas, the tennis courts, the bowling green, and the football pitch. Without needing to consult, they both turned left.

Martha had played on the ladies police football team, and Kirsty found her feet pulling her in the direction of the pitch. 'It will be quiet here,' she said. 'The football practises and matches are all in the afternoon.'

She walked over to the pavilion and sat on the steps. Beatrice joined her, and they sat in silence.

'We should have seen this coming.' Beatrice's voice reflected her misery.

'What could we do? She didn't want our help.'

Once again they lapsed into a sorrowful silence.

Kirsty stared over the empty football pitch. Had it only been last Saturday they both sat here and cheered Martha on? A smile flickered at the corner of her mouth. Martha had been smaller than most of the policewomen and smaller than the other players, but her speed made up for her lack of size and she scored more goals than anyone else. She delighted in anything athletic and was more proficient at ju-jitsu than her colleagues, so she had the skills to defend herself. For Martha to meet her end at the hands of a murderer was beyond the bounds of Kirsty's imagination. Not for the first time that day, tears threatened to overwhelm her. Kirsty blinked hard. Policewomen didn't cry.

'Did you know that Sally was not the only one killed last night?' She stared into the distance, fighting the onset of tears.

'No, the army officer only told me about Sally.' Beatrice paused. 'There was someone else?'

Kirsty's shoulders shook. 'Martha.'

'Your friend? The one we watched play football?'

Kirsty nodded The loss so raw she was unable to speak.

'I am sorry.' Beatrice frowned. 'What reason would he have to kill Martha?'

'She was in the wrong place at the wrong time.' Kirsty struggled to breathe. 'I think she tried to save Sally. She was like that. She never considered her own safety if someone else needed protection.'

'This man, whoever he is, must be caught. He is a vicious killer. Who can tell where he will stop?' Beatrice's voice was harsh with determination.

'The problem is that my sergeant instructed me not to investigate and leave it up to the military.'

Beatrice laughed, although there was no humour in it. 'Do you think the military will be able to find out more than we can?'

'No, I have no faith in their powers of investigation. Their job is to fight, not find murderers.'

'Then that is settled. We conduct our own investigation, but we do not tell anyone what we are doing. If we discover who this killer is we hand him over to the military authorities.'

Kirsty stared at Beatrice. She had never heard the girl so determined before, nor that hint of steel in her voice.

'Right, where do we start?'

'Sally may have had a man friend, but I searched her room, and found nothing to indicate who she was seeing.'

'My search of Martha's room revealed nothing, but I think it is unlikely she knew her killer.'

'I do not think there is any doubt that Sally knew him.'

'What about the other girls in the hostel. Would they know anything?'

'No one owned up to knowing where she was when I asked them at breakfast time. But I have not questioned them individually.'

'We need to do that, but in a such a way our bosses don't latch on to what we are doing.'

'Lieutenant Allen is returning at half-past-two in order to question the girls and the staff.'

'Will they all be available at that time?'

'Yes. The girls in my hostel all work the early shift.'

Kirsty thought for a moment. 'Is there any way one of us

could attend those interviews?'

'I could suggest that it is not proper for females to be interviewed by males without another female present. But it cannot be me because I live in the hostel.'

'What about making the suggestion that the most appropriate person to be present is someone of an official capacity who is already involved and who knew both victims.'

'That might work. If you can come to the hostel at half-past-two I will see what I can arrange.'

'In the meantime, we can keep our eyes and ears open at all times.' Kirsty rose from the pavilion steps. 'And now, I need to get back to my own hostel and get some sleep, so I will be alert during the interviews.'

50

Kirsty

The hammering sound increased, each blow louder than the one before. Her heart beat faster. She had to face the unknown. Face the danger outside. But she couldn't raise her face out of the mud which was smothering her.

'Miss Kirsty, are you awake?' The ear-splitting thumps on the door increased.

Kirsty, rudely awakened from a restless, nightmare-filled sleep, lifted her face from the pillow and rolled over on her back. The nightmare receded into her subconscious, although the feeling of suffocation lingered until she sat up.

'It's all right, Jessie. I am awake now.'

Tiredness remained, and she groaned while forcing her brain, still fuzzy with sleep, and her limbs to do her bidding. With an effort and all the willpower she could muster, she stood in the narrow space in the middle of her tiny room. She stared at the pitcher on her washstand but resisted the temptation to pour the water into the bowl and wash. It would be far better to scrub herself down in the bathroom at the end of the corridor. Her determination to attend the interviews remained firm and she needed to be alert, as well as looking her best.

The coldness of the water made Kirsty gasp when she immersed herself but, afterward, her skin tingled when she rubbed herself dry with the rough towel, and she'd never felt more awake.

Back in her room, she considered what to wear. The uniform would assert her official status, but might also intimidate the girls who neither liked nor respected the lady police. So, she pushed her own need for recognition as a policewoman to the side and picked out a brown skirt and a dark green linen blouse. Brushing her hair only took a moment. Not once had she ever regretted having her waist length hair cut in a Castle Bob style when the dancer, Irene Castle, made it all the rage in 1915. Kirsty never followed fashions, but the ear length bob made life a lot easier. Lastly, she pulled on a brown coat and lighter brown cloche hat. The skirt and coat had been made from the same bolt of material, so they matched perfectly.

'My, miss. You do look lovely,' Jessie said when she passed her in the hall.

'Thank you, Jessie.' Kirsty smiled self-consciously. She never felt comfortable in civilian clothes.

It was only a ten-minute walk to the Mary Queen of Scots' hostel, and Beatrice was waiting at the door for her.

'I cannot recall ever seeing you without your uniform,' Beatrice said. 'You look nice.'

Kirsty wasn't used to getting compliments about her appearance, and a second one within fifteen minutes made her wriggle with embarrassment.

'I much prefer my uniform, but I thought the girls might open up better if I didn't wear it.'

Matron loomed behind Beatrice. 'Ah! This must be the police lady you suggested as a chaperone for the munitionettes while they are being interviewed.'

'This is Miss Campbell,' Beatrice said. 'She agreed to be present to ensure the proprieties.'

'Excellent, if you follow me you can wait in my office until Lieutenant Allen arrives.'

A desk took up most of the space in the middle of the room. Two chairs sat side by side behind it, with another chair in front, while a wooden filing cabinet filled the side wall. Piles of paper cluttered the top of the cabinet, spoiling an otherwise orderly office.

'I've cleared the desk for both of you, and arranged chairs ready for the interviews.' Matron reached up to the cabinet and selected some paper which she placed on the desk. 'For Lieutenant Allen's notes,' she said. 'There are some pencils in the right-hand drawer if he requires one.'

She backed out of the door. 'I will leave you to settle in while I go and wait for the lieutenant.'

Kirsty waited until her footsteps faded down the corridor before she helped herself to paper from the top of the cabinet and rummaged in the drawer for two pencils. Matron obviously assumed Kirsty would only sit and watch while the officer conducted the interviews. However, she had no intention of being a passive observer, she needed to find out as much as possible to facilitate her investigation into Sally and Martha's deaths.

She walked to the door and surveyed the room, trying to imagine she was one of the girls being questioned. That was when she realized the intimidating effect of two interrogators sitting beside each other. It could make some of them aggressive, and frighten others. Walking back to the desk, she shifted one chair to the side and moved the other to a central position. That way she would be better able to assess the outcome of the lieutenant's questions, and if she needed to supplement these it would be easier to make it a friendlier experience.

'I gathered all the girls in the dining room.'

Kirsty whirled around, startled by Beatrice's entrance.

'How are they taking this? Having to be interviewed, I mean.'

'On the whole, they seem to be accepting the need for it. There are always some rebels, though. The Irish girls are protesting, saying it is nothing to do with them. Matron has been firm and told them she will put them on a report if they do not comply. And one thing they dislike, even more, is being fined for misbehaviour.'

The roar of an engine, followed by the squeal of brakes, echoed along the corridor. Kirsty's heartbeat quickened. 'They're here.'

Beatrice placed a hand on Kirsty's arm. 'Good luck. Meet me when it is over so we can compare notes.'

Silence pervaded the room after Beatrice left, but within a few minutes, the sound of a door slamming and heavy footsteps indicated the arrival of the lieutenant. He seemed even taller than she remembered, dwarfing the matron who ushered him into the office.

'This is Miss Campbell,' matron said, 'she will act as chaperone for the girls while you question them.'

The lieutenant placed his cap on the edge of the desk. 'Yes, we met previously.' He thrust his hand out to shake hers.

His hand, warm and firm, enclosed Kirsty's, and she was surprised at the small electric charge which pulsed through her body. She withdrew her hand from his grasp. 'I trust there will be no objections if I occasionally ask a question,' she said in as business-like a manner as she could muster.

'Not at all.' He walked around the desk to sit in the chair. 'Shall we make a start with matron?'

Matron raised her eyebrows.

'Please sit.' He gestured to the chair in front of the desk.

'I thought you would want to question the girls first.' Matron sat on the edge of the seat.

'On the contrary, I think your knowledge of the munitionettes will be of help in order to get the most out of our interviews.'

'I see.' She stiffened her back, apparently uncomfortable at her loss of control.

'What can you tell me about Sally?'

Matron rose and turned to the filing cabinet. She ran her finger over the drawers and pulled one out, it contained a mass of identical folders which she riffled through.

'Ah, yes, here it is.' She placed a brown cardboard folder on the desk. 'I think you will find our record keeping in perfect order.'

She perched on the edge of the chair again. Opening the folder, she studied the contents. 'Miss Scott arrived here in January, there are no fines or admonishments on her record, she is a member of various groups such as needlework, knitting, and physical exercise, and appears to have behaved well.'

'Is that all you can tell me?' The lieutenant sounded surprised.

Matron stiffened. 'Although we are one of the smaller hostels we have approximately sixty-five munitionettes in our care, which makes for a considerable administrative burden. The residents I meet are those who misbehave or break the rules. Miss Jacobs, our assistant matron has closer contact with all the girls.'

'Unless there is something Miss Campbell would like to ask ...'

Kirsty shook her head.

'Then that will be all, matron. Perhaps you might like to send the first girl in?'

Beatrice stood outside the door of the dining room, listening to the buzz of voices. She pushed the door open and the voices ceased as the girls turned their heads towards her.

'It will not be long now,' she said. 'The army motor car has just arrived.'

The girls started to talk again, their voices lower this time, and Beatrice was conscious of surreptitious looks cast in her direction.

'Bloody English army.' A shrill Irish voice soared above the others. 'What right do they have to question us?'

'Pipe down,' another voice hissed. 'We don't want no trouble.'

'I am afraid we have to answer their questions,' Beatrice said. 'One of our girls is dead and the army is in charge of the investigation.'

'Why aren't the rozzers in charge?'

'That's right, Mary Ellen. What do bloody soldiers know about investigations? All they're good for is fighting and killing people.'

'Quiet girls.' Beatrice waved her hands in a shushing motion. 'The reason for the army's involvement is because this is a munitions factory in the charge of the War Office, therefore the military are responsible not the police.'

'I don't answer to any bleeding army officer, and it's not my war. So why should I be questioned.' The belligerent mutter originated from within the cluster of Irish girls at the end of the room.

Beatrice stiffened. She needed to control the subversive elements. In a quiet voice, she said, 'You work here, you accept your wages, therefore, you are required to abide by the rules of the establishment. You know that as well as I do.' She paused for breath. 'One of the girls who lived in this hostel has been murdered, and we need to find out who killed her. Does anyone disagree with that?'

The silence that followed was broken when the door opened and matron said, 'Lieutenant Allen is ready to see the first girl.'

51

Kirsty

Kirsty closed the office door after the last munitionette left. Interviewing the girls had taken a considerable amount of time, with little result, and she bit her lip to prevent her frustration boiling over.

'The investigation seems to be no further forward.' The lieutenant laid his pencil down and frowned at the sheet of paper in front of him. 'Miss Scott does not appear to have made many friendships among the girls.'

'There was that one girl, Maggie McKenzie.' Kirsty bent over the desk and ran her finger down her list of notes. 'Yes, here it is. She said they'd gone to the cinema a few times after Sally first came to Gretna, but that Sally had been avoiding her for the past few weeks.'

'That does not tell us anything, though, does it?' Lieutenant Allen gathered his papers together and rammed them in his briefcase. 'If we understood why Miss Scott was killed, it would help.'

'I think perhaps she knew something about her killer that made her a risk to him.'

The lieutenant didn't yet know about the Silvertown connection, and Kirsty had been waiting for an opportune moment to tell him.

'I doubt that.' His tone was brusque and dismissive. 'It is more likely to be,' he hesitated, 'a romantic liaison that went wrong.'

Despite her annoyance at having her suggestion dismissed so summarily, Kirsty tried, and failed, to suppress a wry smile at his obvious avoidance of the word sexual.

'Thank you for your help, Miss Campbell.' He halted at the door. 'Perhaps, after all this is over, we might meet again.' He hesitated, giving the impression he was searching for a reason. At last, he said, 'We could discuss the outcome of the investigation.'

He turned and marched up the corridor, leaving Kirsty wondering what he meant.

Lieutenant Allen touched the peak of his cap in an informal salute to Kirsty before he climbed into the motor car. The female driver winked at her, revved the engine, and drove off. Kirsty, still wondering about the lieutenant's last comment, stood at the door until they were out of sight.

The matron joined her. 'No one informed me the interviews were finished. I had intended to offer the lieutenant some hospitality.'

'I think he was anxious to return to his duties.' Kirsty cast a sidelong glance at her and was surprised to see her blushing. She had assumed the matron had wanted to interrogate the lieutenant on the outcome of the interviews, but it seemed that the woman was not immune to his charms.

'Would you care to partake of some tea? I am sure cook has made something special to go along with it. Her baking is quite exceptional.'

Kirsty was on the point of refusing, but there was no sign of Beatrice. So she forced a smile, and said, 'That would be delightful.'

The dining room was empty, but the matron led Kirsty to a table next to one of the windows. It was already laid out with china cups and saucers for two, a silver teapot, and a tiered cake stand, resting on a spotless white tablecloth.

Matron had evidently intended to entertain the lieutenant, and the only reason she asked Kirsty to join her was to find out the results of the interviews. It would be a pity to disappoint the woman, although the interviews had revealed nothing of interest.

'Please, sit,' the matron said.

Kirsty pulled one of the chairs out. 'Will Miss Jacobs be joining us?'

'I think Miss Jacobs will be settling the girls down after their distressing experience in the interviews.'

'Distressing? Hardly that.' Kirsty selected one of the rock buns. 'I think they took the whole thing in their stride.'

'You must tell me all about it.' Matron leaned forward.

'Certainly.' Kirsty suppressed a smile as she thought of how disappointed the woman would be with the information she was about to relay.

52

Beatrice

Beatrice, mindful of keeping her promise to meet Kirsty after the interviews but wanting to avoid the matron, slipped out of the hostel as soon as the last girl had returned to the dormitory. Now, she paced up and down at the end of the road, while keeping an eye on the front door. What was delaying the policewoman? The military car had long since gone, and Kirsty was still inside.

She stopped pacing when the door opened, but it was only some of the girls escaping to catch the last of the spring sunshine. Giggling and laughing, they turned in the direction of Central Avenue, on their way to window gaze at the shops, or to sun themselves on the beach bordering the Solway Firth. A pang of envy hit Beatrice who usually avoided the beach, unwilling to witness the simple pleasures of girls separated from their families through choice. Her own separation was much grimmer because her own parents had been prevented from escaping with her, and their lives, firstly in German-occupied Belgium, and now in the refugee camp in the Netherlands, must be fraught with risk.

After what seemed an eternity, Kirsty left the hostel.

Beatrice waved to her. 'What kept you?' she said when Kirsty reached the end of the road.

'The matron caught me before I could escape and marched me to the dining room for tea and cakes.'

Beatrice laughed. 'Tea and cakes?'

'Yes, I suppose it is ridiculous when we're in the middle of a murder inquiry.'

The two young women walked along the road, side by side.

'Were the interviews of any use? Did you find out

anything?'

'There was only one girl who knew Sally well, but even she wouldn't talk.'

'Let me guess. That would be Maggie McKenzie. I do not think Sally made any friends apart from her.' Beatrice walked on, deep in thought. 'Why would Maggie not tell you anything?'

'I thought she seemed scared, and the formality of the interviews didn't help.'

'Do you think she might talk to me?'

'She might. She knows you. She doesn't know me, and the lieutenant is an authoritarian figure representing the military. If she'll talk to anyone, it would be you.'

'I will try to get her on her own and see if she will open up, although it may not be a good idea to rush her.'

'You're probably right.' Kirsty stopped walking when they reached the end of the road. 'I will leave you here. I need to return to my hostel to prepare myself for night shift. But after last night ...' she didn't continue.

'Finding Sally like that must have been terrible.' Tears filled Beatrice's eyes and she turned away from Kirsty so the policewoman would not see them.

'Yes.' Kirsty's voice was little more than a whisper. 'But tonight is my last night shift for a few weeks, and we're allowed two days off to recover before starting the early shift.'

'Until tomorrow,' Beatrice said. 'Maybe we can meet in the afternoon, and I will try to speak with Maggie before then.'

Beatrice watched Kirsty until she was out of sight, then retraced her steps to seek the privacy of her room where she could shed tears for Sally and Martha, without anyone observing her.

For the first time in her police career, Kirsty didn't want to be on duty.

Inside, the mixing station seemed no different, the lights

shone as brightly as they ever did, the girls continued to stir their devil's porridge while they shouted, laughed and joked with each other over the top of the large lead drums that contained the mix.

But outside, the darkness of the night felt ominous, and Kirsty couldn't forget Sally's body lying face down at the bottom of one of the hillocks.

She opened the door several times when the urge to go outside to investigate Sally's death became too strong, but always, she drew back and closed the door again, unwilling to venture into the darkness.

53

Beatrice

Beatrice woke the following morning with gritty eyes and a heavy head. She had slept badly, tossing and turning all night, while a faceless man stalked her dreams. He exuded menace and she could not escape, but when she turned to confront him there was nothing but mist. However, she could not shake off the urgency and dread that seeped into the nightmares, nor the strange feeling she knew this man. But that was impossible, because no one knew who Sally was walking out with after she finished work.

Weak sunshine struggled through the window and the dream slipped away, leaving only a sense of loss and an overpowering urge to understand why Sally had to die at the hands of a killer. She swung her feet out of the bed and threw the pillow, she had been trying to strangle, onto the floor. It was time to face the day; time to start work, in an attempt to expose the evil that had occurred; time to find the killer in their midst.

After the girls left the hostel, Beatrice braced herself to pack Sally's possessions.

'Do we have to do this so soon after her death?' Beatrice had asked the previous evening.

'I am afraid so,' the matron said. 'We need to send Sally's belongings back to her mother, besides the cubicle will be needed.'

Beatrice had nodded, reluctant to speak in case she accused the matron of insensitivity.

Now, standing in front of Sally's cubicle, she was overcome with sadness. How would the girl's mother cope with the loss of her daughter?

She pushed the thoughts out of her mind, pulled aside the

curtain that separated the cubicle from the dormitory, opened the suitcase she had rescued from the storeroom, and started to gather together Sally's meagre possessions. Each item she placed inside, she noted on a piece of paper. The list was painfully small.

'Sally loved that dress. She bought it from the dress shop in the avenue.' The voice behind her sounded tearful.

Beatrice paused with her hand on the blue silk dress. 'Yes, it is lovely. Sally must have looked beautiful in it.'

Maggie nodded. 'She only wore it once, when she went to the dance hall.' She shifted from foot to foot and grasped her arms around her middle. 'I forced her to go. She didn't want to, but I said she should get out more ...' her arms tightened and she rocked backwards and forwards. Tears rolled down her cheeks. 'If I hadn't made her go she would never have met him. And now she's dead. And it's all my fault.'

Reaching for the girl Beatrice folded her arms around her. 'Hush now. It is not your fault.' She guided the sobbing girl to the edge of the bed. 'Sit,' she said, 'and tell me all about it.'

Maggie sobbed for a while, but after a time the tears ceased and she stared at her hands as they twisted and pulled at the material of her nightgown. She seemed to have moved into another time and place. Beatrice wondered what she was seeing, and whether it was a product of her tortured mind.

At last, Maggie looked up. 'I can't get his face out of my head,' she whispered.

Beatrice's eyes widened with astonishment. Whatever she had expected Maggie to say, it was not this. 'You have seen him?' She almost choked on the words.

Maggie nodded. 'It was the day after he scared Sally at the dance hall. He was waiting for her at the train station when she finished her shift. After that, she said she made a mistake and he was really nice.' Maggie sniffed. 'He waited for her again, lots of times, but he always stayed out of sight after that first time.'

'What did he look like?'

Maggie stared at her hands again. 'He looked nice. If he'd asked me I'd have gone out with him. Just goes to show you can't tell what they're like.'

Beatrice assumed that what Maggie meant was that the man was handsome, but that was not enough to go on. 'How tall was he, Maggie?'

'A bit taller than Sally, and quite slim for a man.'

'How much taller?'

'He was taller than most of the girls, miss.'

Beatrice grabbed the list of Sally's possessions, turned the paper over and scribbled on the back. 'Can you remember the colour of his hair?'

'Brown, and he had dark eyes. When he looked at Sally, I remember wishing he'd look at me that way.' Maggie shuddered.

'Is there anything else you can tell me about his hair?'

'Short, miss, with a bit of a wave. He looked like a film star.'

'What about his face. Did he have a moustache or beard?'

'No, miss. He had lovely skin.'

Beatrice scribbled some more details on the piece of paper. 'Anything else you can remember, Maggie?'

The girl shook her head. 'That's all, miss.' She stared at her hands again. 'Do you think he'll come after me?'

'I do not think so. But I want to share this with my friend, Kirsty. She was the one who was with the lieutenant when they questioned you.'

Maggie stood, the alarm reflected in her eyes made her resemble a frightened rabbit. 'If the lady police and the army know, then he'll find out.'

'No, he will not. We will keep this between ourselves, but you have to help us. This man must be caught and put in prison. He must pay for what he did to Sally.'

Maggie nodded, but Beatrice saw she was not convinced.

The night had passed slowly. Kirsty ached all over and the walk from the station to the hostel had never seemed so long before. Thank goodness that was the last of her night shifts. It was just as well there would be two days to recover, because adapting to day shift from working nights was always more difficult than when it was the other way around.

She grasped the handrail and, with an effort, pulled herself up the steps into the hostel. Once inside she stumbled down the corridor to her cubbyhole of a room and collapsed on the bed.

Before lapsing into a troubled sleep she wondered whether Beatrice would have any success with Maggie.

54

Dietger and Beatrice

Dietger arrived in Gretna at a quarter to six, just as the sun was peeking over the horizon. He opened the carriage door when the train slowed, and hopped out the minute it stopped at the platform.

Women, early shift workers, thronging the platform surged towards the doors, but he was already walking to the rear of the train with his collar pulled up and his cap brim pulled far enough forward to shade his face. As soon as the workers were on board, and the carriage doors closed, the train left the station bound for Eastriggs and the munitions factory. Only then did he feel safe to leave the station.

Beatrice's hostel would now be empty except for the staff. But he could not approach her there, he would wait until she emerged. And he was certain she would come out sooner or later, in order to report to Melville.

While he walked, his mind buzzed with disconnected thoughts: the fragmentation of all his carefully laid plans; the murder of the girl and the policewoman, and whether their deaths were necessary; his loss of control; and Beatrice, dear Beatrice.

He had always been a disciplined person, that was why he had worked so effectively in the past, so this loss of control alarmed him, and made him question whether the plan he had spent so much time formulating should be aborted. However, it was too late now. The plan would go ahead, despite the possibility of disaster.

With his head down and his hands stuffed into the pockets of his trousers, Dietger traversed the same deserted streets over and over again, worrying all the time that his presence would arouse suspicion. At nine o'clock the shopkeepers opened their shutters and rolled up their blinds, and the streets became busy with early shoppers. No longer feeling so conspicuous, he mingled with them on Central Avenue, stopping now and again to stare into a shop window. His eyes, however, did not focus on the goods for sale, paying more attention to the crowds hoping for a sight of Beatrice.

A surge of pleasure flowed through him when he spotted her turning the corner into the avenue. Her smart tan costume, the jacket waist pinched in by a narrow belt and the full flared skirt, would not have looked out of place on a Paris boulevard, while the wide brimmed darker brown hat only served to highlight her beauty.

He waited until she passed him before turning and following her. She glanced neither to left nor right and carried on to the train station. The swing of her skirt as she walked enhanced her ankles, and he could not help thinking the new shorter styles most women now wore, were exceedingly attractive. He sighed, if not for this awful war, things might be a lot different and he could court her. But the war made that out of the question.

She started when he touched her arm. 'Dietger? I thought you had gone.'

'I could not leave without seeing you again,' Dietger meant what he said.

The train pulled into the station, enveloping them in a cloud of steam and smoke. He opened a carriage door and offered Beatrice his hand. 'May I?'

Beatrice's face went pink, but she accepted the proffered hand. 'Thank you.' She sat down, arranging her skirt with more care than Dietger thought necessary.

An uneasy silence developed between them as they travelled towards Carlisle. In ten minutes they would arrive, and Dietger had not said what he wished to say, and now he was in her company he was disinclined to probe her for information.

At last, he said, 'You have an appointment in Carlisle?'

'Yes,' she murmured.

'Melville?'

'Yes.'

The train steamed into Carlisle station. He rose, pulled the leather strap to lower the window, reached out and turned the handle to open the door before leaping out to the platform. Beatrice remained seated until he held his hand out to help her alight.

Retaining her hand in his, he said, 'Have you told him about me?'

She made no attempt to remove her hand. 'No, not yet.' She did not look at him.

'Will you? Tell him I am here?'

'Not unless I have to.' She removed her hand from his. 'Now, I must go. I do not want to be late.'

'Meet me afterwards.'

'Where?'

'I will wait beside the Castle, that is easy to find. Will you come?'

'Perhaps,' she said.

Dietger watched her leave the station, her skirt swinging provocatively around her ankles. He had placed his life in her hands. He hoped he had not misjudged her.

55

Beatrice

Beatrice resisted the urge to look back. She fought against her increased pulse rate and the alarming beat of her heart. The effect Dietger had on her was unwelcome. She must not succumb. Melville believed him to be a German spy. But was he? Her duty was to report his presence, but her thoughts were jumbled and confused and she found it difficult to believe that a Belgian would spy for Germany. If she did what Melville expected of her, that would mean a death sentence for Dietger.

As she entered the Station Hotel, somewhere in the town centre, a clock struck ten. The empty foyer, stark and unwelcoming, showed no signs of life. Several minutes passed and still no one came. Frustrated, and resisting the urge to search for Melville, she pinged the brass bell push on the reception counter. The third time she rang the bell a weary receptionist plodded from the depths of the hotel.

'We're full up.' The woman peered at Beatrice. 'You've been here before.' Her voice trembled and her body sagged with tiredness.

'That is correct, I do not need a room this time. I am here to meet Mr Melville. Is he in the hotel?'

The woman's eyes sharpened with suspicion. 'I don't hold with young women meeting men in this hotel,' she said in a disapproving tone.

Heat suffused Beatrice's cheeks. 'I am a respectable woman, and my meeting is a business one with my employer. Now will you please inform him I am here.'

She glared at the receptionist and, after a few seconds, the woman looked away.

'Mr Melville is in the breakfast room having a late

breakfast. You can see him there, but I won't condone you going to his bedroom.'

'I have no wish to meet Mr Melville in his bedroom.' Beatrice kept her voice icy.

The woman shrugged.

The breakfast room was empty apart from Melville sitting at a window table. He rose as Beatrice approached and pulled out a chair for her to sit on.

'I hear there have been developments at Gretna,' he said.

Beatrice sighed. 'It has been terrible,' she said in a low voice. 'Sally Scott, the girl we were trying to protect has been murdered, as well as one of the lady police.' She fought against the tears gathering in her eyes.

Melville leaned over the table and patted her hand. 'Do not blame yourself, Leclercq is a devious man, well versed in avoiding detection.'

Her heart thumped so loudly he must surely hear the thuds. 'You are certain it is him?'

'Of course.'

Melville's eyes were watching her. Now was the time to tell him of Dietger's presence, but she remained unconvinced he was a killer.

'Something is being planned for King George's visit, so it is imperative we find him before then.' Melville dropped two sugar lumps into his teacup. 'Will you take some tea?' His hand hovered over the silver teapot.

Beatrice shook her head. The lump in her throat would prevent her swallowing. 'We may have someone who can identify Sally's boyfriend. Her friend saw them together on one occasion, but I do not want it known anywhere else or she will be at risk as well.'

'You have not told the military?'

'No, I thought it better not to. If I tell them the spotlight will be on Maggie, and I do not want her ending up dead. I think we can investigate more discreetly.'

He fingered his moustache, and stared into the distance giving the impression he was weighing up what Beatrice suggested.

'How do you propose to investigate?'

'Kirsty Campbell, you will remember her from the meeting at Gretna, is already involved. I thought we might work together.'

'Ah, yes! Miss Campbell, I remember. What does her superior officer think?'

'She does not sanction an investigation by the lady police.'

'This means your investigation will be an informal one.'

'We think that will bring the best results without endangering Maggie.'

'I see, and did this Maggie provide a reasonable description of the man we are looking for?'

'A vague one which is not too helpful. She says he is slim, with short brown hair and dark eyes.'

'That description fits Dietger LeClercq.'

Beatrice had been trying to quell that thought ever since she had talked to Maggie.

Beatrice left the hotel, intending to go straight to the station and board the first train for Gretna, but her feet led her to Carlisle Castle where Dietger waited for her. She knew it was foolish to meet him, and that if he was a dangerous spy, she was putting herself at risk. But her heart told her otherwise. He had been kind and helpful to her every time they met, and her instinct was to trust him.

'I did not think you would come.' Dietger grasped her hands. 'But I am glad you did.'

Heat rose from Beatrice's neck into her face.

'Shall we walk?' He released her hands. 'There is a quiet spot by the riverside.'

They walked, without speaking, until they reached a bench overlooking the river. He took her hand and guided her to the seat.

'You did not tell him?' Dietger's voice held a note of uncertainty.

'No, I did not tell him.'

Beatrice lapsed into silence and focused her gaze on the water flowing a few yards from where they sat. She had thought other people might be here, enjoying the midday sun, but there was no one else within sight. If Dietger was as dangerous as Melville stated, this would be the ideal spot to do anything he wanted. No one would see. But Beatrice had never felt safer. She trusted this man.

'Dietger!' She hesitated. 'You are aware Melville thinks you are a spy?'

'Yes.'

'He also thinks you killed Sally and Martha.' Beatrice's voice quavered. 'I must know. Did you?'

Dietger stared at the river in silence. At last, he turned to her. 'Ah, liebchen! That you would think that of me. I can assure you that the deaths of those two women were nothing to do with me.'

Beatrice cringed at the disappointment in his voice. She did not believe he was a murderer, and the relief at his denial overwhelmed her.

'I am sorry. I knew deep within me that Melville was wrong, but I had to be sure.'

Dietger grasped her hands in his. 'You think I am a dangerous man.'

'No, no!'

'I am many things, and I may have done some bad things in my life, but I am no killer.'

'I believe you.'

'You are safe with me, liebchen. I would never harm you. And now, I think we should depart.'

They walked in silence until they reached the castle although Beatrice's thoughts were in turmoil. She believed more than ever that Dietger was what he appeared to be, a kind and generous man, who did not have it in him to hurt anyone.

'I will leave you here,' he said. 'It is not far to the train station.' He kissed her fingertips. 'Until we meet again, liebchen.'

56

Kirsty

Cushioned in a nest of grass on the slope bordering the football pitch, Kirsty closed her eyes and tilted her face to the sun. The weather, unusually warm for early May, more like summer than spring, wouldn't last, so she determined to make the most of it.

Her thoughts drifted to her childhood in Broughty Ferry. A time of innocence when the summers seemed longer and hotter than they were now. She wondered how true that was, or whether this was wishful thinking of an idyllic time that existed only in her imagination. Had her childhood been as carefree as she remembered? Was it a way of denying the disastrous events that followed? The events that haunted her and led to the estrangement from her family.

The thud of the ball hitting the goalposts and the roar of the crowd jerked her back to the present. She sat up, shaded her eyes, and observed the goal scorer raise her arms in jubilation. For a moment, the slim figure, in a football shirt and shorts which exposed her legs up to her knees, looked like Martha. But Martha was dead. Killed by some maniac.

She dashed tears from her eyes with the back of her hands. It had been a mistake to arrange to meet Beatrice here. But the days became muddled when she worked night shift, and she'd forgotten the Saturday football match.

She drew her knees up to her chest and wrapped her arms around them. Several bees buzzed nearby. How simple their lives were compared to her own.

'I am sorry to be late.' Beatrice lowered herself to sit on the grass beside Kirsty. 'I was delayed in Carlisle.'

'Carlisle?'

'Yes, I had to report to Mr Melville.'

'The man who came from London to find out what we knew about Sally?' She stared at Beatrice. 'I never did discover why he was involved.'

Beatrice squirmed. 'Maybe I should not have told you.'

'Why?' Kirsty regarded her through narrowed eyes. 'And why do you report to him?' There was something here she didn't understand.

Beatrice hesitated before speaking. 'If I explain, you must not reveal anything I say.'

Kirsty plucked a blade of grass and chewed the end. What was so important about this man, this official from London, that his involvement must be kept secret?

'Of course,' she said.

Beatrice looked over her shoulder.

'It's all right,' Kirsty said, 'I chose a spot where we couldn't be overheard.'

Beatrice leaned closer to Kirsty. 'Mr Melville is part of the Secret Service. His job is to search for spies and enemy agents, and he is concerned about the royal visit.'

Kirsty's eyebrows rose in an expression of surprise. Beatrice had always seemed such an ordinary young woman.

'What about you? Are you a spy hunter as well?'

Beatrice shook her head. 'I am no spy hunter,' she said. 'Mr Melville occasionally employs me as a translator.'

'Then why are you here?'

Beatrice's face saddened. 'He said he wanted me to keep a watch on the Irish munitionettes, but after I was here I found out the real reason he asked me to come. He believes a Belgian man of my acquaintance is a German spy. I am the only one who can identify him.'

'The German spy is operating in this area, I presume.'

Beatrice nodded.

Kirsty studied Beatrice, she had never seen her so miserable. 'Are you happy with your task?'

'I think Mr Melville is mistaken, but that will not prevent me doing my duty.'

'But if this man is a German spy, do you think he might also be our killer?'

Again Beatrice shook her head. 'Mr Melville believes so, but the man I know is kind and considerate, and I do not think he would be capable of murder.'

Kirsty reached out and grasped Beatrice's hands. 'I am sorry, but you must be aware that strange things happen during wartime and that not everyone acts as their character dictates. Why else would ordinary men become soldiers and kill other men on the battlefield?'

'I know this.' Beatrice's voice was subdued. 'But I am hoping, with Maggie's help, we can find the killer.'

Excitement fizzed through Kirsty and she tightened her grasp on Beatrice's hands. 'Maggie can identify him?'

'We talked this morning, and she said she saw him the first time he waited for Sally.'

'That means Maggie is in danger. Does he know she saw him?'

'She thinks not, but she might be wrong.'

'Who else knows?'

'No one, apart from Mr Melville.'

'Will that pose a risk for Maggie?'

'No, he is happy for us to investigate and report back to him.'

Kirsty was quiet for a moment. 'My sergeant hasn't sanctioned an investigation. She proposes to leave it up to the military. But if Melville is involved ...' She didn't finish.

'You forget, Mr Melville is with the Secret Service, which means any liaison with other officials requires to be advantageous for him.'

'And he sanctions our proposal to investigate?' Kirsty mulled this over in her mind. 'Where do we start?'

'With Maggie. We take her to places of entertainment, such as the cinema, or the dance hall. We could make a list of places this man might frequent.'

'I am not sure,' Kirsty said. 'If Maggie is seen with me, it would be like pointing a finger at her. It would make her a target.'

'Yes, I see what you mean. But I could accompany her to places where you are already on duty. That way you will be available for backup should we need it.'

'Where is Maggie at the moment?'

'At the hostel. I left her there this morning before I went to Carlisle.'

Thoughts whirled through Kirsty's mind. Beatrice's proposition made sense but they would have to ensure Maggie's safety.

She scrambled to her feet and brushed grass from her skirt.

'So far there is no reason to think she will not be safe, but that could change once we start looking for him, that means you need to keep close to her at the hostel. I am on an early shift from Monday, and that's the shift your girls work, so I can keep an eye on her at the mixing station. And, once you work something out with Maggie, send me a message and we will get our investigation started.'

Beatrice removed her hat and jacket, laying them on the bed before she went to look for Maggie. Dishes and pots clattered in the kitchen accompanied by the sound of voices, but apart from that the building was quiet.

Maisie scurried out of one of the dormitories, her arms laden with a pile of sheets.

'Have you seen Maggie?' Beatrice asked.

'No, miss. But a crowd of the girls went off to the beach half an hour ago.'

'Did you notice if Maggie went with them?'

'No, miss.' Maisie shuffled her feet. 'I need to run, miss. The laundry truck will be here soon.'

Beatrice turned away from the dormitories. It was evident from what Maisie said that Maggie was not there. But she did not think it likely that the girl had gone to the beach with the others, so she continued her search in the recreation rooms. If Maggie was not in one of them she might be at The Institute which had more extensive recreational facilities.

However, she found Maggie, curled up in a chair, in the reading room with an open book resting on her knees.

She pulled a chair alongside. 'I thought you might be at the beach with some of the girls.'

Maggie glanced up from her book. 'I wasn't in the mood.'

'What are you reading?'

'The Man Upstairs.' She closed the book.

'Is it any good?'

'Not bad. It's short stories by Wodehouse. I searched for a book by Angela Brazil but couldn't find any.'

'If I am interrupting I could leave,' Beatrice said.

'You're not interrupting. I couldn't concentrate on the stories anyway.'

'That does not surprise me.' Beatrice reached over and grasped Maggie's hand. 'So much has happened.'

Maggie nodded. 'I miss Sally. She didn't deserve what happened to her.'

'When we talked this morning you promised to help catch Sally's killer.'

'I'm not sure.' Her voice trembled. 'He might come after me.'

'I know you are afraid, but if we do not catch this man he could kill again.'

'And it might be me.' Maggie's voice was anguished.

'That is why you must help us, Maggie. This is the only way you will remain safe.'

'What do you want me to do?' She sounded resigned.

'We will visit places we think this man might frequent, and if he is there, you whisper it to me.'

'But if he sees me, he will know.'

'My friend Kirsty and I will protect you. We will make sure he cannot get near to you. You will be safe.' Beatrice prayed she was right. If anything happened to Maggie she would never forgive herself.

'I suppose,' Maggie said.

57

Shannon

'It's time to go.'

Shannon woke with a start, blinking her eyes in the sunlight. It was pleasant here, snoozing on the beach. She had been on the booze in Carlisle last night and drank too much, always a mistake when she had to get up for the early shift the next morning. But who cared. Life was for living.

'Five more minutes,' she murmured, closing her eyes again, 'I'm shattered.'

The whack of a towel on her legs stung. She sat up and glared at Vera. 'What did you do that for?'

'Get up you lazy slag. I've a mouth on me, and me dinner won't wait.'

'You're always hungry. I reckon you've got worms.'

'Better a hunger than a thirst,' Vera snapped. 'Your ma would be ashamed of you.'

'Not for long, she won't.'

'Oh! How's that then?'

'As if I'd be telling you.'

Vera stuck the towel in her canvas beach bag, grasped the wooden handles, and walked away without saying a word.

Shannon frowned. Damned if she would go after her. She lay back on the towel and closed her eyes, but she was too angry to sleep. In any case, a mist pulling in from the firth masked the sun, and everyone else had left.

Sand covered her towel and grains fell out of her hair when she shook her head, plus her clothes and shoes seemed full of the stuff. Damn Vera, she must have kicked the sand over her while she slept. She stood up, shook the towel, and slinging it over her shoulder she strode to the fence bordering the railway line. After a quick look around, to check no lady police waited in hiding to pounce, she vaulted it and crossed the rails. A lot of the girls did that, even though they were perfectly aware they should use the bridge.

A group of girls, the only people left in the otherwise empty street, clustered around the cinema boards further up Central Avenue. She slowed her footsteps expecting Vera to be with them, and she couldn't stand any more of her snide remarks.

She scowled. When exactly did Vera become so full of herself? Shannon was accustomed to being the leader of the group, but recently, Vera had been usurping her position. Maybe she had been too distracted lately, seeing too much of Aidan, and Derek. But what if she had? Most of the girls only managed to attract one boyfriend. Could she help it if two men were interested in her?

At the moment, she didn't know which one of them she preferred. When Aidan kissed her, she loved him with all her heart. But when Derek held her in his arms, she loved him more. It was a balancing act keeping them apart. She wasn't sure about Derek, but Aidan had a jealous streak, and she had no desire to see the ensuing fight if either of them suspected she was seeing the other.

She was so deep in thought about Aiden and Derek she didn't notice when he appeared at her side.

'Penny for them?'

'You startled me,' she said. 'You didn't say you would be in Gretna today.'

He pulled her into a side street. 'We might not be able to meet again before the royal visit, and I wanted to know if you still intend to help. It's not too late to change your mind.' He enclosed her in his arms. 'But I hope you won't.'

She relaxed enjoying his embrace. When he held her she had no doubts she loved him, and when he looked at her like that, she would promise him anything.

'I haven't changed my mind. I'll make you, and my ma, proud of me on Friday.'

58

Beatrice

Beatrice stripped off her skirt and blouse and donned the drab brown dress she wore as assistant matron.

Maggie had refused her offer to accompany her to the dance hall. 'Not tonight,' she said. 'Sally is too much in my thoughts.'

They were both, in their own ways, mourning Sally, so Beatrice had not insisted. But the importance of identifying Sally's killer before King George's visit plagued her thoughts.

She arranged the skirt and blouse on a hanger, placed the hat in its box, and tidied her hair in readiness for the evening meal. Comforting smells of soup and something meaty wafted along the corridor when she opened her door. Cook had a magic touch with the ingredients available, and could make a tasty pot of soup or stew from whatever she had to hand.

The front door slammed, followed by the sound of running feet and laughter. The girls were returning. She met several in the corridor. They slowed down, suppressing their giggles and laughter, until after they passed her.

'Watch where you're going.' Cook, emerging from the kitchen with the soup pot, stepped back sharply to avoid a collision.

Beatrice hurried and opened the dining room door for her. 'That looks heavy,' she said.

Cook plonked the pot on the serving table. 'I'm used to it.'

Maisie ran into the room with the ladle and servers.

'I wondered where you'd got to, lass. Now hop back to the kitchen and drain the tatties. I'll dish up here.' She turned to Beatrice. 'That's me ready. You can sound the dinner gong now.'

Beatrice reached the gong at the same time as the front door banged open. 'You are just in time,' she said to the flustered girl who collided with her.

She struck the large brass gong with the mallet. The deep, full, reverberating sound echoed throughout the hostel announcing the evening meal.

Beatrice laid the mallet down, her eyes thoughtful as she watched the receding figure of Shannon. Something about her, the flush in her cheeks, the tousled hair, the speed with which she ran up the corridor with no hint of an apology, convinced Beatrice that the girl was up to something.

59

Planning the Assassination

He leaned against the wooden guard rail at the top of Gretna Station footbridge. The railway line leading to Eastriggs stretched in front of him, the line behind him led to Longtown and then on to Carlisle. It was here the royal couple would alight from the train.

On the pretext of admiring the sunset over the Solway Firth, he mapped out the area below him. The shore side of the railway line he quickly ruled out as being too exposed with the bulk of the train protecting the couple. That meant he would need to mingle with the crowds, either on the station platform or at the end of Central Avenue, at the other side of the fence.

Closing his eyes he imagined the scene. The train arriving, the welcoming officials, and the crowds eager for a sight of the King and Queen. The platform, crowded with officials and security, where the royal couple would linger while introductions were made. There would likely be a brass band, and the presence of the military and the police was a certainty. No doubt the royals would visit various parts of Gretna, probably the infirmary, the school, and some of the hostels. They might even go on to inspect one of the factory buildings, but the timetable remained a close secret. Without access to the itinerary, he could not plan his assassination attempt anywhere else and he would be too conspicuous if he followed them around.

Mingling with the crowd at the bottom of Central Avenue seemed to be his best option. There was safety in crowds and if he could acquire a good spot, with a clear line of sight, nothing could go wrong. He turned his gaze to the timber fence. How high was it? He couldn't determine the height from this angle, although he believed it to be low enough to see over.

His feet clattered on the wooden steps, taking them two at a time, as he left the bridge in order to make a closer inspection and select the perfect spot. Leaving the station, he walked up Central Avenue, as far as the cinema, before retracing his footsteps. He couldn't afford to be seen paying too much attention to the layout of the station.

Approaching the fence he confirmed the height allowed him to place his elbows on it. Ideal for his gun arm. On the pretext of looking out over the firth, he mapped out the best spot for a clear shot at King George. He doubted he would have time to shoot the Queen as well, but if the opportunity arose, he would take it. In the uproar after the shooting, he would disappear into the crowds and make his way to the rendezvous place, where his Irish friends would be waiting with a truck. And with his job here done, he would return to London, and prepare for his next mission.

It was a pity he wouldn't be able to take Shannon with him. He had grown fond of the girl and it would have been a pleasant interlude. But she was determined to martyr herself for her cause, so it couldn't be helped.

60

Shannon

Shannon shivered with anticipation as she alighted from the train at the Wylies. She'd woken that morning knowing this was the day. The day when she would be written into the annals of Irish history. The day she would make the supreme sacrifice for her country.

Her hand closed on the farthing in her coat pocket. She would pop it into her mouth the minute no one was looking. There was no other way she could smuggle it into the mixing station. The lady police searches were so thorough, they even examined hair for concealed hair pins, but they never looked in mouths, and in any case, once she concealed the farthing under her tongue it would never be seen. And when she spat it into the devil's porridge, the explosion would be spectacular.

It was risky, of course, and she hoped they wouldn't ask any questions when they searched her. But a sullen shake of the head should take care of that.

'You're quiet today.' Vera fell into step beside her.

Shannon gripped the farthing even tighter. 'Can't I be quiet if I want?' She hadn't thought about how she would respond to friends wanting to chat. Not that they would tell anyone, the Irish always looked after their own, but if they knew of the planned explosion they wouldn't want to stay around.

'Sure, and you don't need to snap at me.'

'Just leave me be. I think I'm sickening for something, and I'm not in the mood to talk.'

'Too many late nights with your skirt around your ears,' Vera retorted, and with that snide remark she hurried off to the group in front. 'I would stay clear of Shannon today, she's in a foul temper,' she said to them. Several heads turned to stare at her.

That suited Shannon, but to make sure the other girls stayed their distance, she raised two fingers to them and scowled. As soon as they turned their heads away, to concentrate on walking to the mixing station, she popped the farthing into her mouth. She manipulated it into position beneath her tongue where it wobbled for a moment, clinking off the back of her teeth until she pressed the tip of her tongue on the top of them to keep it in place. She knew, from her practice session last night, that she would have to keep her tongue in this position, and that she would be unable to speak without slurring her words until the time came to spit the coin out. Eleven o'clock he told her, was the best time to set off the explosion to create the diversion he needed.

The coppery taste flooded her mouth, but she was determined to retain the coin there for the next five hours until the time came to fulfil her destiny.

Kirsty removed a hair pin from the munitionette's hair. 'You know perfectly well you're not allowed these in the mixing area,' she said.

The girl scowled, and rammed her dust cap back on her head, tucking the strands of hair underneath.

The next one in line was Shannon. Kirsty had been keeping a keen eye on this one ever since Beatrice confided her suspicions about the Irish girl.

'She's a troublemaker,' Beatrice had said, 'and I'm sure she's planning something.' But, apart from the usual tirades of abuse, Kirsty had never been able to detect any wrongdoing on the girl's part. Despite this, she always made sure her searches were thorough.

She ran her hands over Shannon's body, examined her hair, made her take off her boots so she could check inside, and checked her toes, hands and fingers, but once again drew a blank. However, she sensed something odd about the girl today. Normally, she would sneer at Kirsty and offer a comment. 'Gives you a thrill, does it?' Shannon would say when Kirsty searched her. But she said nothing today despite the malicious gleam in her eyes.

After the search, Shannon walked through the double doors into the work area of the mixing station without a backward glance instead of the usual sniggers, laughter, and rude gestures. Unable to shake off a premonition that she was up to something Kirsty determined to keep her under observation for the rest of the shift.

She was still watching Shannon when the time came for the morning meal break. When the second batch of munitionettes returned from the canteen, and it was time for Shannon to go, she made no attempt to leave her work station.

Kirsty marched up to her. 'You have not taken your break yet,' she said.

Shannon shrugged and turned back to the lead tub containing the explosive mixture.

Her misgivings increased, and Kirsty frowned, trying to work out what the girl was up to. The munitionettes were always keen to take their breaks and the difficulty was getting them to return to the work area. Shannon's refusal to take her break was suspicious.

'The regulations say you have to take a break.'

The scowling munitionette shook her head.

Kirsty's suspicions intensified.

'If you do not take your break now you will be a danger to yourself and the other workers, so I will remove you from the mixing station and send you back to the hostel.'

Shannon scowled. She turned and flounced to the canteen. Ignoring the food, she slumped into a chair with folded arms.

Kirsty stood over her. 'Why are you not eating? Are you unwell?'

Shannon glared at her, defiance written all over her face.

'I demand you answer me.'

Sandra, on duty in the canteen, strode over to join them. She stood, feet apart and with her hands on her hips. 'Problems?' she asked.

'This munitionette is not answering my questions, and I think she is hiding something.'

'You will answer my colleague's questions now, or be charged with insolence and non-compliance with the rules and regulations.' Sandra's voice brooked no argument.

Although unconvinced they could charge anyone with insolence, Kirsty didn't disagree because she was sure the girl was up to something.

'Leave her alone.' One of the girls at an adjacent table shouted, and the cry was taken up by the others.

Kirsty ignored them. 'Answer me, why are you not eating, and why are you not talking?'

Sandra stared at Kirsty. 'She's not talking because she can't. She has something in her mouth.'

Of course. Why did she not think of that herself? 'You hold her,' Kirsty said. 'I will have a look.'

Shannon clamped her mouth shut but Kirsty grasped the girl's jaw, in a pincer grip, with her left hand and prised her mouth open with the other. 'I can't see anything.' She stuck her finger in the girl's mouth. 'There's something under her tongue.' Kirsty hooked her finger on it, but as the coin toppled out Shannon's teeth snapped shut just missing Kirsty's finger.

'Well, what have we here,' Sandra said, 'and what would you be intending to do with that?'

'None of your business.'

'Oh, we've found our tongue now, have we?' Sandra turned to face the other girls in the canteen. 'Would you still be wanting us to leave her alone? When she was planning to blow you all to smithereens.'

'Is that what you were planning?' Kirsty asked.

'Now, wouldn't you be wanting to know.' Shannon's tone was mocking.

'Why now? Why today?'

'Why not?'

'Is this something to do with the King's visit?'

Shannon laughed. 'He's your king, not mine. And you won't be having him for long.'

Realization dawned on Kirsty. 'You were going to create a diversion.'

Shannon laughed again. 'Whatever it was, you're too late now anyway.'

'Keep her under guard,' Kirsty said to Sandra, 'and get someone to send for the military. I need to get back to Gretna before the King arrives.'

She ran for the door with Shannon's voice echoing in her head. 'You're too late, you'll never get there in time.'

He picked his vantage point with care and jostled for a better position among the waiting crowd. The gun pressed against his leg and dragged his jacket down at one side, but he resisted the urge to put his hand in his pocket. That would invite suspicion.

The explosion was timed for the royal couple's arrival. When it came, the traitor king, George Saxe-Coburg-Gotha, would be no more. This time, he would not fail.

The band struck up. The horns and trumpets blasted out *Rule Britannia*. They must be coming. It was almost time. The explosion should be any minute now, and panic would surge through the crowd, giving him his opportunity.

Shannon, that stupid girl, had been easy to manipulate. She thought he loved her and she was more than ready to become a martyr for the cause. Her name would join the names of all those who had died before her in the fight against the hated English.

61

Kirsty and Beatrice

The bicycle, sitting outside the gatekeeper's lodge at Eastriggs, had been a piece of luck. Kirsty didn't waste time asking to borrow it, she just hopped on and pedalled to Gretna. Her legs ached with the effort by the time she arrived in the centre of the township but her determination overruled her tiredness.

She heaved the bicycle into the hedge at the side of the road and joined the crowds surging down Central Avenue. Spotting Beatrice, she pushed through the throng of spectators until she reached her.

'It is pandemonium,' Beatrice said, 'everyone thinks if they are far enough forward they will get a better view. They brought soldiers in to keep order, but I think they are fighting a losing battle.'

Kirsty groaned. An upheaval like this would play into the assassin's hands. The soldiers would never spot him in this crowd.

She grasped Beatrice's hand. 'We must push our way to the front, and I need you with me. You're the only one who can identify the men the Irish girls keep company with.'

'Make way,' Kirsty shouted, pushing people out of her way, and pulling Beatrice behind her. The man would need to be at the front to get a clear shot at the King when he arrived.

Muffled curses followed their progress but Kirsty paid no heed and barged on, pushing and shoving her way through the irate throng. Her breath rasped in and out of her chest by the time they reached the barrier separating the crowds from the station area where the King and Queen would alight.

At the far end of the platform a red-faced sergeant major

remonstrated with the brass band members as they tuned their instruments. Civic dignitaries congregated at the mid-point, and the company of policewomen, chosen to be presented to the royal couple, stood at attention in the vicinity of the bridge.

Kirsty, still gasping for breath, avoided the furious eyes of the sergeant in charge, but she could have sworn red-hot needles of the sergeant's glare bored into her. She would be castigated later for daring to intrude on the royal occasion when she was not one of the chosen ones. But her mission was too important to spend time worrying about that.

She scanned the crowd, but no one stood out. Despair overcame her. She had failed.

'What are you looking for?'

Her hand still gripped Beatrice's wrist, but the babble of voices drowned her voice. She tightened her hold, barely aware of Beatrice's gasp of pain.

'Something is up. You need to tell me what it is.'

Kirsty looked around to check if anyone was in earshot and then leaned forward to bring her mouth close to Beatrice's ear. 'There's an assassin in the crowd. He plans to shoot the King.'

Beatrice's eyes widened. 'How do you know?'

'We apprehended Shannon at the mixing station before she was able to set off an explosion.' Kirsty stared into Beatrice's eyes. 'You're the one who knows Shannon and the folk she mixes with, that's why I grabbed you.'

'I did overhear her talking to her boyfriend about being martyrs for the cause.'

'Have you any idea what the boyfriend looks like?' Kirsty's grip tightened even more.

'No, but I have seen her with a group of navvies.'

'Think. Does she pay extra attention to any one of them?'

Beatrice shook her head. 'Not that I noticed.'

Kirsty wanted to shake her. 'Are any of those navvies here?'

The cacophony of brass band sounds changed into *Rule Britannia*, and the cheers of the spectators combined with the sound of the approaching train, pounded in Kirsty's ears. Out of the corner of her eye, she saw soldiers monitoring the crowd, searching for potential troublemakers, but none of them knew what he looked like. Disaster loomed.

The train juddered to a halt. He put his hand in his pocket, feeling the bulk of the Bulldog Revolver nestling inside. His hand tightened on the wooden grip as he waited for the explosion that would create the diversion he needed.

There was no explosion. Something must have gone wrong at the mixing station, either that or Shannon had changed her mind. Damn the girl. But he was here, he had the revolver, and the opportunity to use it couldn't be missed.

The number of soldiers had increased since his arrival, but he kept his gaze fixed on the platform and the train. Even if they spotted him they would have to force their way through the crowd and that would give him time to shoot before they reached him.

His heart thumped, sweat trickled down his forehead, and he focused on the train's doors. He had to be ready the moment they opened. And he must not miss his target.

62

Beatrice and Kirsty

Despair washed over Beatrice. Melville had sent her here to spy on the Irish girls and she could not even identify Shannon's boyfriend. She must be the most hopeless spy ever. Now, because she had failed in her mission, the King would be assassinated.

The train's doors opened and the first of the dignitaries alighted. She could sense Kirsty's anxiety and watched as the policewoman's head twisted and turned, frantically inspecting the throng of people behind her.

Beatrice was barely aware of the chattering voices, women and girls laughing, children squealing and waving little flags, as her eyes searched the crowd with mounting desperation. There was no time left. They were too late, and it was all her fault.

Then, she saw him. One of the Irish navvies standing close to the barrier, several yards to her right.

'There,' she whispered to Kirsty. Shaking the policewoman's hand from her wrist, she pushed through the throng of spectators in his direction.

The man pulled something from his pocket. Without thinking, Beatrice grabbed his hand. She registered the gun, and his look of surprise, in the split second before he punched her in the face.

Stunned, she let go of his hand and collapsed at his feet.

Any fear Kirsty felt at the sight of a gun-wielding assassin was forgotten when Beatrice slumped to the ground. Overwhelmed with outrage at the vicious attack on her friend, was enough for her to spring into action.

Ignoring the screams of the spectators and the frantic bodies attempting to escape, she circled to his right, seized his gun arm and twisted it up. At the same time she punched his knuckles forcing him to release the weapon. Sidestepping behind him, she wrenched his arm up his back in a jujitsu hold, kicked the back of his knees and forced him to the ground. The blood pounded in her head, and she panted with the exertion of holding him, but she refused to let go. She knew her hold would be difficult for him to break, no matter how much he struggled, but her strength was ebbing.

The few minutes seemed like an eternity but she hung on, oblivious to the crowd around them scattering in panic.

Kirsty's grip weakened but still she held on until the welcome sound of pounding feet, running in her direction, thudded in her ears.

'I will take over now, miss.'

When she released her hold she found herself surrounded by khaki clothed soldiers.

Kirsty sat back on her heels and looked up into the eyes of Lieutenant Allen. She wanted to say something, not sure whether she should thank him for coming to her assistance, or tell him she was capable of managing by herself. In the end, she said nothing.

Beatrice moaned. Her jaw felt as if it were broken, and her vision was blurred. She shook her head and the mists cleared. The sound of voices issuing commands impacted on her hearing, and she raised her head in time to see her assailant marched off under military escort.

Kirsty was on her knees a short distance away. Had she been assaulted as well? What happened after she lost consciousness? Was King George safe? Questions buzzed around her mind with increasing intensity.

'Are you all right, miss?' A concerned soldier hovered over her.

'The King?' she croaked.

'He's safe thanks to that young lady over there.' He

gestured towards Kirsty who had now risen to her feet and was approaching them.

'I'm no lady.' Kirsty scowled. 'I am a policewoman.'

'I will attend to the ladies. You sort the crowd out.' Lieutenant Allen dismissed the soldier.

Kirsty scowled at him. 'I am a policewoman.'

Lieutenant Allen seemed to find her statement amusing and smiled. 'Yes, I heard you the first time.'

Beatrice listened to the altercation with interest, there was a spark between them that Kirsty seemed determined to ignore.

'What happened?' Beatrice struggled to her feet.

'Your friend, Miss Campbell, tackled the assailant and forced him to drop his gun. No doubt she prevented an assassination attempt on King George.' Lieutenant Allen turned his attention to Kirsty. 'I've never seen a woman overcome a man before. How did you manage to do that?'

Kirsty stiffened, giving the impression she was annoyed at his remark. 'It's part of a policewoman's training. We are trained in the martial arts, and we had an excellent jujitsu trainer.'

Lieutenant Allen turned back to Beatrice. 'You took a nasty knock. Are you all right?'

Beatrice fingered her chin. 'For a moment I thought he had broken my jaw, but I think I will only be left with a bruise.'

'Perhaps one of my soldiers could escort you to the infirmary to get it checked out?'

'That is not necessary. I will put a poultice on it tonight and I am sure it will be all right.'

'If you are sure?' He left the question hanging.

'I am sure.'

'Then I will take my leave of you, for the time being.' He raised his cap to them.

'The lieutenant is interested in you, I feel.' Beatrice observed the colour staining Kirsty's cheeks.

'He's only doing his job. And if he calls me a lady one more time ...' Kirsty spluttered.

'He is a polite man, he is showing you respect.'

'I can do without his respect.' Kirsty pushed through the returning crowd to the fence. 'I am going to take a look at King George. Are you coming?'

Beatrice smoothed her dress, shaking the skirt to rid it of dirt. She puzzled over Kirsty's reaction and her apparent aversion to men. Lieutenant Allen was an attractive man who was clearly interested in the policewoman, but she kept pushing him away. However, Kirsty would not want her to pry, so perhaps she would never find out why the policewoman resisted his advances.

63

Beatrice and Kirsty

Beatrice joined Kirsty at the fence. 'He is smaller than I imagined. Queen Mary is a lot taller.'

The royal couple seemed unruffled as they continued shaking hands with the dignitaries lined up on the station platform. Behind them, the lady police stood at attention, while further down, the men in the brass band shuffled their feet and held their instruments in readiness for the next rendition. Spectators pushed forward to the fence, the fracas forgotten in the excitement of the occasion.

King George smiled and nodded to each person with whom he shook hands, murmuring something to them before he moved on. The Queen followed, inclining her head to them. She appeared less engaged.

'Do you think she's bored?'

Beatrice glanced at the Queen. 'It is difficult to tell, I think she is typical of your upper class. I think she is doing her duty.'

'I thought she would be more stylish.' Kirsty leaned over the fence to see better. 'Her clothes are terribly old-fashioned and quite dowdy.'

Beatrice studied the royal couple. King George was smart in his uniform and top coat. His beard was neatly trimmed and his peaked cap resembled the ones the military officers wore. Queen Mary was larger and taller, and her skirt, which trailed the ground, was covered by a matching dark brown coat with a chunky fur collar. Her hair was piled on top of her head in a severe style and was topped by a wide-brimmed hat complete with feather. Queen Elisabeth of Belgium was far more stylish by comparison.

'Perhaps she wants to present an image of respectability,'

Beatrice said. 'I understand she visits hospitals and does much good work.'

'I suppose we expect royalty to be glamorous, and it's a disappointment when they aren't.' Kirsty turned her back on the fence. 'In the meantime I have a bike to return to its owner and I should get back to the mixing station. Besides, I don't think I can tolerate the sergeant's glare any longer.'

'She can hardly chastise you after you caught the assassin.'

Kirsty laughed. 'I wouldn't count on that.'

Beatrice stayed close behind her as the policewoman forced her way through the crowd, and they finally wound up breathless at the end of Central Avenue. They were still laughing when Melville appeared before them, giving the impression he had mysteriously appeared out of thin air.

'May I congratulate you on a piece of good work. I am sure you changed the course of history by your actions.'

'I did not know you were here.'

Melville could not be aware she had confided in Kirsty. But looking at him she was not so sure. Nothing seemed to go past him.

'I was keeping a watching brief in the crowd. You dealt with the situation admirably.' He beamed at them. 'In the meantime I will take my leave, but I expect you both to be at the meeting I have arranged for tomorrow afternoon.'

'What meeting?' Beatrice and Kirsty spoke in unison.

'You will find details when you return to your hostels. Good day, ladies.'

'How did he know to set up a meeting?'

'He seems to be aware of everything,' Beatrice said.

64

Melville

Melville peered through the peephole in the door. 'He does not look very dangerous now,' he said to the lieutenant.

'Appearances can be deceptive, sir.'

'I would like to question him before he is transported to London.'

Lieutenant Allen gestured to one of the soldiers to open the door. 'Stand guard,' he said, 'in case the prisoner presents a danger to Mr Melville.'

'Yes, sir.' The soldier saluted and opened the cell door.

Melville stepped through, followed by the lieutenant. The door slammed shut behind them, although Melville remained aware of the soldier's rifle pointing through the peephole.

'You are not the person I expected. What is your name?'

The man stood, his hands clenched at his sides. 'As if I would be telling you that.' The defiance in the man's voice and posture was unmistakable.

The lieutenant took two steps forward. 'Sit down, or I will have you placed in irons.'

The man flopped on the bench at the rear of the cell and glared, his eyes full of menace.

Melville leaned against the wall. 'Ah, well! I am sure we will find out who you are before long,' he said. 'But I suspect you have an accomplice, and I want you to tell me about him.'

The man laughed. 'Do you see anyone else here?'

Melville sighed. He was sure of Leclercq's involvement in this.

'The man I am looking for is called Dietger LeClercq,' he said, 'although he might be using a different name.'

The prisoner shrugged. 'Don't know anyone of that

name, but if you find him he's welcome to take my place.'

'There is another matter. Two women have recently been killed at Gretna. What can you tell me about their deaths?'

A flicker passed over the man's face. 'Why would I know anything about that?'

Melville sighed again. 'It appears our prisoner does not wish to be forthcoming,' he said to the lieutenant. 'Will you be kind enough to make transport arrangements to take him to London. We have better facilities for interrogation there.'

Lieutenant Allen gestured to the guard to open the cell door. 'Certainly, Mr Melville. Will you require the other prisoner to be transported to London as well?'

Melville hesitated in the doorway to glance back at the prisoner. 'Of course,' he said. 'She's already admitted her intention to create a diversion during King George's visit.'

The cell door slammed shut. The ease with which he had avoided answering the questions of the man with the bushy moustache had provided him with grim pleasure. But the man's last comment deflated his sense of achievement in thwarting someone from the English Government. He would never forget the smug look of triumph on Melville's face when he left.

He clenched his hands, knuckles tight and fingernails digging into his palms. Shannon was here. Would she hang for treason as well? But how could it be treason when England wasn't even their country! He spat on the ground. Bloody English! They had the effrontery to accuse him of murder when they were the biggest murderers of all time. Those they had already sent to the gallows were all honourable men, fighting for what they believed in. When they set him on that path he would go with head held high, defying them, as he prepared to join the ranks of the martyrs.

A door slammed somewhere close by, and the mutter of voices drew nearer. Shannon stopped pacing back and forth to stand and listen. The voices were louder now, and a key rattled in her cell door. Throwing herself on the bench, which also served as a bed, she leaned against the wall, oblivious to the sharp edges of stone pressing on her back. She would show them they couldn't frighten her.

The door creaked open. A man in a shabby brown suit entered, closely followed by an army officer.

Despite his ordinary appearance, the man exuded menace. His eyes narrowed and she imagined they could see right through her munitionette's tunic and trousers. She suppressed a shiver and hoped he hadn't seen it. But those eyes looked as if nothing would go past them and she was sure he sensed her fear.

He propped his walking stick against the wall and sat on the bench beside her.

She pressed her back further into the hard stone.

'Ah! Shannon!' He fingered the end of his bushy moustache. 'This is a fine mess you've got yourself into.'

She could almost swear he'd adopted a slight Irish accent. But he wasn't Irish. He was a filthy Englishman.

'And are you going to be telling me why you intended to blow yourself and your friends to kingdom come?'

Shannon compressed her lips and glared at him.

'We have him, you know.' The man seemed pensive. 'He has already told us all about your part in his plan.'

'I don't believe you.' She couldn't stop the words spilling out.

The man shrugged. 'Believe what you want, but that won't stop you being hanged alongside him in London.'

She pulled her knees up to her chest and hugged them hard. 'I don't care,' she mumbled. 'Aidan will go down in history as a martyr and so will I.'

'Ah! But that's where you are wrong. Aidan will hang as a common murderer, and you as his accomplice. Of course, if you turn King's evidence you might escape the hangman's noose. Either way, you won't be an Irish martyr.' The man stood. 'I will leave you now, but while you are waiting to be transported to London, you might want to reconsider your position.'

Shannon didn't move until after the door slammed shut behind him. What did he mean – murder? She knew nothing of any murders. But a vision of Sally rose before her eyes, and she threw her head back and howled.

The howl reverberated down the corridor, bouncing off the walls to create echoes. It sounded like an animal in pain.

Melville smiled. Shannon would be easily broken once they got her to London. As it was, she did not even realize she had supplied him with a name for his other prisoner. Aidan, he rolled the name around in his mind, it would not take him long to find out everything about the man.

'Thank you for your help,' Melville said to Lieutenant Allen. 'Make sure the prisoners are well guarded until they are transported to London. How soon can you arrange it?'

'Transport can be available tomorrow if you wish.'

Melville's brow creased while he considered this. The only evidence he had was the attempt on the life of King George. There was no actual proof he had murdered the women, and that needed to be verified. Courts and juries could be unpredictable.

'I would prefer the day after,' he said. 'I think I know of someone who might be able to identify our prisoner as the killer of the munitionette and the policewoman.'

'As you wish,' the lieutenant said.

'I will make arrangements for the identification at tomorrow's meeting.'

65

Kirsty

'I did not give permission for you to leave your post yesterday.'

Kirsty compressed her lips. Sometimes she found the discipline of the Women's Police Force difficult to endure. But endure it she must. Rebellion was not an option.

'Nevertheless, you did a good job.'

She waited for the sergeant to say 'I am proud of you,' but this was not forthcoming. Expectations of this kind of response from such a disciplinarian as Sergeant Duncan were unrealistic.

'Thank you, ma'am. I was only doing my duty.'

'Above and beyond,' the sergeant said. 'I have been asked to commend you.' She frowned and shuffled some papers on her desk. 'In response to the request, a commendation will be sent to Commandant Damer Dawson.'

'Thank you, ma'am.'

'Dismissed, Constable Campbell.'

Kirsty saluted and left the office. She scurried down the corridor to her own quarters, clamping her lips shut until she reached the privacy of her room. Closing the door behind her she let out a whoop of delight and danced a jig. Who would have thought it? A commendation, no less, to be sent to the woman she admired above all others, Margaret Damer Dawson, the woman responsible for forming Britain's first women's police force.

A tap at the door jolted her out of her euphoric state.

'The gentleman is here for the meeting, Miss Kirsty, and the sergeant said I should fetch you. She will join you both in a few minutes.'

'Thank you, Jessie. Have you shown him into the dining room?'

'Yes, miss. Cook is making him a pot of tea.'

Kirsty straightened her jacket and smoothed her skirt before following Jessie.

Melville rose as she entered. His eyes, overshadowed by shaggy eyebrows, were piercing, and Kirsty guessed nothing much escaped his gaze. He held out his hand and shook hers in the same way he would do with a man.

'You did well, yesterday, Miss Campbell. The King is most appreciative.'

'I only did my duty, sir.'

'Yes.' He fingered his moustache. 'Your duty. But it was more than that. You averted a serious incident. One that possibly changed the course of history.'

'I am a policewoman, sir. I am expected to intervene in criminal activity.'

Cook clattered into the room carrying a tray. She transferred a teapot and two plates of sandwiches to a table already set with cups, side plates, and cutlery.

'This plate is egg sandwiches, and this one cheese.'

'Marvellous,' said Melville. 'We do not see many eggs in London nowadays.'

'The ministry makes sure we're well supplied with rations. They say the workers are important for the war effort and need to keep their strength up. And the farmers around here make sure we're never short of eggs.' Grasping the tray, she hurried out of the room.

Melville pulled out a chair. 'Sit down, Miss Campbell. I wish to discuss something with you.' He lifted the teapot and poured tea into a cup which he passed to Kirsty before pouring some for himself.

Kirsty added milk and stirred her tea. 'Surely the time for discussion is with the rest of the group once they arrive.'

'I admit there is much to discuss once everyone arrives, but there is something I want to offer you. It could be the opportunity of a lifetime, and a career unlike any of your colleagues.'

Kirsty placed the spoon in her saucer. What on earth did he mean?

'I would like you to come and work with me.' His eyes pierced her, waiting for her reaction. 'You know who I am and what I represent. You would make a good undercover agent.'

'I have a career, sir, in the Women's Police Service.'

'I rather think once the war ends, Scotland Yard will have no further use for a Women's Police Service, therefore, your description of a career might be somewhat optimistic. What I am offering is a career in MI5 where you will be appreciated, and which will continue beyond the end of the war.'

His offer tempted her, but Kirsty was happy as a policewoman. She was helping less fortunate girls and women, and protecting them from the dangers the modern world presented. Every girl she saved from a life of vice was a triumph. But Melville was right, she had no guarantee her chosen career would continue. Resentment from the male police force existed now, what would it be like when the war ended. They wouldn't want women usurping police jobs once the men returned. On the other hand, an undercover agent as he termed it, was simply another name for a spy. If she accepted, that would mean she would no longer be able to protect women and girls from themselves, and the dangers all around them.

'An immediate answer is not necessary. I will be in Carlisle a few more days. Think about it. This opportunity may never come your way again.'

Kirsty pushed her cup away, she no longer felt like drinking the tea, nor did she wish to continue this conversation.

'I thank you for your offer, but I do not need to think about it. I am committed to my career, and I will continue to work as a policewoman as long as I am able.'

'Such a pity,' he said. 'You would make a good agent.'

66

Beatrice and Kirsty

The mist, what the Scottish girls called a haar, rose from the Solway to cloak everything in damp tendrils that seemed to get everywhere. Beatrice turned her collar up and quickened her pace until the welcome sight of the hostel hove into view.

Jessie opened the door. 'This way, miss.'

Beatrice, shaking droplets of water from her hair, followed her to the dining room. Melville and Kirsty were deep in conversation, but Kirsty looked up at Beatrice's entrance and rose to greet her.

'You're wet.'

Beatrice shrugged. 'That mist gets everywhere. And to think, only yesterday we were basking in the sun.'

'Tea, Miss Jacobs?' Melville's hand hovered over the teapot.

She nodded her acceptance, although she preferred coffee.

He poured the tea into a cup and pulled out a chair for her. 'Sergeant Duncan and Lieutenant Allen will be joining us shortly.' He waited until she was settled before passing the cup to her.

Beatrice winced when she sipped the hot liquid. Her face still ached from yesterday's assault. She laid the cup down again, it hurt too much to move her jaw.

'The others are in here, sir.' Jessie's voice wafted into the room as she opened the door to usher Lieutenant Allen inside.

His eyes immediately fixed on Kirsty, and it was a moment before he acknowledged the rest of them.

'I hope I am not late,' the lieutenant said as he joined the group.

'Not at all. We're still waiting for Sergeant Duncan to join us. Ah, here she is now,' Kirsty said as the door opened once again.

Beatrice leaned back in her chair. The tea, which by this time would be cold, sat untouched in front of her. The others were busying themselves with cups and sandwiches which gave her time to wonder about the purpose of the meeting. Surely it was all over now the assassination had been prevented and the killer of Sally and Martha was in custody. But she knew Melville had been fixated on Dietger, and she hoped he would give up the hunt for him now that he had been proved wrong. She had always known in her heart Dietger could not be a murderer, even though she was starting to wonder whether he was, in fact, a spy.

Melville struck the table with the flat of his hand. 'I called this meeting to pull all the threads of yesterday's events together. As you know, the assassination attempt on King George's life was admirably subverted by these two young ladies. So, firstly, I want to commend them for their actions. Secondly, I want to confirm the assassin, and his accomplice, are now locked up in the detention block at the army barracks. However, I am under the impression another accomplice may still be on the loose although the prisoner did not offer up any information when I interrogated him.'

Beatrice's heart thumped. He was referring to Dietger.

'We will be transferring both prisoners to London for further interrogation, and I am sure we will get the information we need, sooner or later. In the meantime, although I am certain the prisoners intended to assassinate King George, we lack evidence to charge the male prisoner with killing the women whose bodies were recently found. In order to acquire evidence I need a witness to identify him as the male friend of one of the victims, Sally Scott.' He turned to look at Beatrice. 'I believe such a witness exists, and that Miss Campbell and Miss Jacobs, can be instrumental in gaining her agreement.'

Deep in thought about Dietger, she became aware of a

sudden silence and Melville looking at her for a response. What had he been talking about?

'You mean Maggie McKenzie,' said Kirsty. 'Sally Scott's friend.'

Beatrice did not realize she was holding her breath until she let it out. She shot a look of gratitude to Kirsty who had obviously guessed she had not been listening.

Melville nodded. 'We will need her to identify the prisoner. Can that be arranged?'

'She is very young,' Beatrice said, 'and she is afraid the killer will come for her if he knows she saw him with Sally.'

'She need not fear. He is in custody.'

'But you said there is no evidence he is the killer. If he is not she will still be at risk.'

'There is that possibility, but I am sure we have our man.'

'If he sees her and subsequently escapes, then the risk still remains.'

'That is unlikely, but we can ensure the prisoner does not catch sight of Miss McKenzie.' Melville glanced at Lieutenant Allen. 'Perhaps you can inform us of any likelihood the prisoner will escape.'

'Impossible,' the lieutenant replied. 'He did attack one of the guards when his cell was entered this morning, but he was soon overpowered, and we shackled him to prevent any re-occurrence. When we move him to London, he will be in irons.'

'Is that satisfactory?' Melville raised his bushy eyebrows.

'I will ask her if she is willing to identify this man when she returns from work this afternoon.' Beatrice pushed her cup away. Maggie would not be easy to convince.

'I am afraid that choice is not hers to make,' Melville said. 'She is a witness, and if necessary she can be forced to comply. Lieutenant Allen will make arrangements to transport you to the detention block, and I will meet you there.'

Beatrice bit her lip to prevent her anger spilling out in an unwary comment. She had promised to protect Maggie, and Melville was forcing her to break her promise. 'In that case, the collection point should be here. She would not feel safe if other people knew she could identify him.'

Melville nodded.

'I will arrange for a car with a civilian driver to be waiting here at three o'clock,' the lieutenant said. 'There is no need for anyone to know where she is being taken.'

'Thank you,' Beatrice said. Now all she had to do was persuade Maggie to identify the prisoner.

Kirsty sensed Beatrice's anger and followed her to the door of the hostel. 'Do you think Maggie will cope with the identification?'

Beatrice shrugged. 'It does not look as if she has much of an option. But I worry about her. She wanted to put all this behind her and forget about it.'

'I will come with you to the identification, but I won't wear my uniform. If anyone sees us leave they will think we are off on a jaunt. And it will be extra support for Maggie.'

'That would be good.' Beatrice smiled at Kirsty before descending the steps. 'I will see you this afternoon,' she called over her shoulder before she hurried down the road.

Kirsty watched until she was out of sight. She sighed, although she knew Beatrice worried about persuading Maggie to identify the prisoner, she shared Melville's view that the identification needed to be done. Because, if he was not the man they had been looking for, it would mean the killer was still on the loose.

'Can I be of assistance, Miss Campbell?'

Kirsty started. She had not heard the lieutenant come up behind her. 'Thank you for your concern, Lieutenant Allen, but I was thinking about Maggie, and how this will affect her.'

'I can assure you, we will take every care necessary and I will ensure the prisoner does not know of her presence, nor will she be identified to him. All he will know is that an identification has been made.'

'But what happens after he is removed to London? Will

Maggie be required to give evidence?'

'That I cannot say. However, I am sure you are aware judges and magistrates are resistant to women appearing in court, therefore, the eventuality may not arise.'

'You are right.' Kirsty pondered over her own attempts to be heard in court and had to admit they had not been successful. 'We can only hope they have enough evidence to convict.'

'I am sure the courts will be reluctant to discharge a potential assassin and saboteur.'

'When will he be moved to London?'

'Early tomorrow morning. The roads are less busy on a Sunday.'

'And Shannon?'

'She will be transported to London as well.'

'I can't help feeling sorry for Shannon. I think she was bewitched by this man.'

'He does seem to possess a charisma that makes him attractive to women. However, his charisma will not help him where he is going.'

Kirsty hoped he was not mistaken because her job as a policewoman was to protect women and girls from predatory men, although sometimes it felt like a hopeless task.

He added, 'You have no need to fear, Miss Campbell. He will remain incarcerated and he will undoubtedly be found guilty, so he will hang. No other woman will suffer at his hands.'

She hoped he was right.

67

Beatrice

The mist had lifted by the time Beatrice and Maggie walked up the road to where the motor car sat outside Kirsty's hostel. Maggie's steps slowed when she saw the car and Beatrice sensed the girl's panic.

'It is all right, no one will know you are doing this.' She kept her voice low and soothing, although she shared some of Maggie's fear.

Thoughts tumbled through her mind. What if he was not the killer? Even if he was – what if he escaped? Would he come after Maggie? Her breath caught in her throat. If it all went wrong it would be her fault.

Maggie's footsteps faltered. She stopped and reached out to grasp Beatrice's hand. 'Are you sure?'

Beatrice nodded. 'I am sure.' She almost choked on the words.

The girl squared her shoulders. 'In any case, it doesn't matter. I must do this for Sally. I want justice for her. I want him punished.' She pulled her hand from Beatrice's grasp.

The car was an open-topped model with a wide running board, stretching between the heavy mudguards, and doors which reached halfway up the body. The khaki green exterior shone as if newly polished, and inside, the buttoned black leather seats were pristine. The driver lifted her hat off the bonnet of the car and rammed it on her head before jumping to attention, on their approach, and opening one of the doors.

'After you,' Beatrice said.

Maggie, smaller than Beatrice, grasped the door to pull herself up onto the running board. When Beatrice followed her she understood Maggie's predicament, because the

255

running board was high even for her.

They had hardly settled themselves in their seats when Kirsty hurried from the hostel. 'I was watching for you.' She clambered into the front seat and, once she had eased herself into a comfortable position, turned her head to look at Maggie. 'Are you all right with this?'

Maggie nodded.

The driver leaned into the car. 'Make yourselves comfortable.' She grasped the steering wheel and pushed a lever behind it into the up position, then turned a switch on the square box at the end of the steering column. She grinned at them. 'Get ready.'

She walked around the bonnet of the car, grabbed the edge of the mudguard with her right hand and the crank with her left, and exerting all her strength she turned the handle. The engine shuddered into life. Releasing the handle, she jumped in, moved the switch on the square box in the opposite direction, pushed the lever behind the steering wheel into the down position, manipulated another lever at the other side of the wheel, and drove the vehicle along the road.

Beatrice rested her arm on the door and leaned back, enjoying the wind on her face. It brought back memories of Belgium before the war, family picnics, and her father driving his Model T Ford. Her brother, Paul, always claimed the front seat beside their father, while she and her mother sat in the back with the breeze blowing their hair and caressing their faces. As they drove, she and Paul would sing the popular songs of the day while her father tutted and her mother smiled. It was such a carefree, joyous time. What were they doing now? Would she ever see them again?

She pushed thoughts of the past away when Maggie grasped her hand in a vice-like grip. The girl shook and huddled into the seat, unable to mask her fear.

'Have you not ridden in a motor car before?'

Maggie shook her head.

'Do not be frightened. No harm will come to you.'

'It is so fast.' The girl cowered even further into her seat.

'I am sure our driver is competent, and we will soon be there.'

She held the girl's hand until they reached the army barracks, situated at the western end of the munitions factory.

'I think we have arrived,' she said, staring at a series of wooden huts, laid out in a military style, behind a heavy wire fence. They did not look much different from the smaller wooden buildings in Gretna Township.

The driver brought the motor car to a halt at the barrier. She waved to the guard on duty, and when he raised the bar she steered the car into the compound, following the road until they drove through an opening into a quadrangle. Wooden buildings flanked three sides of the square with a sturdier stone building at the far end.

Lieutenant Allen strode forward to meet them, while Melville puffed on his pipe outside the door to the stone building. The lieutenant opened the car door and offered his hand to help Beatrice descend, and then held it out to Maggie. Kirsty jumped out while he assisted the girl to alight, which made Beatrice wonder if she was deliberately avoiding his touch.

He led them to where Melville stood, flanked by two guards with rifles.

Beatrice grasped Maggie's hand. 'You will be all right. I will be at your side.'

The girl nodded and focused her eyes on the ground, seemingly frightened by the presence of soldiers. Her hand tightened in Beatrice's grasp, but she did not look up.

'Come.' Melville opened the heavy wooden door and ushered them in.

Another guard sat at a desk inside. He rose at their entrance and escorted them through a door, which he unlocked, and along several passages each barred by a series of locked doors. Finally, he stopped outside a brass studded one and slid a section of wood aside, revealing an oblong peephole. He stood back to allow them to view the prisoner.

'Are you ready?' Melville took his pipe out of his mouth

257

and pointed it at Maggie.

She nodded but did not move forward.

'He can't see you,' Lieutenant Allen said. 'The viewing slot is so small it will hide your face.'

Beatrice tightened her grip on Maggie's hand. 'I am here. I am with you,' she said.

Maggie nodded again and moved forward to the peephole. Catching her breath, she peered through.

Beatrice felt the girl's body stiffen. She seemed incapable of movement. At last, a breath of air passed her lips and she staggered back.

'Well?' Melville waved his pipe. 'Is it him?'

'Yes,' Maggie whispered. 'That is the man I saw with Sally.' A tear rolled down her face. 'Can I go now?'

68

Kirsty

Kirsty had never doubted that the assassin she and Beatrice caught, was the killer of Martha and Sally. Maggie's identification confirmed this. But bringing him to justice did not provide her with the pleasure she thought it would. Martha and Sally were still dead.

Images of Martha swirled through her brain as she followed Beatrice and Maggie, and she wished she could vent her feelings in the way Maggie did, instead of having to maintain a professional front. She felt a moment of envy as she watched Beatrice put her arm around the girl's shoulder to comfort her, but knew in her heart she would have rejected any expression of sympathy if it had been offered.

At last, they reached the exit. The guard jangled his keys as he unlocked the door.

'The car is waiting to return you ladies to Gretna,' he said.

Kirsty glared at him. She resented being called a lady, particularly as the Gretna policewomen were commonly referred to as the lady police.

A smell of fumes, from the staff car's engine, enveloped her when she exited the prison block, although Beatrice and Maggie didn't seem to notice. She ran around the front of the car and jumped into the passenger seat. The driver's seat was still empty, but the engine continued to rumble in readiness for their departure.

She swung around to face Beatrice and Maggie. 'There's no driver.'

'Maybe she is still inside,' Beatrice said.

A door slammed with a resounding thump. 'That's probably her now.' Kirsty faced front again.

'Are we ready to go, ladies?'

Kirsty stared in astonishment at Lieutenant Allen in the driving seat.

'Don't look so surprised,' he said. 'My driver is otherwise engaged, so I decided to drive you home myself.'

During the drive back to Gretna Kirsty focused on the road, although tempted to sneak glances at the lieutenant.

'Not this way,' she snapped when she realized the lieutenant was heading for Beatrice's hostel. They had been so careful to avoid the car collecting Maggie from the hostel because she was terrified the Irish girls would find out she was involved in the identification.

'Maggie can't be seen arriving in this car. It would announce to the other residents what she'd been doing this afternoon.'

'Where then,' he said.

'The policewomen's hostel. Beatrice will escort her home from there.'

Within a few minutes, the car drew up. Kirsty jumped out and helped Beatrice and Maggie down.

'I will see you later.' Beatrice grinned at Kirsty. 'I think Lieutenant Allen wishes a word with you.'

Kirsty frowned. Beatrice had this idea that the lieutenant was attracted to her, and she wasn't ready for that kind of complication in her life. Ignoring him, she walked to the hostel door.

'Miss Campbell,' the lieutenant called after her. He leaned over the passenger seat.

Kirsty stopped at the bottom of the steps leading to the door. 'Yes?'

'I wondered, may I call on you?'

Not knowing how to respond Kirsty gave a brief nod before climbing the steps. Once inside, she leaned against the door. Why on earth had she nodded when she had meant to shake her head? And how was she going to handle it when he came calling?

69

Melville and Shannon

The rumble of engines, marching feet, and shouted orders, broke the silence after a long and uncomfortable night, where nightmares frequented Shannon's sleeping and waking hours.

A key rattled in the lock, and the door clicked open. It was the man who questioned her yesterday, but today he displayed no semblance of the menace she had sensed then. Today he seemed more benign, more like a grandfather with a comforting appearance. But it was probably a trick, and she still didn't trust him.

She shrank further back into the corner, hands clasping her knees to her chest. The wooden slats below the thin mattress pressed on her aching buttocks, and the rough stone of the wall she leaned against chilled her spine.

'I am so sorry you find yourself in this situation,' the man said.

She didn't answer.

He removed the unlit pipe from his mouth. 'They tell me you haven't spoken to anyone else, but I couldn't let you leave without coming to explain what you are facing.'

She flicked her eyes away from him and studied the wall.

'The transport is waiting outside to take you to London where you will stand trial beside your boyfriend.'

The man looked at her, and she thought she detected a tear in his eye. But why would he cry for her?

'He will hang, you know.'

'He'll die a martyr,' she mumbled without looking up.

'Ah! That is where you are wrong. He will be hanged as a common murderer, for that is what he is.'

She looked up. He'd said that yesterday and she didn't

believe him then, nor did she believe him now. She suppressed the doubt that surfaced in her mind. He was playing with her.

He waved his pipe in the air. 'Hanging is not a nice way to die.'

Unable to help herself, she shuddered.

'I understand you are under the impression you acted for the good of Ireland. For the good of the cause.' He rammed the pipe into his mouth and sucked the stem. 'What you were doing was aiding a murderer.'

'It was an assassination attempt, not murder.' Anger surged through her and she swung her legs off the bed to turn and glare at him.

'I am afraid I was not talking about the assassination attempt.' He looked back at her with a sad expression on his face. 'I was referring to the murder of three innocent women. They were not part of the fight for your cause.'

She struggled for breath. The doubt resurfaced. Surely he couldn't be talking about Sally's death. It was hard for her to believe Aidan was responsible for that. But when the man said three women. What did he mean?

'Ah! You do not understand. The man you regard as a hero and a patriot is a killer of women and girls.' He tamped the tobacco in the bowl of the pipe with his index finger before continuing. 'The first one he killed in London was no more than a girl, not yet fifteen. After that, he came here and killed Sally and the policewoman. For all we know there might be more. So, not a hero or a patriot, a common woman killer.'

Shannon stared at him in disbelief.

'He did intend for you to die in the explosion. I have no doubt he said you would be a martyr to the cause. If by chance, you survived, your use to him would be over, and you would have become one of his victims.'

Shannon found it difficult to answer.

The man's gaze was sympathetic. 'You don't have to hang beside him.'

She stared at the floor refusing to meet his eyes. 'I don't

want to die.'

'You don't have to. All you need to do is testify against him. It would still mean a prison sentence, but you wouldn't hang.'

Conflicting thoughts raced through her brain. Could she inform against Aidan? If she didn't she would hang. If she did, she would never be able to return to Ireland. And those women he murdered, that was never part of the plan. How many more would he have killed if he hadn't been caught? And finally, the most horrific thought of all, would he have killed her?

'I'll do it.' She sounded defeated.

'That is a sensible decision,' he said. 'The transport is waiting to take you to London I wish you well.' He banged on the door and signalled to the guard he was ready to leave. 'You will be travelling separately,' he said, 'we don't want him to kill you before you arrive.'

Over the years Melville had developed a hard shell but Shannon had penetrated that, and her image remained with him after he left the prison block. He hoped it would not haunt him for too long.

He stepped outside, breathing in the clean air which was refreshing after the claustrophobic cell where Shannon was imprisoned.

The scene here was a far cry from the factory buildings where the workers manufactured munitions. He leaned against the wall enjoying the warmth of the spring sun on his face. Shouted orders drifted to his ears as a squad of soldiers drilled at the opposite end of the quadrangle. Were they glad to be serving here? Or did they itch, like a lot of the young men who joined up, for the horrors of the trenches at the front?

He straightened. He did not have time to enjoy such luxuries as the spring sun. His job here was done for the time being, and after a few days winding things up in Carlisle he would be on his way back to London and all that entailed.

He dragged his gaze away from the drilling soldiers and focused on Alice Blake leaning on the bonnet of the staff car parked a few feet in front of him. He beckoned to her.

She straightened, said something to the driver and walked over to stand beside him.

'I have finished interviewing Shannon, she will be leaving for London shortly.'

'After I've taken her there and completed my mission, will you want me to return to Gretna to continue as Beatrice's contact?'

'No, I think your job here is finished now that Beatrice knows what is expected of her.'

Lieutenant Allen walked up to them. 'Maguire is on his way to London,' he said. 'The prisoner transport left while you were inside.'

'Good, I did not want them to catch sight of each other. Did he go quietly?'

'Not really, he lashed out at the guards, but they had no problem restraining him. I do not think he will give them any more trouble.'

Something in the lieutenant's voice made Melville wonder how much restraint was applied, but he decided not to ask.

'How was your interview with the girl?'

'She will testify.' Melville did not elaborate on his time with Shannon.

'He'll hang then.'

'Without a doubt.' He tapped his pipe on the wall, before refilling it with tobacco.

'And the girl?'

'Most likely a prison sentence.' Melville scraped a match on the stone wall and applied the flame to the bowl of his pipe.

'Will you travel with her?'

'No, Alice will accompany her to London. I will follow in a few days. There are some ends I need to tie up before I go.'

70

Beatrice and Dietger

Beatrice closed her eyes and leaned back on the bench enjoying the warmth of the late evening sun on her face. The River Eden flowed past in front of her, the water lapping at the river bank a few yards from her feet.

A lot had happened since she travelled north to be William Melville's eyes and ears, and she was unsure how successful she had been at this task. She certainly had not given him everything he wanted. Nor had she told him about her meetings with Dietger on this Carlisle bench which was at a safe distance from Gretna, and far from the prying eyes of those who would ensure his capture. But she had to face up to the truth. Dietger was a spy working for the enemy. Did that make her a collaborator?

She sighed, well aware of her duty to inform Melville about Dietger. Her duty was clear. He had to be prevented from sending more information to the enemy, thus damaging the country she now called home. But they hanged spies. Could she live with the knowledge she had been responsible for his death?

'A penny for them?' Dietger's voice was little more than a whisper as he slid onto the bench beside her.

Opening her eyes she looked at him. His hair was untidy, and the flat cap did not suit him, but he was still as beautiful as ever. A slight smile tweaked the corners of her mouth, maybe she should think of him as handsome rather than beautiful, but there was a symmetry to his features and a smoothness to his skin many a woman might envy.

'I was thinking how glad I am you did not kill Sally and the policewoman.'

'I do not kill people. I am not a murderer.'

'No? What about the information you provide to Germany?' She paused to reflect. 'Zeppelin bombs kill people?'

'That is different. It is part of war. There are British spies in Germany doing the same thing.'

Beatrice stared out over the water. 'And that makes it right, does it?'

'You are in a strange mood tonight.' Dietger reached out and took her hand in his. 'Does that mean you do not like me anymore?'

'Of course, I do.' His hands were warm, and tingles of anticipation crept through her body culminating in a hollow sensation in her middle. A feeling which signalled an unrecognized need her body cried out for. Why did this man affect her like this?

'My task is finished here. This is our last meeting.'

'I know.'

'You can come with me if you wish.'

'Does that mean you still plan to leave tomorrow night?'

'Yes.' His hands tightened on hers, enclosing them in his grasp. 'The London train. Meet me at the station.'

Beatrice closed her eyes, tempted by the offer she could not accept. 'I cannot betray my country.'

'As you wish, but the war cannot go on forever.' He kissed her on the lips. 'We will meet again, liebchen, in happier times.'

Tears filled her eyes as he strode up the river bank. His image remained imprinted on her memory and she stared after him, for a long time, after he vanished from view.

There would be no happier times. She had to betray him and she would have to live with that for the rest of her life.

71

Kirsty and Lieutenant Allen

'Miss, miss!' Jessie burst through Kirsty's door. Her face flushed with excitement. 'Lieutenant Allen is waiting in the hall, he brought you these.' Jessie thrust a bunch of flowers into her arms.

Kirsty pushed the flowers back to her. 'Put them in some water and place them on the hall table. I am sure he meant them for all of us.'

Jessie jiggled her feet. 'He's waiting to see you.'

She grabbed her jacket. Whatever Lieutenant Allen wanted to say would have to be said outside. There would be enough gossip without Jessie eavesdropping on their conversation.

Kirsty's pulse quickened a little when she saw him, standing in the hall, with his cap tucked under his arm and an expression of embarrassment on his face.

He smiled when she approached. 'I thought I would call and update you on our progress.'

Perhaps she misread the situation. He was simply reporting back. But then she remembered the flowers. It was something entirely different and the reporting back was an excuse.

She was aware of Jessie hovering at the end of the hall. 'That is most considerate, but it is a lovely day so I thought we might discuss this outside.'

'Yes, that would be pleasurable.' Placing his cap on his head he offered his arm to her.

Kirsty ignored the arm and walked out of the hostel in front of him.

'So, what is happening?'

'Both prisoners are on their way to London and Shannon

has agreed to testify.'

'That's the end of it then,' she said. 'The killing is finished.'

'Yes.'

'I am glad.'

They walked in silence. Early afternoon shoppers thronged Central Avenue, flitting from shop to shop. Anyone visiting would think the war didn't exist. However, she sensed the lieutenant wanted to speak, but was reluctant to do so with so many people around.

'We should find somewhere quieter.' She wanted this over and done with, hating what she was about to do to him.

'The beach,' he suggested, pointing towards the end of the avenue.

'It will be busy today. The sun is shining and that's where a lot of the munitionettes go to sunbathe.'

'Where do you suggest?'

'The sports fields. The football pitch should be quiet.'

They left Central Avenue behind them and the streets became less busy the nearer they got to the sports area. Several people were on the bowling green, and a foursome played tennis on the town's courts. But Kirsty was right, few people were at the football ground. The only ones in sight were sunbathing at the far end.

'We can sit here.' She pointed to the pavilion steps.

The lieutenant removed his hat and sat. He stared into the distance and seemed to be having difficulty knowing what to say to her. The awkward silence stretched, seeming endless.

At last, he said, 'I am not very good at this. I do not know how to talk to women.'

Kirsty cringed. She didn't want him to continue, but she couldn't stop him.

'In normal times I would be more circumspect, but these are not normal times. The war forces us to throw caution to the winds and to grasp at happiness where we can find it.' He hesitated. 'My time here is coming to an end and I am being called to the front.'

'I am not sure whether to congratulate you or say I am

sorry,' Kirsty said.

'Before I go, I would like us to have an understanding.' His words sounded prim and forced.

'Don't say anything more.' She tried to cut him off.

'I must. Once I am gone it will be too late.'

Kirsty's breath caught in her throat. Would it be so bad to agree to an understanding? Give him some hope before he left, something to sustain him in the midst of battle. But that would be dishonest.

He continued to speak before she had a chance to say anything.

'I am aware we have not known each other long, but I would be honoured if you would consider marrying me.'

This was worse than she thought, and now she must refuse him. 'You are right, we don't really know each other, therefore I cannot accept.'

He grasped her hand. 'But you like me, I can tell.'

She quivered at his touch which invoked a mixture of longing and revulsion. Unable to bear it she withdrew her hand and clenched it at her side. How could she explain to him that what happened eight years earlier had scarred her and prevented her from seeking male company? She had trusted that boy eight years ago and he betrayed her trust so viciously, she could never contemplate forming any kind of relationship with a man. That was one of the reasons she tried to protect vulnerable young women, who did not understand how rape changed a woman's life.

'I do like you,' she said, 'but I am wedded to my job, and I can't think about marriage to any man.'

The look in his eyes reminded her of a dog that had been kicked. She looked away. She wasn't proud of what she was doing to him, but she could not accept his proposal. He would not want a wife who couldn't bear his touch.

'Perhaps through time, you will change your mind.'

'No, and I think it best if we do not see each other again.'

'As you wish,' he said, standing up.

She watched him walk away. Nothing in his appearance suggested he'd been rejected. His shoulders were squared, his frame erect, and his footsteps firm and unwavering.

A pang of regret crept through her mind, but she resisted the urge to call him back, because it would never work. She would not have been able to suppress a shudder every time he touched her, and as far as anything else was concerned that was completely out of the question.

She turned her back on his retreating figure and determined to concentrate on her career. It was for the best.

72

Dietger
Dietger surveyed the station platform. As he expected they were all waiting for him. Melville, Beatrice, and a horde of policemen and soldiers.

'Ah, Beatrice, what have you done?' His voice was no more than a murmur.

The London train arrived at the platform in front of him, but he turned his back on it and crossed the bridge to board the Glasgow train.

No one paid any attention to the regal looking woman, with the large hat, who carried a Paisley Terrier to whom she whispered endearments as she walked. A porter, clutching her valise, scurried behind her.

'Goodbye, Beatrice,' Dietger whispered as the Glasgow train steamed out of the station. 'Perhaps we will meet again when the war is over.'

Historical Note

Silvertown Explosion

On Friday 19th January, 1917, at 6.52 pm, a massive explosion at the Brunner-Mond munitions factory destroyed most of Silvertown. This explosion has been described as the biggest explosion ever to have taken place in London.

Silvertown, in the east end of London, was an industrial area on the north bank of the River Thames, opposite the Greenwich Peninsula, and south of the Victoria Docks.

The Brunner-Mond factory at Silvertown, was an old established chemical works which had been adapted, at the start of the First World War, to manufacture TNT (trinitrotoluene) a highly explosive substance.

The explosion occurred after a fire broke out in the melt room shortly after the workers had finished work for the weekend. It destroyed the factory and obliterated a large part of Silvertown. It is recorded that the sound of the blast could be heard as far away as Sussex, and red-hot lumps of metal rained down on other areas, starting fires wherever they landed. A gas holder, across the river on the Greenwich Peninsula, was hit and shot 8 million cubic feet of gas into the sky in a massive fireball. This gas holder was in the area now occupied by the Millennium Dome.

A local reporter, writing in the *Stratford Express*, wrote: *"The whole heavens were lit in awful splendour. A fiery glow seemed to have come over the dark and miserable January evening, and objects which a few minutes before had been blotted out in the intense darkness were silhouetted against the sky."*

It is estimated that between 60,000 to 70,000 properties were damaged, 73 people were killed, and over 400 were injured. The toll would have been even greater had the explosion occurred during working hours.

Rumours were rife about the cause of the explosion. Some thought it was a Zeppelin attack, some said it was sabotage, but these were ruled out and the cause was confirmed as an accident.

Gretna Munitions Factory
The site of Gretna Munitions Factory was a large, sparsely populated, green field area, on the shores of the Solway Firth. The land was acquired by the Ministry of Munitions at the start of the First World War, and various farms situated there were taken over by compulsory purchase orders.

The first surveys of the site were completed in early 1915. Construction work commenced in August 1915, with work going on round the clock. Several thousand Irish navvies were drafted in as construction workers, 600 rail trucks loaded with building materials arrived daily, and there were approximately 30,000 people working on the site at any one time. Production in some areas started in June 1916, and the factory became fully operational in August 1916.

The factory was two miles wide and over nine miles in length, beginning at Dornock in Scotland, and following the coast of the Solway Estuary to Mossband near Longtown, in England.

There were thirty Paste Mixing Houses – six to each nitroglycerine section – where nitroglycerine and guncotton were mixed together into cordite paste at the Dornock end of the factory. The paste was then transferred to the Mossband area to make into cordite, a propellant.

The factory was self sufficient with its own water mains, steam boilers, a hydraulic plant, a refrigerating plant, a power house for generating electricity, and a railway system within the site which also connected up with the main North British and Caledonian Railways. In addition, two new towns were built.

The Townships

Two complete townships were built by the Ministry of Munitions to service the factory. Eastriggs was built on a 173 acre site, while Gretna's site occupied 431 acres. There were over 1,000 permanent cottages built on these sites by the end of the war.

Eastriggs serviced the Dornock area of the factory and is 4.5 miles west of Gretna, although many of the munitionettes lived in the Gretna hostels and travelled daily to either the Dornock site in the west, or the eastern Mossband site over the border in England. When considering the geography of the area it is important not to confuse Gretna Township with Gretna Green village which is 1.2 miles north of Gretna. As most people know, Gretna Green is famous for its over the anvil weddings.

Many of the buildings in Gretna were made of wood, and it was soon nicknamed Timbertown. The wooden houses, set out like a military grid, contained between three to five rooms and were for families or groups. However, there were also larger brick built hostels used mainly for unmarried women. All the hostels were named after military leaders and famous people. Wellington, Kitchener, and Wolfe, were situated on Victory Avenue and Burnside Road as was The Pensions Hospital, and the Maternity House Hostel. Clive, and Gordon Hostels were on Central Avenue, while Mary Queen of Scots Hostel, which features in *Devil's Porridge*, was located on Dominion Road. The hostels in Victory Avenue were all the larger brick-built ones, but the buildings in Dominion Road were wooden. Likewise, the women police were based in a large wooden hostel.

Both Eastriggs and Gretna were self sufficient, providing everything needed within a town. For example, Gretna Township's facilities included a central shopping area, a cinema, a dance hall and concert hall, churches, bank, post office, bakery, laundry, assembly halls, sports grounds, hotels and clubs.

The Ministry of Munitions controlled all the towns in the area including Carlisle, and they imposed draconian measures to curb drinking that were applied to all hotels and public houses. This included early closing times, no drinks served without meals, and no treating. It was an offence to buy someone else a drink.

There was nowhere else in Britain quite like Gretna Munitions Factory and the surrounding area.

Women Police

The first women police appeared in London in 1914. They were recruited, trained and employed by voluntary organizations and worked independently of the all-male police forces. Although the women police were not employed by the police authorities, these organizations were given approval by the Police Commissioner, Sir Edward Henry, to provide police women to patrol the streets of London. They worked closely with the police forces in London and around the country.

There were two voluntary organizations providing a police service. The first of these was the Women's Police Volunteers (WPV), founded in 1914 by the two main suffragette societies, the Women's Social and Political Union (WSPU) and the Women's Freedom League (WFL). The second was the Voluntary Women Patrols, set up by the National Union of Women Workers (NUWW).

Women's Police Volunteers/Women's Police Service

Margaret Damer Dawson (WSPU), an anti-white slavery campaigner, was the chief of the WPV. Nina Boyle (WFL), a militant suffragette was her deputy. Many of the women they recruited were suffragettes and in September 1914, the first person to appear in WPV uniform was probably Edith Watson, suffragette and columnist.

One of the aims of the women's police service was to change the attitudes of the police towards women and to provide protection to other women who suffered at police hands, namely prostitutes.

When Damer Dawson and Nina Boyle parted company over a disagreement about the level of co-operation with the male police (Damer Dawson favoured co-operation with the men, Nina Boyle did not), Mary Allen was appointed deputy. Their titles were Commandant and Sub-Commandant. Mary Allen became Commandant in 1920 when Damer Dawson died. Mary Allen had been a militant suffragette who was imprisoned three times, one of these occasions was after throwing a brick through a Home Office window.

In 1915, the Women's Police Volunteers was renamed the Women's Police Service (WPS). Damer Dawson and Mary Allen were subsequently awarded the OBE for services to their country during wartime.

At the end of the war, Scotland Yard tried, unsuccessfully, to disband the Women's Police Service, and in 1920, it was renamed the Women's Auxiliary Service. It remained operational until 1940.

Voluntary Women Patrols/Special Patrols
The second police service set up during the war years was the Voluntary Women Patrols.

The women patrols wore armbands, and their main aim was to safeguard, influence, and if need be, restrain the behaviour of women and girls who congregated in the neighbourhood of army camps.

New Special Patrols were formulated in 1916, in an endeavour to check unseemly conduct in the Royal Parks, and to assist the police in making enquiries into the machinery for the sale of cocaine among women and soldiers. They still did not wear uniform, but their armlets were replaced by those of the regular police. They had no power of arrest, but they were allocated a constable to escort them through the streets.

Mrs Sofia Stanley was appointed Supervisor of the Special Patrols in March 1917. At the time of her appointment, there were 37 Special Patrols in central London and 29 in the suburbs, most of them working one or two nights a week.

This organization was made up of women who were

mostly middle class. Members of the WPS, who prided themselves on their professionalism, thought they were do-gooders.

Women's Police Patrols

In 1918, the Commissioner of the Police, Sir Nevil Macready, set up an official body of women police, the Women's Police Patrols, and appointed Mrs Sofia Stanley as Superintendent.

The policewomen's pay was poor, and they were employed on a yearly basis. They wore uniforms but were neither sworn in nor given power of arrest, and one of their main duties included prostitute control. The first recruits were ex-Special Patrols, closely followed by women from the WPS.

Their training included instructions in police duty, education, first aid and foot drill. They were also taught jujitsu as a form of self-defence.

Their uniforms of high-necked tunics and long skirts were made by Harrods, and their footwear was hard knee-length boots of solid, unpolishable leather (old land-army issue considered too heavy for work). A heavy, shallow helmet completed their outfit.

Although the male police resented them they found the women police useful for escorting lost children and dogs to the police station, and fetching the barrow for the conveyance of drunks.

In 1922, a decision was taken to disband the Women's Police Patrols, but this met with resistance and instead their numbers were reduced to 25. Mrs Sofia Stanley was one of those who lost their jobs. The threat of disbandment, however, was a prime factor in Sergeant Lilian Wyles' acceptance of an offer to be the statement taker for the CID.

She became the first woman detective in the Metropolitan Police Force.

Also by Chris Longmuir

DUNDEE CRIME SERIES

Night Watcher

Dead Wood

Missing Believed Dead

THE KIRSTY CAMPBELL MYSTERIES

Devil's Porridge

The Death Game

HISTORICAL SAGAS

A Salt Splashed Cradle

NONFICTION

Nuts & Bolts of Self-Publishing

CHRIS LONGMUIR

Chris is an award winning novelist and has published three novels in her Dundee Crime Series. Night Watcher, the first book in the series, won the Scottish Association of Writers' Pitlochry Award, and the sequel, Dead Wood, won the Dundee International Book Prize, as well as the Pitlochry Award. Missing Believed Dead is the third book in the series.

Chris also publishes a historical crime series, the Kirsty Campbell Mysteries, featuring one of Britain's first policewomen.

Her crime novels are set in Dundee, Scotland, and have been described as atmospheric page turners. Chris also writes historical sagas, short stories and historical articles which have been published in America and Britain. She confesses to being a bit of a techno-geek, and builds computers in her spare time.

Chris is a member of the Society of Authors, the Crime Writers Association, and the Scottish Association of Writers.

www.chrislongmuir.co.uk